# Rosie Won't Stay Dead

Brothers of Texas, Book 2

Tamara G. Cooper

## Dedication

To my editor,
**Jo Gallagher,**
for her expertise and
encouragement. I wouldn't be
where I am today
without her incredible gifts.

## In Appreciation

To my husband,
**Michael T. Cooper,**
whose love, support, and
encouragement have been so
invaluable to me on this writing journey.

Thank you, Trudy Hewitt, for
your great eye for detail and your
willingness to read and read and read.

**Books by Tamara G. Cooper**

**BROTHERS OF TEXAS Series**
*Who Killed Brigitt Holcomb?*
*Rosie Won't Stay Dead*
*Deception at Fairfield Ranch*
*Brothers of Texas Trilogy*

**SOPHIE O'BRION MYSTERIES**
*The Vacant House*
*The New Neighbors*

**ROMANCE**
*Love, Again*

This is a work of fiction. Names, characters, places, and events are from the author's imagination or used in a fictitious manner. Any resemblance to actual persons, living or dead, or actual events is purely coincidental.

# Table of Contents

ONE 1
TWO 14
THREE 21
FOUR 30
FIVE 39
SIX 51
SEVEN 55
EIGHT 62
NINE 69
TEN 77
ELEVEN 91
TWELVE 102
THIRTEEN 118
FOURTEEN 126
FIFTEEN 135
SIXTEEN 148
SEVENTEEN 160
EIGHTEEN 165
NINETEEN 178
TWENTY 187
TWENTY-ONE 197
TWENTY-TWO 207
TWENTY-THREE 221

# Rosie Won't Stay Dead

# ONE

Luke McKenzie shoved his overstuffed backpack into the bed of his pickup, secured the hard cover, and looked around the ranch. Sparse trees and vegetation surrounded him as cattle dotted the land and oil rigs slowly dipped and rose against a breeze rushing through the spring grass.

Luke loved this ranch, this part of the Texas panhandle.

But he needed to get away for a few weeks.

He hadn't slept well in a long time and leaving McKenzie Ranch and the stress since Dad's murder might help. Everywhere he looked, he saw his father, and he needed a break from the guilt and the loss.

Luke wanted to hike in the Colorado Rockies with only his golden retriever, Molly, for company and soak in the beauty that always nourished his soul. And, first thing, he wanted to hike Bear Camp Trail where he'd spend a night or two in the cave he'd discovered years ago. The trail was closed to hikers until the fifteenth of May, which meant he'd have it all to himself.

"Let's go, Molly girl. Time's a-wastin'." He laughed when his golden retriever bounded over to him and danced around his feet. He wasn't one to show his emotions much, but Luke was as excited about leaving as Molly.

Behind him, his younger brother Mac, the owner of McKenzie Ranch, came out of the main house and said, "You about to leave, buddy?"

Luke turned around, grateful Mac had seen his need for a break. But if anyone should be getting away, it was Mac. He and his wife had faced off against a gang last December that the sheriff had called 'pure reprobates.' The one week Mac and Marianne had spent on their honeymoon in February hadn't been enough of a break, Mac had told him, so they planned to get away in the fall to the family cabin in Little Texas, Colorado, that Luke was headed for today.

"Just about ready, but I hate putting more work on you by going."

"I have plenty of help. Now, go. You haven't had a vacation in two years, so have fun. Hike. Enjoy being alone. If you don't, I might have to send you back out there." Mac squeezed his shoulder. "Really, buddy. The ranch 'll survive without its foreman for a month. Take six weeks, if you need to."

"'Preciate it, bro'." When Luke opened the driver's door of his truck, Molly jumped inside the cab and barked at him. "I know, girl. We're fixin' to leave."

He turned back to Mac to say goodbye. It was harder than he thought it would be to leave the ranch, his life, his responsibilities. But he needed to get away more than he needed to stay. Maybe in the Rocky Mountains, he'd find some peace about Dad's murder. That would be his number one goal—and maybe a little forgiveness, too, for not being there when Dad needed him.

Luke hugged his brother, then got in the truck and started it.

"Be careful and have a great time."

"I will, Mac. See you in a month." Luke backed up his truck, waved, and headed for Little Texas, Colorado, in the high country of the Rockies.

At two o'clock in the morning, Sarah Morgan loaded the last of her luggage into her car. Kansas had been unusually warm for May, and the garage was stifling hot. But if the man who'd attacked her twice six months ago was outside watching her house, she didn't want him to see her packing to leave. She would hide in here until the very last moment.

Her mother was standing in her pajamas by the door leading to the kitchen, arms crossed, a worried expression on her face.

Sarah touched her arm. "I'll be fine, Mom. I have to do this."

"I know." She gripped Sarah's hand. "Just be careful, honey. Never stop watching for him."

"I won't. Where's Dad?" She reached up and opened the kitchen door. "Dad, come on. I'm leaving."

Sarah didn't want to see worry on his face, too, but there it was as he walked down the steps and gave her a hug.

"You sure you don't want us to go with you? Help keep you safe?"

"That would defeat my purpose, Dad. Can you catch the lights, so they won't come on when I open the garage?"

Her father flipped a switch.

At least in the middle of the night, it would be easier to spot someone following her. If she suspected he was, she'd call 9-1-1 and drive straight to the nearest police station.

"Okay, then." She looked from her mother to her father. "Group hug." She felt their deep love and concern for her in the especially long, tight hug. Pulling back, she said, "I have to go. The Rockies are calling me. Oh, Mom."

Tears were rolling down her mother's face, and Sarah grabbed her in a tight hug and held her for a few seconds. She felt her father's hand on her back. "I know this is hard for you, but I'll be careful and smart. I promise."

She smiled at both of them, trying to reassure them that she'd be fine. "I love you both. I'll call you at every stop until I get to Little Texas."

Luke arrived at McKenzie Cabin a little before nine that night. He took his things inside the cabin, showered, and went to bed. He was tired, but not too tired to wake up before five and get out on Bear Camp Trail, his favorite hike.

The alarm sounded at 4:30. He'd crammed everything he needed into his backpack in Texas, and he was ready to go a few minutes before five.

He stepped outside and took a deep breath.

It was always the same on his first morning in Little Texas, Colorado. He relished the thin air, the crisp morning, and the glorious beauty of snow-capped mountains. He would never admit to anyone at McKenzie Ranch that their tough-guy foreman needed this. For him, the old saying was true: there's no place like home. He loved Texas. The panhandle was the only place he ever wanted to live, but he loved these mountains, too.

At straight-up five o'clock, he locked McKenzie Cabin and slowly made his way to his pickup as he admired the panoramic beauty around him. Molly was standing by the driver's door of his truck, her whole body wagging in anticipation. "Me, too, girl. Me, too." With a quick laugh, Luke opened the door. She jumped inside and made her way to the passenger window. He rolled it down, and she leaned out and sniffed the cool mountain air.

He drove about five minutes to the dirt road leading to Bear Camp Trail. As he passed the only cabin on this stretch, he thought the owner had one of the best views in the area.

He parked down a bit from the trail's starting point and opened his door. Molly jumped out, made a quick right turn, and passed a sign that said, "Trail Closed for the Winter." Good. He'd be alone and could hike at his own steady pace. Just too much to see to rush through this day.

Sarah tried hard not to be afraid. She'd made the trip in just under five hours, had taken everything into her parents' cabin, locked all the doors, and was sitting on the chair closest to the fireplace, ready to jump out of her skin. She took a deep breath and blew it out. No one had followed her. *He* hadn't followed her, to be more specific. Now, she just had to relax enough to enjoy being here.

Tomorrow, she decided, she'd get up early and head out to Bear Camp Trail, just around the corner from her cabin and down a bit. She would be brave and hike by herself.

But right now, she needed a nap.

She took two long naps, ate a little supper, crawled into bed, and called her parents for the third time that day. She set her alarm for four o'clock, so she could be ready to hike by five.

She awoke before the alarm, got dressed, braided her long hair, and checked her day pack. She was ready to go.

She opened the cabin door and looked outside.

It was still dark. With no streetlamps near her family's cabin, she couldn't make out specific shapes. If the killer stood beside a tree, she wouldn't see him.

But he didn't follow her here. She'd been very alert, very careful. She was as sure as she could be that he wasn't here, despite the fear she'd heard in her parents' voices every time she called them. Both of them thought she was still in danger. *"If you want to come home, honey, just call me. I'll fly out and drive you home"*—her father. *"Honey, just be careful. Keep me posted. Don't forget to lock your doors"*—her mother. Their constant worrying and hovering was a good enough reason to get away.

She needed her independence again.

She stood still and enjoyed the quiet morning, listening, watching. The longer she stood there, the more she could see; the black of night was becoming a deep gray. She narrowed her eyes, searched the area around the cabin, and took one step outside. A bull elk lying in the grass blended in with the pewter-brown colors of a tree. He turned his racked head toward her, rose to his feet, and bounded off.

She looked up. A few stars were still visible, but the sun was on its way. Her bicycle leaned against the cabin. No more treadmill or indoor cycling or stair stepping. Nodding, she turned on the flashlight. Just a few hours of hiking today. Three hours up. Three hours back.

She pulled the locked door shut. Something moved behind her. She spun around, fumbled her flashlight, and dropped it on the pavement. She swiped it up and turned it on. It didn't work.

Her heart pounded as she backed into the door and grabbed the knob—but it was locked! Frantic, she searched the yard as she imagined her attacker sneaking around the corner of the cabin and grabbing her.

A squirrel's head popped out from behind a nearby pine tree. He stared at her. When Sarah moved her hand, he hurried behind the tree.

"Okay. It was only a squirrel." She took in a deep breath and let it out. "Just a squirrel."

She'd taken to talking to herself lately. Sometimes, the words were a prayer. Other times, she needed to hear someone—herself—telling her she'd be okay again. She was determined not to let the attacks define her, but she had so many questions about that night. It had been dark. She'd been in bed. Her house had been locked up tightly. With no broken windows, how had he gotten inside without a sound?

And how had he overpowered her so quickly?

She would have been dead like his other two victims if her roommates hadn't come into the house, laughing and calling her name. When he heard them, he leaned over her and whispered, "Later, sugar plum."

The police came and left. Her parents insisted she stay with them that night. She did, but he found her there—later—five hours after the assault.

Sitting in the dark in her old bedroom, wide awake, holding pepper spray and wondering how in the world she would ever fall asleep again, she heard something. Not knowing if it was one of her parents or him, she rushed behind the bedroom door. Her whole body quaked as someone crept into her room. When she saw him, she sprayed the back of his head and continued spraying as he turned around.

And then she screamed. God help her, she screamed until she had no voice left. Her father raced into her downstairs bedroom with a rifle, but the man was gone.

The police questioned her again. She had nothing for them—not his description, his weight, or skin color. He was taller than her, but that wasn't saying much. She'd completely focused on the back of his head and the pepper spray.

The media had dubbed him the Darkslayer because he'd murdered his victims in their own bedrooms in the dark. Sarah was the only known survivor.

Most of her life, she had scolded herself for being afraid of the dark. But never again. She knew now what the dark could hide.

She didn't want to think about that night right now.

Her total focus needed to be on the bike ride. Down this street. Around the corner. About five hundred feet to the dirt road. Another half mile to the trail.

Then she'd focus on hiking for a few hours. Early, on a closed trail, so no one would bother her. She wanted to take a long nap under a tree, climb up to a great view of the mountains, and sit and enjoy her picnic. She wanted to *live.*

"Okay. It's time."

With all the courage she could muster, she hurried to her bike and rode toward the trail.


Man, it was good to be in the Rockies!

Luke breathed in deeply, held his breath, and blew it out. He looked up the trail. It was an easy, steady climb—except for the altitude. Five minutes of hiking, two minutes of catching his breath. Start and stop, start and stop for the first hour. Home was about eighteen hundred feet above sea level. Starting out at eight thousand feet and heading up was a big jump for him. But he would enjoy the pauses for catching his breath as much as he'd enjoy the hike. It was just his way.

Maybe he should have waited a couple days to acclimate to the high altitude before hiking. Most hikers would have. But he'd needed to be out here. "You doin' awright, Molly girl?"

She barked and ran ahead of him.

They came to a sign that said "Scenic Overlook" with an arrow pointing east. They climbed up to it, enjoyed the view, and then headed back down to the trail. By late morning, they'd reached the first pasture. Luke felt a couple of raindrops, looked up, and laughed. "This day's just gettin' better and better, isn't it, girl? C'mon. There's a place to settle in right over here." He headed for an outcropping of rock, sat under it, and watched the rain show. This was just what he needed.

He thought of a nap—some of the best rest he'd ever had was in high altitude. The air had cooled, and the lack of sleep from his long drive yesterday was catching up with him. He covered himself with his jacket and lay his head on his backpack.

He could already tell he was starting to relax here. Just seconds after putting his head down, his eyes felt heavy with the need to sleep. As he started to doze off, he thought how good it was to be in the mountains again. Molly curled up next to him. He draped an arm over her and drifted into sleep.

Sitting under a Ponderosa pine tree, Sarah grinned to herself. This day had been perfect. She'd done everything she wanted to do.

Picnic. *Check.*

Climbing up to a lookout point and admiring the view. *Check.*

Waking up under a tree after a solid two-hour nap. *Check.*

The rain shower was a bonus. Everything smelled sweet and fresh now. She loved how the first signs of spring had dressed up the valleys a little bit, but the mountains still wore their caps of snow. Was there any place as delightful as this?

She was alone—yes!—and so very brave. *Check and double check.*

She chuckled at herself and stuffed her things into her daypack.

Listening to the mountain stream below her had helped her to fall asleep. She stood and walked to the trail's edge. Above her, the mountains loomed, great and beautiful. Below her, the stream playfully bubbled over rocks as if it were thrilled to finally be out of the hard winter freeze. This world was exactly what she'd needed to learn to live again.

Smiling, she leaned over to better see the stream when footsteps sounded behind her. She gasped and started to turn around, but hands pushed hard against her back, forcing her over the edge.

A short, piercing scream popped the silence like a whip.

Luke jerked awake and sat up. "Did you hear that, Molly?" He rubbed his eyes and tried to shake the sleep out of his head, but the high-altitude grogginess held on. "Sounded like somebody screamed."

Molly whimpered and inched closer to him. Her whole body was shaking.

"C'mere, girl." He picked her up and stroked her side as he glanced around. "It was probably an animal. Cougars scream. Coulda been a cougar."

Molly's head snapped toward the gaping mouth of the woods that swallowed up their hiking path. She scrambled to her feet, lowered her head, and growled, low and steady.

"Or a red fox." Luke looked up. "Storm's gone. We got three hours yet to make it to the cave 'fore night gets here. So let's go—"

Like a shot, she raced through the tall grass and stopped at the opening to the woods, barking and dancing as if asking his permission to run inside.

"No, Molly. We just came from there. We need to keep go—"

She disappeared into the foliage.

"Well, great. Is 'go' the only word you understand today?" He grabbed his pack, slipped it on, reached for his water bottle and placed it in his waist pack as he sprinted toward Molly. He'd planned this day thoroughly and *running toward trouble* wasn't on his to-do list. But he knew something was wrong by Molly's behavior. He'd check it out and then get back on the trail.

He slowed down as he stepped into the quiet forest. Only in the Colorado Rockies could an afternoon rain draw such scents from the trees and brush. He wanted to stop and take a good whiff, to savor the beauty of these mountains, but Molly's persistent barking pulled him on.

He jumped over bulging roots, dodged low-hanging wet branches, and eased between pointed rocks that seemed to shoot up out of the ground. He rounded a tree-lined switchback into a narrow valley. All was silent but for the aspen leaves shivering in the breeze.

He spotted Molly and jogged toward her. She was struggling to keep her paws planted on a slippery slope as she barked at something down below.

"Okay, girl. What'd you find?" Luke grabbed her collar, tugged her back, and leaned over. About ten feet below them, a woman sprawled face-down in the tall grass, her head not five feet from the rushing mountain stream. A long blonde braid rested on top of her small daypack. Her arm lay across the small of her back, twisted in the straps of her pack.

"Well, I'll be." He'd never known a hiker who'd fallen off such a wide trail. Maybe her foot slipped on the wet incline.

Molly yelped and nudged Luke's leg several times as if to say, "Hurry! Help her!"

The woman lifted her head, rolled over, and screeched when she saw them. With the agility of an athlete, she jumped to her feet and then winced and fell to one knee, struggling against the straps of her daypack. She teetered and fell back. Her head jerked toward Luke. Her wide eyes watched him as if he was holding a bloody knife.

"Are you hurt?" Luke started the slide down and tried to keep his gaze on her, but it was difficult to plant his feet on the slick hill. He slipped and grabbed a tree. "Do you need help?"

As he continued down, she rolled to her right side. Her left foot dug into the wet grass, propelling her awkwardly through the tall thick brush bordering the stream.

"Look. I'm not going to hurt you." He reached the bottom of the ravine. "I'm trying to help you." But the terror in the woman's eyes told him to stop, to back up. So, he did.

Her gaze never left him. Her eyes were the same color as the amber-gold stone on one of his belt buckles. Her right foot touched the ground, and she sucked in a breath and reached for her ankle.

"Leaving your boot on will help support a sprain." He took a step toward her as she struggled against the straps of her small daypack. "Would you like some help with that?"

Her clothes were wet. *Dry, warm, hydrated.* The three musts in a hiking accident. "You're wet. You must be cold. Do you have a jacket?"

She didn't blink or even acknowledge she'd heard him.
Another step.
Her full lips firmed into a straight line, although she shook like a leaf.

"You p-pushed me."

"No, I didn't."

Another step.

Her body shook so hard, he thought he could hear her teeth clattering. He talked to her as he would an injured horse: softly, with unwavering eye contact. "Does anything else hurt besides your ankle and your shoulder?"

Two more steps forward.

Her hand trembled as she brushed strands of blonde hair from her face and stared at him. A tiny woman, she couldn't weigh more than a large sack of feed.

"I felt you push me."

"I couldn't have. We were asleep under a ledge. Your scream woke us up."

"This trail is closed. No one else is hiking here."

"Someone is, if you were pushed."

"There is no 'if.' I was pushed."

Molly nudged her hand, and she jerked. Then she smiled for the first time and patted Molly's head as if she could sense the dog wouldn't hurt her. "Hello." She glanced at Luke as she held up the dog tag, then read it. "Molly. It says, 'McKenzie Ranch, Texas'." Another glance at Luke, as if she were afraid to take her gaze off him. "Are you a cow-herding dog, Molly?"

Good. With the woman's attention on Molly, Luke might be able to help her and then get back to the trail and his plans. "Here, let me get that strap for you."

He gave her time to get used to the idea by slipping off his pack and setting it against a tree. With his hands in the air, he approached her. "I'll just loosen this—" The woman leaned to the side, her wary gaze on him. Molly settled next to her. "—and you'll be on your way." He gently untwisted the straps and then stepped back about five feet. "There. Better?"

"Yes," she muttered. "Thank you." She rubbed her shoulder, still staring at him. "I felt hands on my back. Someone else is here if—if it wasn't you." Her arms went around Molly's neck, and she tugged her closer as if they'd known each other for a while instead of a few minutes.

"My truck's the only one parked at the trailhead. Not another place to park for at least a couple miles. 'Course, he could have hidden a bicycle somewhere. Or parked after I did. Or come off another trail."

The woman's body told him she was afraid of him. Her gaze fastened on everything but him. Her hands rubbed her lower arms and found their way to her shoulders. And, of course, her body vibrated as if she sat in ice.

"You're—you're not in cahoots with him, are you? Not part of some... some c-cowboy gang preying on women or... anything?"

"'Course not. Even if I had such inclinations, Molly wouldn't let me give in to them. It's not in her nature to stand by while someone's being hurt. *She's* the one—" Luke lowered his voice when the woman's lips pressed together as if she tried to hold back tears. "—who came to your rescue."

In profile, her chin quivered. Her gaze connected with his for a moment, and then she shut her eyes and turned away from him as if she could make him and her troubles vanish.

The trail ridge above them disappeared into thick pine and aspen trees. Nothing but dense shrubs and weeds on the way up. "We'll have to bushwhack out of here. The brush is too thick to walk in, much less carry someone."

Her head snapped up. "I can walk."

"Good." He held out a hand, moved his fingers in a come-on-give-me-your-hand gesture, and she took it. Her hand felt soft and small in his.

She took a step, sucked in a breath, and clutched his arm. "Okay. So, I can't walk."

"Yeah." Irritation gnawed at him like a burrowing tick. Just a simple trek in the mountains. That's all he'd wanted. A man and his dog enjoying the untamed mountains of Colorado—alone. Being alone had been his top priority for hiking today. And here he was, *not* alone and responsible for an injured woman. He wanted to ask her what in the world she was doing out here by herself. Every seasoned hiker knew not to hike alone. And because of her foolish decision, he was stuck with changing his plans on his first day here!

"I'm not asking you to stay."

He scooped up her sleeping bag and clipped it to his backpack. "I wouldn't leave an injured animal stranded, much less a woman. I'll have to carry you back to the trailhead."

Her jaw dropped, and she shook her head. "You can't possibly." She glanced around as if she hoped to find a trail-ready gurney with wheels leaning against a tree. "It's too far."

"And not getting any closer while we stand around and yap about it." Actually, it wasn't a bad idea to head back. Dark clouds lined the horizon. If he didn't miss his guess, snow lay thick in them—snow that hadn't been in the forecast.

"You need to get dry clothes on." He held up her daypack.

"I intended to." She took it and lifted her chin. "Turn around."

He did. "Make it quick. We'll lose light in another couple hours." Clothing rustled behind him. The woman drew in a quick breath and moaned. Must be her shoulder or her ankle. He'd have to be careful with both when he carried her out.

"I'm ready."

"Great." He clipped her pack to his. "Let's go."

He slung his backpack on and picked her up. "Arms around my neck, shift some of the weight. Better yet, straddle my waist—" She inhaled sharply. "—and I'll support your back."

A blush. The woman was blushing. Her chin eased up as her mouth pinched. "I most certainly will not."

She reminded him of his ninth grade science teacher, Mrs. Harrigan. Anyone who disrupted her class with even the slightest hint of humor was called "Mr. Hooligan" or "Miss Hooligan." She'd said it disdainfully, with the same puckered mouth and raised chin he faced at the moment. "Which part of what I said will you most certainly not?"

"I'll not...not...and you...you probably pushed me so...so you could..." Her lips pinched even more. "Put me down. I'll manage by myself." Her queen-of-the-rodeo stance probably would have worked had she not blushed all over herself again.

"Suit yourself, lady. I hope you came prepared to spend the night. That ankle will need healing time before you head back and that means no standing on it." He unclipped her pack and her sleeping bag, set them on the ground, and started walking away. He had no intentions of leaving her alone. He'd stay back. Watch her. Protect her if it came to that, but he couldn't force her to go with him.

He hadn't taken five steps when Molly stopped and looked back at her.

"All right. I'll do it."

He stopped, too, but didn't turn around. A part of him wanted to keep walking, but the stronger need to help her won out.

"I said I'd do it," she added in a louder voice.

"Then let's go. Time's a-wastin'." He walked back, attached her gear, and came as close to grumbling out loud as he possibly could without actually making a sound. The woman reminded him of a newborn colt—skittish, unable to plant her feet, and scared of everything.

Just what he needed for his vacation.

"Can't we leave your pack? I could ride piggy-back."

"No." He winced at the force of the word and made the next ones come out more gently. "We might need it. These mountains are unpredictable." As the coming storm indicated.

He settled the woman on his waist pack. Another blush crawled up her neck and face. She placed her arms to her side, but he knew she couldn't balance herself like that for long. "You're going to have to hang onto me. I have to use both hands to grab trees to get us topside. But first things first." A strand of her hair teased his chin, and he swatted at it. "I'm Luke McKenzie."

Another pinch took over her mouth as her perky little nose lifted a couple inches.

"Do you have a name?"

"Why do you want to know?"

"It's a custom in the state of my birth, actually. We exchange names in Texas, usually in a friendly manner. That way, we can communicate."

"We can communicate without names."

"Fine. I'll call you Myrtle."

She laughed. "Okay. I'm Sarah."

He looked into her eyes. Little specks of black made them interesting. "Dimples. Nice," he said. "So, Miss Sarah, I guess I can't expect a last name with that."

She raised her chin, a look with which he was becoming all too familiar. "You're perceptive, Luke McKenzie. I like that."

"Peachy," he muttered and reached for the nearest tree.

# TWO

"Let's rest." Luke set Sarah on a huge boulder. "Despite the fact that you're as tiny as a mole, you're getting heavy." He checked out the trail ahead of them as he slid his pack off.

"I'm not that tiny. You're just big."

"How much do you weigh? A whopping hundred pounds?"

"Plus five."

"That's tiny. And you're what? Five foot?"

"Five-two. You?"

"Six-three."

"A foot taller. I'm impressed."

"Then you impress far too easily."

"You'd be surprised," she mumbled, unscrewing her canteen's lid. "How much farther?"

"We've been hiking an hour. It'll be long after dark before we get back."

"I brought extra rations and came prepared to spend the night if necessary."

He took out his water bottle and drank. A black squirrel sat on a branch above them, swishing its tail, staring him down. The little booger was probably wondering when they'd be getting out of here so he could scamper to his heart's content. "I'm with you on that, buddy," Luke mumbled and glanced at Sarah.

He took a moment to study her. She was small, with a long, thick braid down her back. Real blonde, like it didn't come out of a bottle. An appealing mouth with full lips and a perky nose that seemed to enjoy the air since she put it up there so often. Her body was slim and well toned. Maybe a tennis player or a swimmer. Or a hiker. It was her hair that caught his attention. Really thick and long. Not great hair for ranch life, and that made him wonder what she did for a living.

But he wasn't interested enough to ask. He just wanted to get her home so he could get home himself, rest, and try this hike again in the morning.

He turned his back to her. They were buried in a switchback where the mountains weren't visible. The sky was covered up with tall pines and aspens.

It was then that he noticed the quiet.

No birds sang. No ground squirrels popped out of hidden havens. He looked up; the black squirrel was gone. Something had caused him to leave—or the person who'd pushed Sarah was still out here.

Luke glanced around as his hand slid to the hunting knife on his belt. He held his breath and turned a slow circle, searching from tree to tree for someone watching them, crouched to strike, ready to finish what he'd started with Sarah.

Sunlight crawled across the area where he stood as more clouds separated. Luke unsnapped the knife case and eased the blade out. A spurt of wind caused the aspen leaves to quake above him.

In the quiet, he didn't move for several moments.

Then the hair on the back of his neck suddenly rose.

He squinted into the deep green shadows surrounding them. "Sarah," he spoke slowly, softly. "You're sure someone pushed you?"

She looked up, and their gazes locked. "Yes," she answered and glanced around warily.

"But why push you? Why leave you? Did he follow you down, check on you?"

"I don't know to all of your questions."

Luke sheathed his knife. "We need to get out of here. Now." He reached for his backpack and stopped, his arm in mid-air. Uneasy, he quickly glanced over his shoulder.

Molly whimpered and looked down the path with worried eyes.

Everything seemed to be on pause, waiting for something to happen.

"Get down, Sarah."

A gun fired. Bark flew off a tree a couple feet from them. Sarah yelped and swatted at her ear.

"Get down! Down, Molly!" Luke tackled Sarah by the waist and plunged them both behind the boulder as the leaves on the ground jerked and danced to more gunshots.

Sarah gasped and clutched Luke's arm. "He's back, Luke. The man who—"

Bullets stabbed the tree above them. Debris fell on their backs as they squatted. They couldn't stay in this position much longer. Luke's legs were already starting to cramp.

"Be still," he breathed into her ear. With his shoulder, he nudged her over a few inches, then they both turned around and sat. Luke drew up his legs and positioned his body protectively beside her. He opened his fanny pack holster and checked his gun. It was loaded with the safety on.

"Is that legal here?"

"Actually, yes."

They were sitting ducks. Nowhere to hide but right where they were, out in the open in this idiot's line of fire.

Unless...

He looked through the trees. It took him a few seconds to locate the brush covering the cave. This boulder was the marker he'd used to spot the hidden opening on previous hikes. Every year, he intended to explore it but had never done it. He'd been inside far enough to know that it had potential to be a deep cave.

"—and Lord, keep us safe, please," Sarah whispered. "And thank you. Amen."

Humbled by her words, Luke nodded. "Amen."

Silence enveloped them. Luke turned his head and strained to listen but heard nothing. "Do you have any idea who's after you, Sarah?"

"Maybe you're his target, and he didn't want a witness, so he pushed me out of the way."

Bullets sprayed a branch, causing it to fall across the boulder. It created a triangular opening just above Sarah's head. Luke waited a few minutes after the firing stopped, eased up, and looked through the opening, searching every bush and tree for the sniper. But the fullness of the leaves simply swallowed the gun and the person shooting it.

If the sniper changed his location in either direction, he and Sarah were dead.

Luke listened for anything that sounded like a footstep or brush being moved aside or a gun cocking. Anything that might signal where the gunman was positioned.

Sarah looked at her watch. "It's been over ten minutes since the last shot." She shifted away from him. "You're crowding me."

He waited a couple of seconds before he leaned over and said, "Would you rather he had a clear shot at you?"

"No." She scooted closer to the boulder and to Luke.

Everything was silent. Something crawled on Luke's arm, and he brushed it off. He patted Molly's head. "Have you ticked anyone off lately?"

"Why do you think this guy's after me?"

"He pushed you."

"If it's the same guy."

"You're thinking there are *two* homicidal maniacs? I've hiked this trail for years and never saw anything even remotely suspicious on it and you're saying—"

"I'm *not* saying—"

"That there could be *two* nut cases out here?"

"Maybe he's trying to scare you off."

"So he can have you all to himself?" He noted that her face suddenly went pale. "If that's his intent, he's a lousy shot."

A bullet zinged off the top of the branch angled across the boulder above them. Wood chips fell in Sarah's face, and she slapped at it.

"Just keep still, Sarah, and we'll—"

"We'll what, Luke? What if he comes closer? What if he changes positions?"

"Lower your voice."

Her body shook against him. "We can't fight a man with a gun, especially if we can't see him."

"I don't suppose you brought a cell phone with you."

"I realized I left it in my cabin when I got here and didn't want to go back and get it."

"A lot of good that does you."

"Where's yours?"

"Dead, in my truck."

"A lot of good that does you."

"Yeah, well. There was no service up here the last time I visited. Why were you hiking alone?"

"I could ask you the same question."

"I'm not a shrimp. I have Molly, and I can take care of myself."

"So can I."

"Oh, it shows." Arguing would get them nowhere. "When it's fully dark, we'll make a run for it. Let's hope he's gotten his jollies by then and moved out of here."

Time ground on. As long as Luke didn't move, no bullets sprayed at their feet. He listened and watched—wary of the hunter lying in wait for them and dreading the coming night.

At the only cabin on Bear Camp Road, Gertie Jansen slung her tattered rug over the weathered wooden rail outside her back door and ruthlessly beat it with a canoe oar.

Pausing to catch her breath, she looked toward Bear Camp Trail. The shiny red pickup was still parked a few yards below it. Did the driver honestly think he'd fooled anybody into thinking he wasn't hiking that closed trail?

She remembered the golden retriever leaning out the passenger window this morning, its ears and tongue flapping in the cool May wind, and that made her smile. She felt the same exhilaration sometimes, when the wind played in the trees and a storm threatened. She'd stand on the back porch and lift her face to the crisp, fresh wind and thrill to it wafting across her face.

But her smile disappeared when she thought about the truck's owner spending the whole day on that trail, and here was night and cold and snow on its way in, and him still out there.

"Stupid hiker," she mumbled and slapped her rug again. She didn't see many visitors until the tourists intruded around the first of June. They'd 'discovered' Little Texas in the '80s. After the townspeople realized the intruders also wanted to spend money, they made hay while the sun shined and were shed of most of them by mid-September. Gertie could bear the June-to-September rush well enough, but she'd just as soon live without the tourists herself.

Her relatives, the Jansens, were one of four Texas families who'd settled this area in the 1890s. In a hidden valley nestled high in the Colorado Rockies, Little Texas was an enclave of Texans. Everybody was very protective of the town's heritage; no one wanted to see it grow with 'outsiders.' A natural rock border prevented much growth, anyway. She would tolerate what had to be tolerated, until September.

She glanced at the truck again and shook her head. Foolish tourists didn't respect nature. As sure as she was standing here, they'd simply walked around the sign that said *Trail Closed for the Winter* and headed right into a spring snowstorm.

Well, she couldn't take care of every brainless hiker who ventured into the Colorado Rockies.

She reared back and slugged the rug again. It was as clean as she was going to get it, so she tugged it off the rail. With one last glance over her shoulder, she stepped inside her cabin and let the screen door slam shut behind her.


Something moved. Sarah squinted into the meager evening light, spotted a red fox, and breathed a sigh of relief. It scampered across a fallen log and disappeared into the foliage. "Not exactly how I wanted to spend my day."

Luke didn't say anything.

"I really appreciate your willingness to help me. I hate that this man ruined your plans, too."

"Our plans are the least of our worries."

"I know that. Still, I wanted to say thank you."

"You're welcome." Luke twisted around and looked through the opening made by the branch on top of the boulder.

"See anything?" For an hour, no movement had come from the gunman. In any other setting, with the moon shining bright around them and the cool crisp breeze nipping at their noses, it would have been a perfect night for campfires and ghost stories and hot chocolate.

"No. Do you think you can use your foot?"

"It's better. I've been off it for a while now." She gasped and looked past him.

Luke turned toward the shadows slithering across the trail and sat again. "Just a deer," he murmured. "Look, Sarah. I found a cave a few years back, but I've never been deep inside it. Right over there." He nudged her arm, but it was too dark to see where he was pointing. "We could get out of this cold wind."

"A cave? If the sniper's still here, he could trap us inside."

"We're not trapped now?"

"Not if he's gone."

"We wouldn't be trapped in there either if he's gone. At least we wouldn't be sitting ducks. We'd have a place to stay until morning, and we'd be warmer." Leaves and brush rustled in the bitter night breeze. "We'd be sitting on the other side of the entrance. That would be an advantage."

Bullets spat at them. Luke braced his back against the boulder and scooted Molly out of firing range with his foot.

Sarah struggled to think. She was absolutely freezing. The temperature had probably dropped at least twenty degrees since they'd been pinned behind the boulder.

Luke leaned toward her. "He's got to sleep. We'll wait awhile and then head inside the cave and out of this wind. Did you bring a flashlight?"

"Yes, two. Although, I dropped one. Not sure it's working."

"I brought two with extra batteries and flares."

"Flares! Why haven't you used them? We could signal someone. Some rangers!"

"And they'd find our bodies riddled with bullets when they got here. That shooter could've killed us a long time ago, but he didn't. That tells me he wants one of us alive. If we're both going to get out of this still breathing, we have to stay sharp and outsmart him."

"We could make a run for it."

"How do you think he saw us just now in this dark?"

She groaned. "Night vision goggles." She eased her head back against the boulder. In the small opening at the top of the trees, clouds floated across the bottom portion of a bright moon. It wouldn't be long before the snowstorm was here. "He's well-equipped."

"And we're not. At least, not for this. Let's get into our sleeping bags and wait until the time is right to try for the cave. You sleep. I'll keep watch."

"I can't sleep."

"Try. It might be a long night. Snow's on the way in, which might work in our favor. If he didn't come prepared for it, he might leave. At least in the cave, we'll be out of it."

# THREE

*No!* Sarah grunted and squirmed. *His hands—all over her! She pushed against him and screamed, "Noooo!"*

"Sarah. Be quiet."

*His hand pressed against her mouth. She couldn't breathe! She fought him, wildly shaking her head, kicking, thrashing. The dark. Trapped! Oh, God, help me!*

"Sarah."

*All over her, grabbing her, hurting her. She shoved against him, and he grunted. "A little thing like you, sugar? You couldn't budge a flea." Sweaty hands. Beer breath. The black, black dark. She jabbed his chin with the heel of her hand. He ripped her blouse. Arching her back, she fought him, kicking, clawing.*

"Sarah, wake up!"

*His hand tightened. She... couldn't... breathe!*

"Sarah!"

Yes, she could. The hand over her mouth tightened its grip, but she could breathe. Another hand pressed against the back of her neck.

"Come *on*," he urged. "Wake up!"

Luke's voice reached her, and she startled awake, squirming against his hand until he removed it. "Luke?" The dregs of the nightmare hung on, making the night seem darker, colder, and scarier. She shivered, and her feet dug in as she pushed back against the boulder. She took big gulps of the frigid air to even out her breathing, but her heart continued to race.

"You were dreaming."

*From one nightmare to another.* She shook her head and closed her eyes against the memories. *Oh, God, will this ever stop?*

She had tried so hard. The old Sarah was going to be back. She'd be brave and adventurous and enjoy nature and go with the flow of the day. She'd make her day *count*. She took a chance hiking alone, but she needed to prove to herself that she could do it, that she could be the strong woman she'd been before the attack. That she could leave the fear behind.

But it had met her here instead.

"It's been a while since he shot at us." Luke's voice sounded gruff.

He probably thought she was weak, that she couldn't hold her own out here. Let him think what he would. She knew who she was—who she used to be. She just had to figure out how to tap into that woman again.

"Let's see if we can get to the cave. Are you awake enough to move out?"

"Yes."

"Who hurt you?"

It was none of his business. The one dogged purpose of this trip had been to rediscover Sarah Ann Morgan—whatever that meant anymore. And here she was, with a man she didn't know, facing God only knew what, with a psycho firing *bullets* at them, and she was thinking about going into a cave that might end up as her grave.

"Is it him, shooting at us?"

She closed her eyes and shook her head. "Let's just leave, Luke. Now. Please."

"Look, I need to know if—"

"I don't know. It happened in Kansas. I don't know who this man is, all right?" The cold wind against her neck woke her completely, and she scooted away from Luke enough that their bodies weren't touching anymore.

"Let's try for the cave. Be quiet and roll up your bag. Stay low."

Grateful for something to do, she eased out of her sleeping bag. The shock of the cold made her want to crawl back into the warmth, but she knew they had to move quickly. She rolled up her bag and attached it to her pack. She let out the air of her pillow, rolled it up, and stuffed it into her backpack. If only she could stuff the memories away as easily as that. Then she'd hurl them into oblivion and never have to face them again.

She dug for her gloves and jacket, put them on, and then slipped on her pack.

The rustling beside her stopped. "Ready?"

She took a deep breath and made herself say, "Yes." She would not let her fear of the dark keep her from staying alive. "Just to get out of this wind."

"Shhh, Molly. Let's go." Luke took Sarah's hand. "Come on."

Bending over, they slipped into the night.

Inside a minute, they stepped around huge brush covering a small outcrop of rock. Luke led her around to the backside of it, which put them at an angle to the sniper's last position.

Luke tugged her to her knees, crawled under the brush to a cave mouth, and crouched at the opening. She was right behind him.

She looked inside the cave and shivered, not because of the cold but because of the blackness in front of her—like a vacuum ready to suck the life out of her. Squatting, she reached out to steady herself and connected with cold, rough rock.

"Bottom left pocket on my pack. Grab the fold-up walking stick and flashlight. We'll need both before we can go forward."

She was so cold, she could hardly move her fingers, even with her gloves on. But she found the pocket, fumbled with the zipper, and pulled out the walking stick and flashlight. "I think it's below freezing."

"Yeah." Luke unfolded the staff and inched inside the mouth of the cave, tapping the floor and wall and ceiling. "I can't turn on the light. He might see it. Stay low and right behind me. I was in here once. The ceiling rises in about ten feet."

She glanced over her shoulder at the shadows behind them, and bullets showered the brush. Sarah gasped as Luke tugged her inside the opening and against the cave wall. She felt the dust-up from several bullets landing in the dirt near her feet.

"Man, this guy doesn't quit. Molly, here!"

Sarah pressed against the rough wall, trying hard to control her breathing and calm her heart. "He changed positions."

"He's letting us know he's watching us every second."

"Luke, this man's a good shot. He aimed right at the tree above us and hit it. The branch and hit it. Our feet, and never hit us. He's taunting us. He's had every opportunity to kill us, so why are we still alive?"

"Maybe he likes scaring people. Maybe he came out here to hunt an elk, we scared off his prey, and he's getting back at us. Maybe we're target practice. I have no idea. But if we go in deeper, he might go find something else to practice on."

"Or follow us in here."

"Maybe, but I don't think so. At any rate, we have to decide if we're going in deeper or if we stay here. This cave might end in twenty feet, or it may go on for a mile."

She didn't know what to do, so she prayed silently for a few moments.

"Okay. Let's look at our options, Sarah. One, we stay right here, although he knows where we are and could meet us here in a few minutes. Two, head inside, wait a little while and see if he's gone, although he's shown no indication he's done with us. Three, make a run for it in the dark; are you willing to take a chance on getting shot? Four, go in deeper. That's our best option."

She shivered, so cold and hardly able to think. Kansas could be cold but not this into-the-bone cold here.

"Feel that draft, Sarah? Sometimes when there's a draft, there's another way out. It just might be large enough for us to fit through. C'mon. Let's at least go a little further inside." He turned on the flashlight. "Then we can decide."

They inched along the wall into the unknown as Luke tapped the walking stick against solid ground, wall, and ceiling. Within a short distance, they were standing.

The thought of going down into the very bowels of the earth terrified Sarah. How long would it take to get out? Would their flashlights last? Would they die? Her family would never know what happened to her. Did she have enough food, enough water? Would she ever see the light of day again?

"We need to keep moving, Sarah."

"Do we? Why don't we stop here?"

"Because he's stayed with us all afternoon and into the night. I don't think he's going to quit. We can search for another way out. If there isn't one, we'll wait him out and head back here."

"Okay. I hope you know what you're doing."

A long pause.

"I need to give you my credentials?"

"I don't know you, Luke."

"You're right. Sure." He shined the light on a creature crawling on the wall. "Every year, my family came up here for summer vacation. My brother Greg, the oldest, started caving with a church group from Estes Park years ago. He loved it. The next year, he took me along. I loved it. When we came up here, we included caving. A couple times, one of my other brothers would join us. One year, all of us went with Dad. I've probably explored fifty caves. Some, virgin. Others, crawling with people. Every cave is different. Every cave is the same."

"What's the mortality rate for cavers?"

"About three deaths a year in the U.S., mostly from drowning. It's a very safe sport."

"I'm with an experienced caver. That's comforting."

"If I don't think it's safe, we'll turn around. We're trying to save our lives here, not have an adventure. So, we're good to go?"

"Yes."

"Then stay directly behind me as much as possible." He shined the light around. "I'm only checking the space in front of me. There could be holes in the floor, so stay close."

"Maybe getting us in here was part of his plan."

"This cave isn't visible from the trail."

"You found it."

"I know what to look for. Most people don't."

She flicked one last glance over her shoulder, moved closer to Luke, and slipped a finger through a loop on his pack.

"Don't pull."

She grabbed the edge of a lower pocket on his pack.

"We'll use only one flashlight until it runs out. Be careful where you walk. It's so dark, we won't be able to tell the difference between the black of open space in front of us and the black of the cave floor. If I start to fall, let go." Luke chuckled.

She was so not in the mood for humor. "It's warmer than it was outside."

"Probably stays around fifty degrees, even at the cave's heart."

"And no wind, thank God. What about Molly? She might fall."

Luke turned around. "You've never had a dog, have you?"

It was slow going. A few steps. The tapping of the walking stick. The light scanning the walls and floor. A few steps. The tap-tap-tap of the walking stick. The light moving about.

After a while, Luke stopped so suddenly, Sarah ran into the back of his pack. "What is it?"

"Shhh." He turned around, gripped her arm. "Listen."

"I don't hear—"

The light went out. "Shhh," he whispered.

She froze. *He's behind us! Oh, God!* Her heart raced. She tried to swallow and couldn't, to speak and couldn't, to breathe and couldn't. Blackness beyond anything she had ever known surrounded them, and a madman was behind them. She imagined his hand, reaching out of the dark, grabbing her. Molly's nose nudged her leg, and she just about jumped out of her skin. Tense moments pounded along with her heavy heartbeat.

"Okay." Luke's light came back on. "Let's get your flashlight out of your pack." His hands landed on her shoulders and turned her around. "Where is it?"

"Wait a minute. What do you mean, where is it? Why did you stop? You scared me half to death!"

"I thought I heard something."

"Well, then, *tell* me. You don't have to grab me and scare the living wits out of me."

"I reacted. I thought he might be behind us."

"Then turn the light off. That'll be our signal to stop and be quiet. Great day, Luke, I'm not difficult to scare senseless in this netherworld."

"Point taken. I didn't mean to scare you. I needed to listen and figure out what was going on. Grabbing your arm was my expedited signal."

"Well, try it my way next time. A bit of restraint would be nice." A little huffy, she presented her back to him. "My flashlight's in the middle compartment." Was that a snicker behind her? Was he laughing at her?

She turned around. Yes, it was laughter. "What's so funny?"

"Not funny. Surprising. You are. Well, maybe a tad funny."

She crossed her arms, having decided to stay miffed despite his laughter. "Explain."

"I thought you were a little mouse, but you roared like a lion."

Now, she grinned. She couldn't say why his look of approval meant something to her. "I did, didn't I? A lion. I like that. You can get my flashlight now." The zipper snarled open and then closed.

"Here." He nudged her with it. "Don't turn it on. Be prepared to use it as a weapon—which I have no doubt you will."

She took it and smiled. She loved this. He thought she was a lion.

He nudged her behind him, flicked on his light, and reached toward the ceiling.

"Do you think he's behind us?"

"There's no indication of a light of any kind."

"He has the night goggles."

"You have to have some light to use them, and it's way past dark in here."

"Couldn't we be furnishing the light for him?"

"At a distance, yes, but he'd have to turn on a light to see where he's walking." His light scaled the walls and floor and stopped on a sloping area. "This looks like a good spot to eat a few bites and rest. No more than a couple minutes." Luke dug into a compartment and pulled out a baggie as he cradled the walking stick in the crook of his arm. "How's the foot?"

"It hurts a little, but I can stand it. Hold this." She handed him her flashlight and rummaged for her sandwich.

"Your shoulder?" His mouth sounded full.

"It hurts, too, but I'm tough. Little, but tough." She took two bites. "I'm starving."

"Eat only a third."

Nodding, she watched him give Molly a big bite of food and then pack the rest away. She did the same. When the man said two minutes, the man meant two minutes.

A short distance later, he stopped and leaned over. "Look. The walkway ends right here." The light trailed over the smooth, ridged ledge. "Flowing water created this. We've been walking at a downward slope since we entered the cave, the path the water would have taken. Feel how smooth this is."

On her knees, she let him guide her hand to the spot. "Where does it go?"

"Right there, see? That's the bottom of the shaft. That's what? Eight feet? Hard to tell with little depth perception." He pulled something out of his pocket, dropped it. "Yep, penny says six feet or so. Molly and I will go first and make sure it's safe. If there's a problem, Molly won't let me go down. I'll secure the rope."

"Are you leaving it here?"

"Yes. We might need to get back up. I have two more in my pack."

He tied it, yanked on it. "Here's my flashlight. Use it and put that one in my right bottom pocket." He turned around. She put it away.

He reached for Molly and placed a vest on her, slid the rope through several rings, and slipped on his gloves.

He lowered Molly first and then slid down the rope. Sarah held the light on what they thought was a landing. Within seconds, Luke grunted and stomped. Molly barked and sniffed around.

Luke's grinning face lifted toward her. "Solid rock." He slipped off his backpack. "I need to look around. It'll only take a few seconds."

Gripping the rope, Sarah watched and waited and made herself *not* look over her shoulder at the darkness pressing against her back. She made a quick mental list: she would stay brave; she would be strong; she would pray a *lot*. And she might roar like a lion.

Light shined in her eyes. "We can keep going. Drop the light." He caught it. "Come on down when you're ready."

Gritting her teeth, she scooted to the edge. "I can't hold the rope. My shoulder still hurts. Get ready to catch me." She stepped off and landed in his arms.

"Gotcha! Piece of cake." He set her on her feet.

"Thank God." She leaned against the stone wall and sank to her bottom. It was such a relief to have solid wall at her back. Just past Luke's feet, the ceiling was lower. She looked up, shined her light on the ledge they'd just come from, and imagined seeing the sniper's head and his gaze on them. But nothing was there.

She took a deep breath, grateful for the reprieve. "Listen. Is that a waterfall?"

"The river that made this cave." Luke looked under the low ceiling. "Molly and I saw another shelf below us. About three feet down. We'll take a look, see where it goes." They disappeared. A thud. Molly barked once.

"Whoa." Luke's voice sounded muffled below her. "This room is huge. What I can see is absolutely gargantuan, the size of three football fields. Not many caves like this, but I've read about 'em."

She scooted to the edge and shined her light below. Only Luke's boots were visible. "Can we keep going?"

"Yeah. It's about four feet from the bottom. Push both our packs over and join us. There's a ledge where we can catch some Zs."

The packs landed with Sarah close behind.
"Hopefully, we'll find another way out soon. Let's get to that ledge."
"I am so ready for some sleep, Luke."

# FOUR

Sleep was out of the question.

Gertie Jansen glanced at her windup clock tick-tocking on her bedside table and groaned at the *1:53*. She wished to high heaven she hadn't seen that red truck parked over at the trailhead.

And because she had, she was wide awake. Easing the quilts off, she slid her old bones out of bed and her feet into her slippers. "How am I supposed to get any sleep with a hiker on the loose?"

She plucked her high-powered flashlight off the shelf, moved the stepladder to the kitchen sink and took the two steps up to the window. The flashlight clicked on. A sword of light sliced into the snowy night, landing on the red pickup now covered with seven inches of snow. The light moved past the wooden gate several yards down to a tree. What was that shape? A wheel? Two wheels?

"A bicycle," she muttered, shaking her head. "So, there's two morons over there."

Well, she couldn't do anything about it now. But come morning, she'd bundle up and get up to the phone at Alva's store and gas station and call Jim Banks at the Little Texas Search & Rescue. Sure wasn't the first time he'd have to rescue a lame-brained hiker, and it wouldn't be the last.

She stepped down, put away her light and stepladder, and headed for bed. She didn't figure on getting much sleep, if any. She was too worried about those hikers, out on a cold snowy night in the Colorado Rockies and not a single soul knowing where they were.

"Nincompoops, that's what hikers are," she mumbled and rolled onto her side, away from the ticking clock. Maybe it was time for her to buy herself a phone. That way, come morning, she could just pick it up and call Jim Banks instead of having to trudge through this heavy spring snow to Alva's store.


"Another fatality," Jim Banks mumbled to no one in particular at Search & Rescue as he slapped the paperwork on his cluttered desk. It went without saying it was senseless. Another hiker, walking right past a large sign announcing a trail was closed.

He reached for his umpteenth cup of coffee, realized it was cold too late and, without so much as a grimace, swallowed it. He dutifully set his cup on the Elvis coaster his secretary, Elva Lee, gave all the rangers to use. "I'm his namesake," she'd said the morning she had set them out. "Mama's crush on Elvis is never ending. Today's his birthday, and she bought these for all of us."

As if on cue, the thick wooden door opened and slammed shut. His secretary, Elva Lee Ward, stomped her feet. "Brrr! It's cold out there, boys!"

Jim looked up and studied her. *Well, well, well, if she wasn't losing some weight there.* She shook out her short, curly brown hair and fluffed it in the back like she always did, with those long, fake purple nails Jodee put on her about three months ago. Her typing was pretty good before that, but now she hunted and pecked like she'd never seen a keyboard before.

Her short legs were covered in thick black tights that ended in clunky, brown hiking boots with lacy pink socks peeking over the tops. Her red sweater hung clean down to her knees and had what looked like pink toilet paper wads clinging for dear life at the hem. Elva Lee called them her spring flowers.

She walked to the dual coffee pots and switched off the burner under the empty pot. "More coffee, Jim?"

He flashed her a guilty smile. "That'd be fine. 'Preciate it."

"Where did they find those two hikers?"

"Near the split between Devil's Gulch and the Branch cutoff. People today don't know how to read." He sighed. "At least one of them is still alive."

Lying in her sleeping bag in the dark, Sarah let herself imagine she was camping near a lake with the sun about to appear above the mountains; fish jumped eagerly in the mountain lake; early birds flew overhead; a deer stood nearby, watching them.

But none of that was true. They were in an underground cave system without any sign of an opening out of here.

Beside her, Molly whined.

"Come here, girl." Sarah lifted the corner of her sleeping bag, and the dog settled next to her. "Tell you what, Molly. We'll stick together, you and I. Mr. Pushy Giant here can fend for himself. He's a big ol' brute and monsters never go after the big guys, do they?"

The blackness rumbled with a deep chuckle. "I've dealt with a couple monsters in my lifetime."

"Humph. We don't believe that, do we, girl?" Sarah tugged Molly closer and burrowed her face in the dog's neck.

"Third grade. Mickey Zamora. Jumped me every day and stole the sandwich out of my lunch bag."

"Now that's scary."

"He was in fifth grade and big, and I was scrawny. I wanted my brothers to help me out, but I couldn't bring myself to tell them a bully was getting the better of me."

"What did you do?"

"I hit a mean growing spurt that summer. He never bothered me again. 'Course, it also helped that my seven brothers were all taller than me. The tallest, Mac, is six-five."

"You have seven brothers?"

"Six now. My brother Joey died when he was sixteen."

"Oh, I'm so sorry, Luke. How awful. How long ago was that?"

"Years now. About nineteen. I was nine when it happened."

"Who's the second monster?"

Luke was silent for a moment. "He murdered my father fifteen months ago."

"Murdered?" Pain wrapped around her heart at his words. She couldn't imagine that kind of wound. "Luke, oh, my goodness. What happened if, y'know, you want to talk about it?"

"My father was coming home from a cattle auction. He pulled over to the side of the road to find the radio station where my brother Kyle was being interviewed. It was dark. He was out in the middle of nowhere. A man walks right up to him and shoots him, point blank, between the eyes." He sighed. "No clues. No idea who did it. Nothing."

"I'm so sorry." They had something in common, then. They had both suffered at the hands of evil people.

The throbbing quiet surrounding her was soothed by the distant murmur of the waterfall. Molly lifted her head and rested her chin on Sarah's arm.

"Luke?"

"Umm?"

"Are you afraid down here?"

"Not afraid. Cautious."

"Does anything scare you?"

He didn't answer for a few moments. And when he did, he simply said, "Yes." Another few seconds, and he added, "Someone trying to hurt my family or someone I care about."

Although he couldn't see her, she nodded and stroked Molly's head.

"Like my dad. I wasn't there to help him."

"Would you have been able to save him?"

"He wouldn't have pulled over to find the radio station if I'd been with him. None of it would have happened."

"You think."

"I know."

"Well, if this man was intent on killing your father, he'd have found another way."

"I've thought about that. He had to have targeted Dad. When Dad pulled over, he was in the middle of nowhere. Just a spot to pull over. My father didn't see lights or hear a car drive up behind him. The man just appeared at the driver's side and shot him. My brother Kyle heard the whole thing."

"How awful for him."

"Yeah. So, you're probably right. It would've happened anyway."

"Then you can't blame yourself for his death."

The words hung between them. All was silent except for the tranquil sounds of the waterfall below them.

"Thanks for that, Sarah. I needed to hear it."

She thought he turned toward her but couldn't be sure. He didn't say anything else. "I think I'd go mad in this blackness."

"It's easy to get disoriented." His sleeping bag rustled, and she assumed he sat up. Light appeared and, in a few quick strokes, he transformed his flashlight into a lantern and set it near her feet. "Did you sleep, Sarah?"

"A little bit. Too many creepy things to worry about."

He looked over at her. "What's your last name?"

It seemed silly not to tell him. "Morgan. Sarah Ann Morgan."

"How old are you?"

In the faint light, his eyes seemed black. "Twenty-five. How old are you?"

"Twenty-eight. Twenty-nine in July."

Their gazes locked, and her heart thumped heavily. It was no secret why. Luke McKenzie was undoubtedly the most beautiful man she'd ever seen. Tall, tanned, thick black hair, incredible blue eyes, square jaw, and well-built, as if he worked hard every day.

She looked away. This trip was about pulling herself together, not falling for some gorgeous hunk she'd known only a few hours and wouldn't know much longer. She was on vacation. He was on vacation. This time together in the underworld would end, and she'd go home. As would he.

Rolling to her knees, she folded her sleeping bag.

"Where are you from, Sarah?"

"Riadon, in western Kansas. Where are you from?"

"Mole's Bench, Texas."

She snickered. "I'd be embarrassed to tell anyone I was from any place named Mole's Bench." She tightened a strap.

"Has character. Anyone pining for you back in Riadon, Kansas?"

"Pining?"

"Missing you."

The question surprised her. "That's too personal."

"Being alone with me in an underground cave system isn't? But you're right. It's none of my business if you don't want it to be."

Surprised and a little disappointed that he'd given up so quickly, she tossed the bag toward her pack. As she watched him roll up his sleeping bag, she realized that she liked him. She knew from experience that some men were capable of horrible acts against someone they could dominate physically. But, like her father, others would never consider hurting a woman. She thought Luke was in the latter category. All he had done was help her, protect her, and try to keep her safe. Maybe he was someone worth getting to know.

She stood, brushed off her pants, and picked up her daypack. "What does one do in Mole's Bench, Texas?"

"Not much," he chuckled as he clipped his sleeping bag to his pack. "But if you're asking about me, I'm foreman of my brother's ranch."

"Is it a big ranch?"

"Sixty-three thousand acres, give or take." He hoisted his pack onto his shoulder and flashed the light into the center of the room below them. A thin, luminescent-green stream meandered through the rock sculptures.

"Do you think that water's drinkable, Luke?"

"I wouldn't use it to brush my teeth."

"I need a bio break."

"A what?"

"The call of nature."

"Oh. You can find a spot down there. You ready to head out?"


At Little Texas Search & Rescue, Elva Lee pushed up her bulky sleeves, set the coffee pot under the faucet, and turned on the water. She'd gotten to know Jim Banks well in the few years she'd worked at S&R as his secretary. And today, he was in one of his moods.

As the head of S&R, he took it to heart when they were unable to save someone. She'd learned a long time ago not to say anything to him when he was moody. She noticed the water pressure was low again, but now was not a good time to mention it.

His chair scraped on the hardwood floor as he stood. She moved over a little, so he could pour out his cold coffee and set the cup in the stainless-steel sink without touching her. Then he headed for the window and stood there, watching the snow falling.

She sighed. It was a disgrace what his wife, Renee, had done to him, running off like that almost a year ago now without so much as a word when she left and not a word since. How could she do that to the very best man God ever created? He seemed to have gotten his legs back under him again and was—

Jim turned around and caught her staring at him. She fumbled with turning off the water.

Scowling, he grabbed his cap and tugged his coat off one of the elk horns on the wall by his desk. "I'll be back," he muttered and slammed the door behind him.

Elva Lee didn't take it personally. Finding a victim dead was hard on Jim. She jumped as the phone rang and finished counting her scoops before she hurried across the wooden floor to catch the phone just before the voicemail picked up.

"Why, hello there, Miss Gertie. What are you doing out in this wicked weather?"

"It's business, Elva Lee. I need to speak to Jim. Is he available?"

"He just left. Let me see if I can catch him. Are you at Alva's store?"

"I am."

"Stay there. I'll have him call you in just a few minutes."


Jim put his truck in reverse and backed up. What was wrong with him lately? Elva Lee Ward had worked with him for four years, and he'd never even looked at her, and now he was noticing she'd lost weight? Oh, yeah, he'd also noticed her hair, her nails, her boots, her pink socks, and those silly flowers on her sweater.

He was just lonely.

No one could understand how much it hurt him when Renee ran out on him, leaving him with everything broken in his life. The questions had eaten him alive. Why did she leave? Where did she go? Was the baby his or another man's? Had everything they'd lived been a lie? All the teasing, the loving, the plans, the little one?

Those questions had gnawed on him for a year now, and in the midst of all that living, breathing pain, he could only see where he'd failed her.

He slammed on his brakes when his cell phone rang. "Banks."

Harriet and Henry Flagstone drove by in their like-new '69 Thunderbird. Henry waved, looked up at the thick falling snow and shook his head at Jim. Nodding in understanding, Jim waved back and listened as Elva Lee told him about Miss Gertie's phone call.

"I'll call her at Alva's." He hung up and did just that. "Hey, Alva. This is Jim Banks. Is Miss Gertie standing there, waiting on a call from me?"

"She sure is. Here ya go, Miss Gertie."

"Jim?" She told him about the two hikers who'd left a truck and a bicycle at the Bear Camp trailhead.

"I'll go on over there, check out that truck, and see if I can figure out who it belongs to. 'Preciate you letting me know, Miss Gertie."

His next call was to Elva Lee. "Get ahold of Tommy and let him know about those two hikers. We can't do much in this weather. I'll check in with you when I get to the trailhead."

He jiggled the sliding bar of the heater. It'd been gasping for breath the last couple weeks, but spring was just around the corner, and he'd put off getting it fixed. Any one of the hundreds of people who had taken his Safety First seminar through the years would be surprised that he'd let the heater go. "Now, Jim," they'd say, "don't I recall you saying that being prepared for bad weather is being prepared to stay alive?"

And his wife, Renee, would have pointed a finger at him, dipped her head, sassily raised her brows, and said something like, "Jimmy, you wouldn't want us to have to rescue you, now, would ja, honey?"

"Well, great," he mumbled against set teeth as he shook off Renee like she'd shook him off. He slammed on his brakes at the blinking red light, jerked his head both ways, and headed down the road toward Miss Gertie's dirt road.

The thick, wet snow fell in straight lines. Jim turned the wipers up and hoped to high heaven those hikers at Bear Camp Trail had had sense enough to bring warm clothes with them.

"Look." Luke shined the light down a walkway. "Another corridor. The draft is strong. I'm pretty sure we're close to the other opening."

Sarah nudged past him and gazed into the tunnel. "I didn't think we'd ever find it." Her voice wobbled. "Hours and hours of searching. Every muscle in my body hurts. Oh, thank you, Lord, for showing us the way."

Even though Luke knew she was close to falling apart, those words said more about her strength than any weakness. "Do you want to go on or stop here to eat?"

"I want out of here. I don't do well all cooped up, especially in the company of crawling things."

"Then let's away, my friend." He bowed, grandly swept a hand toward the opening, and handed her the walking stick.

Shaking her head, she flicked a thumb at him. "No way, Jose.' You first.

Monsters don't go after the big guys, remember?"

# FIVE

Twenty-nine years ago, Little Texas welcomed Lulu Banks into this world, kicking and screaming, and today, she was kicking and screaming to get out.

Ever since her husband Ray Baines had died in a car wreck a year ago, she'd been itching to spread her independent, red-tipped wings, *finally!*, and fly to Denver. Ray had hated big towns, so they'd never ventured past Willow Falls, thirty miles south of Little Texas, a bigger town but no less a sinkhole.

Well, Ray was gone, and, oh! she missed him! But she was itching—she told her best friend Myra Simms, *literally* itching—to get on down to Denver.

Only she couldn't drive. She had never gotten her license. *Just consider me your personal chauffeur, Lulu,* Ray had said, and she had. Working out back, fixing anything with a motor in it, Ray would wipe his hands on a work towel, grin real big, reach for his cap and say, "Come on, woman. You got your green heels on. Must be time to cruise."

She'd laugh and he'd open the driver's door and she'd slide in and wait on him to start the truck so she could listen to country music on a CD.

"High time you got your license," Myra decreed yesterday. She'd cupped her lighter, drew in a breath of smoke, and popped the lighter closed. "You can march yourself down to that driver's license office, take that test, and drive to Denver today." Her big loop earrings with the tiny turquoise beads dangled and jumped when she shook her head and gestured with fingers holding a cigarette. "No man around now to tie you down."

"But I don't know where Denver is, and I can't read a map. Besides, Ray didn't tie me down. I tied myself down, and I don't know why. Come with me, Myra? You been to Denver a lot of times, haven't cha?"

"Well, yeah, Lulu, but Fred would kill me if I went with you alone. You know how he gets when I'm out of his sight. That man is a jealous bean."

So, in front of a warm cozy fire, with the television blaring, Lulu sat in Ray's favorite recliner with her two-inch green heels on, her freshly cut-colored-and-curled hair, waiting for Myra to come pick her up to go shopping in Estes Park.

With her foot wiggling, she decided tomorrow, yessiree, tomorrow she'd get that license and shake this town lickety-split—at least for a day or two.

One minute later, she was dead.

"Rosie," a voice whispered in her ear. A finger lifted one of her green earrings as a tear fell onto her cheek. "Why won't you stay dead, Rosie?" Weeping filled the room. "Why in blue blazes won't you stay dead?"

At Search & Rescue, Jim checked his watch when Elva Lee breezed in a little after one, holding a brown paper sack from Colson's. When she kicked the door shut with her booted foot, keys on the bronze deer-head key holder above the light switch rattled.

"I want everybody to know—" She huffed as she set the sack on her desk, opened her middle desk drawer, and dropped her keys in. "—that I'm on a plateau with my diet. I hate to admit it, but I may be a little difficult to get along with. Forewarned is forearmed, all right?" She hung up her coat and scarf.

Tommy Blakesly was the first to look up. "Wuh, Elva Lee, why are you on a diet, honey? You look pretty as a peach tree as it is." He grinned at Buddy Washburn, who winked at him and said, "Does this mean you're not gonna get us any more donuts on Monday mornings?"

She glared at them. "You just laugh and joke about it. You'll see. This diet's all about eating protein and veggies and staying away from refined carbohydrates. They're the enemy—"

"Who is?" Tommy stuffed a piece of chewing gum into his mouth to hide his silly grin.

Jim was just about ready to throw the lot of them out the door.

"Why, the bad carbohydrates, Tommy. Haven't you been listening to me the last few weeks? They're the enemy. Good carbs. Bad carbs. And the bad carbs just don't sit well in some people's bodies."

"They seem to be sitting okay in yours."

*Well, great. Now you've done it.* Jim turned his back on Elva Lee and put his nose in his paperwork, wishing Tommy had kept his big, fat mouth shut.

He didn't have to turn around to know that the silence pumping in the room had everything to do with tears filling Elva Lee's eyes. Lips are probably quivering about right now, too. Jim stacked his papers, pulled out the bottom drawer of his file cabinet, yanked out a folder, and stuffed the papers into it.

She sniffed, and Jim wanted to groan.

Instead, he slammed the file cabinet drawer, turned around, cut his throat with a stiff hand, and jerked his head toward the door. He'd clearly said "Get out!" as if he'd said the words.

Tommy got the message. He took his skinny self outside, with Buddy and his pot belly following close behind.

What was Jim supposed to do now, for Pete's sake?

Elva Lee pulled out a Kleenex from the wooden box on the edge of her desk, sniffed a couple times, and sat in her squawking chair.

"Elva Lee," Jim ventured. "None of us need those donuts. You just take care of yourself now. That's what's important."

"Thank you, Jim." She neatly folded, tucked, and straightened that brown paper sack as if somebody's life depended on it. She slipped it between her desk and the file cabinet. "What did you find out about those hikers? Their truck still out there?"

Better keep his eyes off her and study the notes he'd made or he might find himself stepping outside to teach Tommy some manners. "Found the registration. Luke McKenzie out of Mole's Bench, Texas. I know the family well."

"Luke? It's been a while since he's been here."

"A couple of years. Man, we go way back. A lot of good memories growing up with that family. I placed a call to Mac, his younger brother. A woman said he was with a mare about to foal and would call me as soon as he could." He checked the wall clock. "That was an hour ago."

Elva Lee opened a bag of something and chomped on it. "I hope we find Luke alive."

"And the woman."

"A woman's with him?"

His gaze connected with hers. "If that bike's any indication," he muttered and turned back around, wondering how in the world they were going to find them in all this snow.

Grateful to be sitting, Sarah took a bite of her sandwich and leaned back against the wall of rock. They'd struggled through tight spots, squeezes, shimmied under low-hanging ceilings, and walked over loose rock for three hours before they stopped to eat. She was famished.

Closing her eyes, she enjoyed the quiet until she surprised herself with an unexpected question. "Is there anyone waiting for you back on your ranch?"

"Not on *my* ranch. Mine's two thousand acres, and I'm in the process of building my house and outbuildings right now. No one waiting for me there or anywhere." An impish grin crossed Luke's mouth. "Why do you ask?"

"Just curious."

He tore off a bite of his sandwich and tossed it to Molly. "Who hurt you?"

Sarah lowered her eyes. It was none of his business. "I don't know what you mean."

"Yeah, you do."

Turning away from him as well as the question, she stroked Molly's head. She didn't want him to know any more about her than was absolutely necessary to get out of this place.

"What do you do for a living in Riadon, Sarah?"

"I'm a glass artist."

"You mean, the long pole, bubbles, and dripping glass kind?"

"Yes." She took a bite of her sandwich, avoiding his eyes.

"Impressive. What do you do with your works?"

"I sell them in my shop."

"Umm. I'll have to come see that shop of yours some day."

"You'd be welcome, although I wouldn't think you'd take the time or trouble to come and look at glass." She couldn't tell if he was joking or serious, but she needed to thwart any expectations of a relationship outside this cave.

"No trouble." With grinning eyes that told her he knew exactly what she was thinking, he stuffed his sandwich bag into a side pocket and zipped it closed. "Let's go, Sarah. Time's a-wasting."

Jim came out of the supply room and plopped into his chair as the phone rang. It was just about quitting time.

"Search & Rescue. This is Elva Lee."

For some reason he couldn't explain, he spun around in his office chair to watch her. She covered the mouthpiece and nudged the phone at Jim. "It's Andrew Jackson, Jim. Line one."

He chuckled. His parents named both their sons after presidents. His older brother, A.J., knew everything there was to know about the seventh president. Sibling rivalry caused Jim to study up on his namesake, James Madison, the fourth president. They'd enjoyed verbal wrestling as kids, spitting facts about each president at each other to see who would win the I-know-more-than-you-do game. Usually, A.J. won.

Jim picked up the phone, leaned back in his chair, and rocked as he said, "Hey, A.J. Whatcha know good?" A long bout of silence followed his greeting. "A.J.?"

"You need to come over to Lulu's house."

Jim stopped rocking. "Why?"

Leaning forward, he rested his elbow on his desk, eased his head onto his hand, and listened, unbelievingly, as his brother, the chief of police here in Little Texas, told him their cousin was missing—or worse.

Jim squeezed his eyes shut. Took a deep breath. Blew it out.

With a hand splayed over his face, he said, "All right. Be right there." He hung up.

Without saying a word, he stood, reached for his hat and coat, and stalked out the door.


Tilted forward to keep the pack from pulling her back onto the dirt floor, Sarah waddled under the low ceiling.

Panting, she flicked her light on Luke, who was waddling, too. She wanted to laugh at the ridiculous posture but couldn't bring herself to make the effort. Her knees cramped, her back ached, and her ankle pounded a steady rhythm of pain. "Do you think he's behind us?"

"Following?"

"Yes."

"No. He may be at the other opening, waiting for us."

"I'd actually thought of that. Are you ready to rest?"

"And stretch a bit." He shined the light down the path. "Wait. It looks like the tunnel's opening up. Leave your pack on."

Another twenty feet, and the low ceiling disappeared.

"Ah, this is nice." She stood and stretched.

Luke shined the light to the right of them. "There's another room. C'mon." It was small, about the size of seven or eight stalls. "Look at that jagged fissure." It looked like a giant had stabbed the wall with a serrated knife and ripped it open, going down and to the left about three feet. It ended about chest-level on Luke. "I wonder if anyone's ever ventured inside that."

"It's big enough, but I sure wouldn't. I'd be too claustrophobic. I need to take a bio. Then, let's sleep a little. I'm exhausted."

Luke shined the light behind her. "Look. Back there. A hole large enough for all three of us to sleep."

"A cave within a cave." She turned on her light. "I'll be back."

When she returned, they both took the time to pull out their sleeping bags to rest. Molly snuggled with Sarah. In seconds, gentle snoring from Luke helped her to fall into a deep sleep.

She awoke to a hand gripping her mouth!

Her nose was stuffy, and she could hardly breathe! She tried to shake off the hand and gripped its huge wrist, feeling a warm breath as a whispered, "Shhh," sounded in her ear.

Luke. She almost relaxed but tensed again as she heard it.

Singing.

*Singing?* She quickly nodded. Her heart raced as Luke took her hand, squeezed it, and let it go.

A lustrous, rowdy song about mommy kissing Santa Claus echoed in the distance. The voice was getting louder as it headed in their direction.

*What in the world?* Sarah leaned forward. Molly nudged her arm. Behind her, Luke whispered a "Shhh" to Molly.

The loud tenor voice was now wishing them a Merry Christmas.

A jerking beam of light appeared. As it rounded a corner, Sarah heard a dragging sound. Her breath caught. Luke reached for her hand and squeezed it.

Across the wide expanse, into the great room, came a man. Or Sarah supposed it to be a man by the voice since she couldn't see anything but the laser-like shaft of light floating around the room.

The dragging stopped.

The singing turned to humming as the light moved behind a huge boulder. In a matter of seconds, it re-appeared. A click sounded, and a large circular light popped on. It shined on the jagged crack they'd seen earlier.

Sarah began to shake and covered her mouth in case she whimpered. Luke tightened his grip on her other hand. She clearly got the message: *be quiet.*

The flashlight bounded behind the boulder again and came out a few seconds later. Another circular light appeared. *Like stage lights.* The man moved behind the big rock, reappeared, and placed a three-rung stepladder under the crevice.

*What is going on?*

Molly's wet nose nudged Sarah's elbow, and she jumped. Luke patted Molly, then took Sarah's hand again and kneaded it. She was grateful for the comfort he offered.

In silence, the man disappeared into the blackness behind the lights.

The dragging began again.

It stopped.

Sarah held her breath as the man stepped into the lights and climbed up to the top rung of the ladder. He leaned into the crevice. "Hello? Anybody down there?" Then he laughed and jumped to the ground.

After a few moments, he moved into the lights again with a gunnysack draped over his shoulder. Something heavy was in it because the man struggled to get up to the top rung of the stepladder. Then he hoisted the bag onto the lip of the crevice and pushed. A woman's leg with a green high heel shoe on her foot caught on the edge of the fissure. The green shoe fell to the ground as he forced the leg into the hole. The man shoved the woman down the fissure as he worked the sack off her.

Then he jumped down, picked up the shoe, laughed as he threw it into the crevice, and said, "Oh, Rosie. You're such a kidder."

He meticulously folded the sack and tucked it under his arm.

*Oh, God.* Sarah covered her mouth. *Oh, God.*

Suddenly lightheaded, she felt her hand slip to her lap. She'd fainted only once in her life... and knew... she was—

Jim couldn't remember a time he'd dreaded anything as much as he did walking up the sidewalk to his cousin Lulu's house. Where was she?

In the quiet, he rested his foot on the bottom step of the porch and tugged on the front of his cap, just for something to do with his hands. So many memories here. The porch swing where he and Renee had kissed for the first time. He used to smile at the memory. Now it only made him sad.

In his mind's eye, Lulu's husband, Ray, came out of the house, the screen door slamming shut behind him.

*"Ray," Lulu hollered, "you better catch that door, mister!"*

*He winked at Jim. "Ain't she the cutest thing?"*

Like as not when Ray spotted him walking toward their house, he would have said, "Well, cousin, you *do* remember where we live. Sit it down, friend, and fill my ear with some news."

Instead, Jim's grim-faced older brother, A.J., opened the screen door and held it with the toe of his scuffed work boot. He avoided Jim's eyes. "Come on in, then, and have a look-see. Make sure I haven't missed anything."

Jim slipped his hands into disposable gloves. He'd been a policeman for six years in Denver. Everybody in Little Texas wondered why he'd come back home after he'd hit it big in the city, but Jim wouldn't say, and nobody asked. Well, nobody asked *him*. There'd been plenty of asking going on behind his back, but he'd never told anyone outside his parents and A.J. that Renee simply didn't like living in Denver. They were trying to get pregnant, and she didn't want to bring up a child in a big city. That was enough for Jim. They'd moved back home.

His brother, A.J., had wanted Jim on the police force with him, but he had already decided to take over Search & Rescue. But when he could, he helped his brother out.

He caught the closing door as A.J. went inside first. Jim stopped on the threshold. "I smell blood."

A.J. nodded toward the chair nearby. "Ray's recliner. Got samples off already. You know Lulu liked to sit there."

Jim took two steps inside and spotted the blood. He closed his eyes and took a deep breath to fight the sudden nausea. "God help her." He looked around the room. "Don't recall Lulu ever being so neat."

"Myra said she was itching to get her license and head down to Denver, so she went on a cleaning spree. Lulu said she just had too much energy and wanted to make good use of it. They planned to go to Estes Park today, but Lulu was gone when Myra got here."

Jim listened to his brother and continued searching, wishing his cousin was here to visit with him.

"Myra said Lulu had her nails and hair done earlier down at Jodee's Salon."

Jim walked to the window overlooking the carport, touched the lace curtain, and drew it back. He remembered Lulu drawing back this curtain when Ray would pull into the carport. She'd announce, "He's here," as if Jim hadn't heard that souped-up engine himself.

"Did she get the license?" It seemed strange to see the riding mower sitting all alone in the big carport Ray built onto the house for his truck. Ray had always been good with his hands.

"No. She decided to get it tomorrow and drive to Denver where a good time was waiting on her, according to Myra."

"Alone?"

"It doesn't sound like Lulu, does it? Pipe dreams, I'm thinking."

Jim stood in the doorway to Lulu's bedroom. The bed was ruthlessly made, pillows piled high, not a speck of dust to be found on the headboard or the dresser or the chest of drawers—as if she had known they'd be in her house later looking at everything.

Ray's rifle stood in the corner where it always stood, probably loaded if the open shell box on the windowsill meant anything. His slick waders rested beside his rifle, folded over.

Jim could see Ray grinning like a 'possum when he caught himself a big one a little before dawn out at Palmer's Creek. That last trip, the summer before he died, was crystal clear to Jim, like it had happened yesterday. Gripping that bass's mouth, holding it up as if the King of all creation was watching and very proud of him.

Jim poked his head in the bathroom; nothing personal on the counter.

Voices echoed from in here.

*"Get your own beer, Ray! I'm putting on my face."*

*"Laws, woman, don't let me interrupt you doing that. I'm partial to a woman with a face!"*

Ray would laugh and Lulu would come out to the hallway and point her eyelash thing at him and try to look mad, but she ended up laughing instead.

*Laughter.* That's what Jim remembered most about this house.

He stepped into the kitchen and stood still, listening to days gone by. His Aunt Charlotte saying to him and Lulu, "I swanny, you two are like two peas in a pod. Now get on outside, both of you, 'fore I make use of all that energy and put you both to work." Maybe that's where Lulu got the notion to work off her excess energy.

Jim sighed, opened the back door, and looked through the snow-sprayed screen door. Footprints in the snow. "A.J."

"I saw 'em."

"Where do they go?"

"To the road. Could have been the milk man. I'm checking on his route. You know Lulu loved her whole milk and ice cream."

Standing in the cold air, nose almost touching the screen door, he studied the tree in the yard, the clothesline, the storage shed. "Why Lulu? Who would ever want to hurt her? She was so tiny, wouldn't—couldn't—hurt a fly. Just like Renee. Tiny just like Renee."

"No bigger'n a minute," A.J. mumbled behind him.

"You know what? When Buddy Washburn's wife left him out of the blue a couple years back, I felt sorry for him, but I didn't know what it felt like. I sure didn't know what to say to him. I got a little smug, figuring Renee'd never do that to me. But she did."

Jim shook his head. "And now Lulu. Same pattern. Car—or truck—gone. No sign of a struggle. Clothes packed. Her gone, but nothing making sense." He turned around and faced his brother and the truth. "Maybe Renee and the others didn't leave. Maybe there's a pattern here that's just come to light."

He looked at the old plastic lace doily sitting under the big clay frog he'd made for Lulu in third grade, now stuffed with ivy coming out its back. Leaves curled around the base, so its pink-painted toenails were hidden.

"Maybe they didn't just up and leave one day." His gaze locked on his brother's. "Maybe they were all taken—or worse. Let's get out of here, meet at the station, and try to figure out what's going on."

"I'm heading to Casey's home to tell her about her sister being missing. I'll meet you in a bit."

"I'll go with you."

Sarah squirmed. Darkness surrounded her and lay heavy on her skin. She jerked when she remembered the green shoe on the woman. She tried to sit up, but arms were around her—Luke's arms. Something touched her ear. "Shhhh," he whispered.

In the pounding silence, nothing moved. Sarah couldn't stand the loneliness or the absolute quiet or the blackness anymore. She turned, pulled Luke's head down, and whispered in his ear. "Is he gone?"

A long pause, then, "Yes."

"I could have ended up like her."

"What do you mean?"

"I was traumatized, almost raped. He insisted on it being dark."

"*This* man?"

"No." She shook her head. "I don't know. A stranger. He broke into my home."

"The nightmare."

Nodding, she sniffed and made herself continue, to get it out in the open. "My roommates came home. He heard them and ran. The police came. They told me I was lucky, that he was probably the serial rapist and murderer that had beaten, molested, and killed two women the previous two nights." She shook her head and cried silently.

Luke's arms tightened around her. "He beat you?"

Leaning back against his chest, she nodded.

"I'm so sorry, Sarah."

She couldn't speak for a few heartbeats. "They never found him. I've struggled with getting my life back. That's the reason I'm here in Colorado—to try to find myself, to get over what he did to me. Twice."

"Twice?"

She nodded and told him about the second break-in.

"You think this man could be him?"

"I don't know. I didn't get a good look at him in the dark."

For the first time, the darkness didn't frighten her. Luke's arms were around her.

His head rested against hers. "You'll never get over it, but you will learn how to deal with it. Hopefully, it won't have the hold on you that it does now. You'll get stronger."

She realized she was lying back against him, in his arms, comfortably talking, without worrying that he was a man. It was... okay. Like her father. A friend.

"I know about loss, Sarah. I'm learning to live without my dad. It's not easy. I have a long way to go yet."

"I don't know what I'd do if I lost my father like that."

They were quiet for a few moments.

"This poor woman. I wonder who she was."

"I don't know. We'll report all of this to the police." He helped her up, essentially ending the conversation. He turned on his light and stood. "We'll be out of here soon."

Sarah didn't want to think about the crevice in the wall and what lay at the bottom of it. "Luke. I-I've felt God here with me, with us, ever since we came in here. Even when that monster was in here."

"It doesn't seem right that He'd be in such a place at such a time." His voice was quiet, reverent.

"But He was. He is. How do we explain that?"

"We're here. He's here."

She nodded. It was that simple.

"We've given this man plenty of lead time, Sarah. It won't be long before we're up top."

"And the sniper welcomes us to another nightmare."

"We'll find out when we get there."

## SIX

Jim drove to the office. He dreaded telling Elva Lee that her best friend's sister was missing, but when he arrived, she already knew. She was crying at her desk.

He set a box of Kleenex beside her. "Here, Elva Lee."

She took one and wiped her face and then started crying again.

Jim's head hurt. He watched Elva Lee fall apart and wanted to fall apart, too, and let somebody else handle this.

He sighed. He was out at Lulu's just two days ago, having supper with her. Both of them had lost their spouses. They'd always been close, but they'd gotten closer over this last year. Lulu saw to it that Jim ate with her at least twice a week; she'd included A.J. after Penny kicked him out. Then, they'd return the favor by taking her out to eat at Penny's Bar & Grill twice a week for supper.

"Elva Lee, it's time for you to go home. You can have the day off."

"I want to stay. It's my job. I might be able to help."

She tugged three Kleenex out so quickly, he was sure they had to be connected. She pressed them over her eyes as her shoulders shook. Her nails looked like spikes growing out of the tissues. He couldn't for the life of him figure out why she'd had them put on.

"Why would anyone want to hurt Lulu, Jim?"

"I don't know, but I have to get back to the station, and I'd like to know you were at home or at your mama's or wherever you need to be." Her green eyes flicked to his, and he wanted to shake that little body of hers and make her go home, because she didn't know what he'd already figured out about the killer's fetish for small women.

"I'll stay right here and do my job." She threw the tissues into the wastebasket at her feet, reached for the ringing phone, and cleared her throat. "Search & Rescue, this is Elva Lee." She listened for a moment, and then her face crumbled. "Oh, Mama."

"Great." Jim told Tommy to get her somewhere safe and left.

Luke approached the soft glow of light emanating from above them in a maze of rock and roots. "I think I see sky and clouds."

"Thank God! I can't get out of here soon enough."

He shined his light up. "See that ledge? There, just below those roots. That's where we're headed. Ready?"

"I'm right behind you."

Luke picked up Molly and climbed to the ledge. He could hear the wind above him. He'd bet the farm it was cold and bitter. It was getting chillier the closer they climbed to the opening. "Almost there."

He crawled up through a root tunnel, shoving Molly ahead of him. "How in the world did he get the woman down this way?" He grunted as he climbed to the last level and poked his head above ground in thick brush. "Spring storm left a couple feet of snow." He shoved Molly topside and then followed her. Turning a three-sixty in the soft morning light, he said, "No one's about." He straddled the opening.

"Any sign of the killer?"

"Drag marks. A few footprints. They head up a small rise. Looks like car lights on the other side of the rise. Let's hope he didn't plan a welcoming party for us. Take my hand. I'll pull you up."

He lifted her out.

"How long were we in there?"

"Sun's rising. What time is it?"

She glanced at her watch. "A little after seven."

"Then, about thirty-six hours. Come on. We have enough light to see. Don't use a flashlight. I don't want to attract any attention."

They gave the drag marks a wide berth. When they topped the hill, twin beams from a van shone on a woman and a man standing in the parking lot. Luke and Sarah walked toward the van until Sarah placed a hand on his arm.

"Luke."

A low growl came from Molly.

"Give me those keys, Matthew Brandon Patterson. You're on restriction from driving for three days. I don't have time to teach you to drive and then you treat me like I'm the dirt under your feet."

In the bright lights, the spikes in young Patterson's hair swayed in the breeze, losing the fight to stay poised and erect and utterly cool.

Lifted brows and rolling eyes indicated Matthew Brandon Patterson was trying to decide whether to obey the woman in front of him. *His mother,*

Luke guessed by his youthfulness and her tone.

"Now." For emphasis, the woman jabbed her already-extended flat hand toward the young man and pinched her lips.

Matthew Brandon Patterson held up the keys, jiggled them, and dropped them above his mother's hand. They didn't make it, though. If she'd wanted to catch them, she would have had to move her hand to the left and from the look in the gaze mercilessly piercing her son even as the keys fell, she wasn't about to.

They landed on the snow-covered road, muffled in the snow. *Oh, man, is he in for it now.*

"Pick them up." An underlying growl accompanied the words and, once again, Matthew Brandon Patterson stood still, staring at her as if he was deciding whether or not to mind her.

"Four days."

Still he didn't budge.

"Five days."

"Ah, Mom. You're being ridiculous!"

Mom didn't bat an eye. "Six."

"Okay, okay. Stop counting. Here are your stupid keys."

"Seven."

His hand disappeared in the snow. He held up the keys, shook the snow off them, and then slapped them onto Mom's hand. Even from this distance, Luke could tell that hurt Mom's hand.

"Eight."

"Jeez, Mom, you're out of control. Get a grip, okay?"

"Nine."

The young man threw up his hands and stalked around the van to the passenger side. He slammed the door.

When the woman snapped her head in Luke's direction, Luke cleared his throat and stepped back.

"Oh." She flapped a hand at him. "I only eat fifteen-year-old boys learning to drive for breakfast. You look a little too old for my taste."

Luke smiled. "Do you know my mother? I think she wrote the script you just rehearsed, and quite flawlessly, I might add."

"We've practiced it so many times, we have our lines down." The woman looked at Sarah, then Luke. "Do you need some help?"

"If you have a cell phone and would dial 9-1-1 for us, we'd sure appreciate it."

The woman's eyes widened as her gaze quickly swept over Sarah. "Are you okay? Is anyone hurt?"

Luke shifted his backpack. "We're both fine. We just need to report a crime to the police. Could we use your phone?"

"Of course." She reached into her pocket and punched the numbers. "Here," she said, shoving the phone toward Luke.

A.J. and Jim walked down the steps of Lulu's house when A.J.'s phone rang. "Hello? Well, well, about time you checked in with us, buddy. Everything okay with you?" He turned toward Jim and listened, and then he frowned, shook his head, and closed his eyes. "All right," he said quietly. "I'll send Officer Larry Traylor out to pick you up." He hung up.

"Who was that?"

"Luke McKenzie. He was in the cave near Gem's Peak Park and wants to report a murder. A woman in green high heels."

Jim cursed under his breath. "Lulu."

# SEVEN

In Officer Traylor's truck, Luke was having trouble staying awake. It didn't help that Sarah's head was heavy on his shoulder, drawing him into sleep with her deep breathing.

"Here we are, folks."

The truck pulled up to a rustic brown building. A sign read "Search & Rescue, Little Texas, Colorado." A.J. and Jim stood outside on the sidewalk.

The chill of the night had turned to downright cold this morning. Luke touched Sarah's shoulder, but she didn't move. He hated waking her, but they had to get this over with before they could both grab some sleep.

"Sarah." He nudged her. Her hair had fallen over her face, and he moved it behind her ear.

Her eyes opened. She sat up and rubbed her shoulder where Luke's hand had been. "Yeah. We've got to—" Her head fell back against the seat, and then she melted against his shoulder again. "I'm so wiped out."

"One more hour and you can go to your cabin and rest." He opened the truck door. "Do you need any help getting out? Stay, Molly."

Larry turned around. "It's all right to bring her in. We have dogs in here all the time."

They went inside. A.J. and Jim greeted Luke, met Sarah, and then they all sat at a rectangular table with six chairs.

A.J. plucked a pen out of his shirt pocket. "Now, tell us what you saw in that cave."

Luke shook his head. "We actually didn't see much. Only a flashlight and the body of a woman. The man's face was in the dark the whole time."

Molly quietly slept while A.J. took the report.

After thirty minutes of questioning, Sarah rested her head on her folded arms and slept. Luke wanted to join her, but it wouldn't be too long before he'd be in bed.

Jim cleared his throat. "So, what we've got here is a diminutive man singing and humming Christmas songs, dragging a woman's body—"

"Lulu's. There." A.J. threw his arms out. "I said it out loud. It's real. She's dead. She's the only woman in this town who owns a pair of green high-heel shoes. Larry's headed to her house to see if hers are gone."

Silence throbbed. Jim sat, unmoving, and stared at the floor. An overhead fluorescent light buzzed and flickered. He started when the phone rang. A.J. picked it up, listened intently, and dropped it in its cradle with a long sigh.

"The shoes weren't there?"

A.J. frowned and shook his head at his brother. "No."

Jim stood, placed his hand on his brother's shoulder for a moment, and turned to Luke. "I don't think it's a stretch to consider that the man firing on you and Sarah might be the man who went after Lulu."

Luke had actually thought the same thing. "Would the sniper have taken the chance of bringing the body into the cave with us in there? We could have easily reached the crevice and witnessed him by the time he arrived."

Jim nodded. "Unless he's never gone far enough past there to discover that the other opening is on Bear Camp Trail. Or he figured you two had doubled back and left while he went after Lulu. Or, there are two of them." He shook his head at A.J.

"But why was he after her? What good reason could he have for killing Lulu, Jim?"

"He could have been after Sarah, and Luke fouled it up for him."

"That might explain why he pushed her over the edge instead of killing her," Luke said, nodding. "She was close to catching up with me on the trail. He wanted her alone. But why didn't he kill me and just take her?"

"We can guess that when he failed with Sarah, he went after Lulu. If Sarah hadn't screamed and caught your attention, she would've been the victim here, not Lulu."

"Me?" Sarah shivered and groggily lifted her head. "But why? I don't know anyone up here but you people."

Luke stood. "Listen, A.J., I don't think we're going to get any more this morning. Could we continue this after we've had some sleep? Sarah needs to get home."

Her head landed on her arms again. "I second that."

"That's fine." A.J. looked over at Luke. "We have two crime scenes to secure. We know exactly where you were on Bear Camp Trail. We've known about that cave entrance for a long time, but I don't think it's general knowledge around here, do you, Jim?"

"No. Do you want me on this? I could meet y'all over there."

"Yeah. We'll need help on both cases. We'd appreciate your assistance, too, Luke."

"You have it." He stood and picked up his pack. "My truck and her mountain bike are at the trailhead. Can one of you drive us over there? I'll take her home."

Sarah's head popped up again. "Us?"

"Yes, us." Luke pulled her chair back and helped her stand. "I made you a promise to get you to the hospital or your home. I intend to keep it."

"Are you staying in my cabin?"

"I hadn't intended to."

"Oh."

"Do you want me to?"

"Well, no, actually. I mean, I would appreciate *some*one staying with me, what with, you know, the sniper *and* the killer out there. The sniper may know where I live. He may have followed me to the trail."

Luke sighed. He was too tired to argue with her. But one thing was clear: surviving until they found the way out of the cave was one thing; staying with her in her cabin was another entirely. But someone needed to be with her until they could figure this thing out. "All right. I'll stay."

"It doesn't have to be you."

"Yeah, it does."

Jim stood. "Y'all sleep all day and all night, then we can meet tomorrow morning, maybe have breakfast before we do."

A.J. nodded. "Let's meet at Penny's Bar and Grill, my wife's place—my *estranged* wife's place. She fixes a mean breakfast and doesn't charge an arm and a leg for it."

Luke asked, "What time? Seven-thirty okay with everybody?"

Jim nodded. "How about we have Penny cater breakfast here at S&R? We'd be pestered to death with questions about Lulu if we ate at the restaurant."

"Sounds great." Luke picked up Sarah's pack. "Seven-thirty here. See y'all then."

Sarah fell asleep after giving Luke her keys and directions to her cabin. After picking up her bike, he drove to his home, gathered some things, and then drove to Sarah's. He unloaded her bike, opened the cabin door, turned on the light, looked around, and then went back to his truck and lifted her out. It seemed surreal, carrying a sleeping beauty into a mountain cabin with aspens shivering in the cold breeze and snow glistening in the sunshine as a heavy-racked elk trotted across the front lawn.

Luke kicked the door shut against the last thirty-six-plus hours. Sarah roused, and he set her on her feet. She fell against him, and, instinctively, he wrapped his arms around her to keep her from falling.

She gently pushed away. "I'm going to take a shower," she mumbled and turned toward the hallway.

"Good. You're rank."

"So are you, McKenzie."

He smiled and looked around. Oak paneling covered the walls. A stone fireplace dominated the small room. A cat's bed sat next to it.

Rustic, comfortable, inviting. Luke melted into a brown sofa, propped his booted feet on a matching ottoman, and prayed for an angel to start a fire in the fireplace. He listened to the shower and closed his eyes.

"Luke?"

Her voice was pulling him out of the darkness.

"Luke?"

"Umm?"

"Your turn, Luke. The shower."

He smelled her before he opened his eyes.

She stood in a white terry cloth robe tied at the waist, clean and fresh, a sweet aroma surrounding her. Her wet-spiked eyelashes framed golden eyes, her damp blonde hair brushed back from a shiny clean face. The few scratches on her face were less red now. Her robe slipped over her shoulder, and his gaze dipped to it.

At his look, she straightened her robe, took a step back, and pointed toward the bathroom. "Shower. Your bedroom. That way." She enunciated slowly, as a mother would to a headstrong child.

Weary, he rubbed his eyes and headed to a hot shower in the hopes that it would wash away the grime of the last two days.

Fifteen minutes later, he found her bedroom. She was asleep. Thick dark curtains shut out the sun. He moved a curtain aside and peered at the snow-covered yard. Outside, nothing moved. All was serene.

He dropped the curtain and flicked off a growling bear nightlight sitting on the rustic table by her bed. It was pretty dark for day time. "Good-night, Sarah."

His room was smaller with a single bed sitting below a single window. The sheets were crisp and clean, and he slid between them, too exhausted to care that his feet hung off the bottom of the bed.

Just as he drifted into sleep, a scream startled him fully awake.

Another scream.

He threw off the covers and raced down the short hall into Sarah's room. In a sleepy fog, he grabbed her shoulders and gently shook her. "Sarah."

She groped for Luke. "Oh. Oh. I—I thought he was in here. I could feel him in here, hovering over my bed."

He held her hands. "I'm here. Just me." He sat on the edge of her bed. "You're safe now, in your cabin. He's not here, and you're safe."

She closed her eyes, then opened them again, but not for long. They wilted closed again, and she began to breathe deeply. He eased off the mattress.

She grabbed his wrist. "Don't go," she whispered and pulled him back down beside her.

Past exhaustion, Luke didn't think he could stay awake much longer. "I'll be in the next room. You'll be okay. Here, let me turn on the nightlight again."

"I don't want to be alone."

"And where will I sleep? In this chair?" He stood. "Look. I'll sit in here until you're asleep."

"Will you be here when I wake up?"

"No."

She rolled over and faced the wall. "I'm sorry, Luke. I wasn't quite awake. Go on back to your room. I'll be all right."

Without a backward glance, he walked out of the room, dropped onto his bed, and knew nothing as he fell headlong into sleep.

They slept all day. When Luke got up some time in the evening, Sarah was still asleep, but he saw evidence that she'd been awake. A cup with a little water in it sat on the counter beside a jar of peanut butter. He found jelly in the fridge and fixed a couple of sandwiches and enjoyed the quiet. Glancing outside, he saw nothing moving. He stayed up a while and went back to bed. He awoke at four, glanced at the clock, groaned, and rolled over.

"Sarah. Come on, Sarah. Wake up."
She lifted her head and stared into a sea of fluffy white. *Wha—?*
"You were dreaming. At least—"
Wide-eyed, she rolled off her pillow and gasped. "What are you doing?"
Luke squinted at her as if he was trying to make sense of her question.
"I said, what are you doing in here?"
"Here?"
"In my bed!"
He frowned at her and shook his head twice. "Not so loud." His patted the air several times. "You had a nightmare last night and asked me to stay—"
"I most *certainly—*"
"Did." He held up a boy scout's hand and crossed his heart. "As I live and breathe. But I didn't stay. When you screamed a few minutes ago, I ran to the rescue again. But—" He started toward the door. "The damsel doesn't need rescuing."
She closed her eyes. "Shut the door on your way—"
The door slammed.
"Nightmare, my eye!" She pulled her knees up and rested her aching head on them. "I didn't have a nightmare. He just—"
She lifted her head. She remembered. She woke up terrified. He came into her room to see if she was all right. She did ask him to stay and then changed her mind when he said he wouldn't do it.
*Great day in the morning!* Even half asleep, how could she have done that to herself—and to him? Thank God, he'd had the good sense to do the right thing. Angry at herself, she headed for the kitchen to fix coffee. But it

was already brewing.

A door shut quietly down the hall.

Thoroughly humbled, she stepped into the hallway to make sure he heard her. "Thank you for making the coffee."

When he didn't answer, she poured herself a cup, sipped a little, and headed for the bathroom. "We need to leave in about forty-five minutes if we plan to be on time."

No answer.

She showered again, took her time dressing, and came out of her room. "Luke? Let's go."

No answer.

"Fine. I'll see you there." She headed outside. She pulled up when she spotted him standing beside his truck wearing a cowboy hat, boots, and a short winter coat. "I know that cowboy hat wasn't in your backpack. Where'd you get the clothes?"

"I went to my cabin." Holding a steaming to-go cup, he said, "Time's a-wasting, Sarah. Let's go."

She slipped inside the truck as did he. "Before we leave, Luke, I need to apologize for my attitude this morning and for last night when you came to help me. I do remember now, and I'm sorry I put you in that position."

"No problem. If that's all you've got to apologize for, then it's a good day already."

# EIGHT

Pancakes, French toast, eggs, bacon, and biscuits and gravy were delivered to Search & Rescue and not the police station simply because S&R had two long tables, one for the food and one for everyone to enjoy breakfast.

Jim sipped his coffee and tried to ignore the tension between his brother A.J. and his estranged wife, Penny. When would those pea-brains get their act together and stop this nonsense of being separated? Jim watched Penny turn around and when she saw A.J. staring at her, she presented her back to him and headed for the coffee station.

Police officers Larry and Roland waltzed in, with S&R's Tommy and Buddy right behind them. Sarah and Luke popped in soon after.

"Good morning, folks." Jim waited until he had everyone's attention. "Luke, you know everybody here. Sarah, let me make introductions real quick. This is Penny Banks, owner of the best restaurant in town and my sister-in-law. Tommy and Buddy work with me at S&R. You know A.J. and Larry. You didn't meet Roland Graves last night. He's a police officer, too."

They all nodded at her. Then Penny poured coffee into cups she'd set at each place on the table.

Luke grabbed one. "Thank you, Penny."

"If everybody's ready to eat, then let's bless this food." Jim bowed his head, prayed, stood back while everyone filled up. It was a quiet group. Not much to say this morning, with police and S&R staying up late, trying to figure out what had happened to Lulu and who could have done it.

Jim caught his brother trying hard not to watch Penny. She was cross with A.J. but pleasant to everyone else. At one point, Jim nudged his brother's foot when Penny walked up behind him with a pot of coffee. But she just poured his coffee and moved on to the next person. Jim wished to high heaven those two would grow up a little bit.

The front door opened. All heads turned toward Miss Gertie as she headed toward them. Chairs scooted back as the men stood.

She flapped her hands at them. "Y'all sit, sit, and enjoy your breakfasts." She turned to Jim and A.J. "I heard about Lulu. I'm sorry for the both of you. She was a sweet woman, as was her mother, a dear friend of mine."

Jim nodded. "'Preciate it, Miss Gertie. Would you like to join us? There's plenty here."

She eyed the dishes. "Well, I just might have myself a couple of Penny's pancakes." Jim tugged a chair out for her, and she draped her little daypack over it.

But she didn't sit. "Just came from my sister's house. She tells me a couple of bona fide nincompoops are in here this morning. Been awhile since I've seen one, and I came in here to do just that." Her gaze stopped on Luke. "Luke McKenzie, don't tell me it was you." She cocked her head, a frayed ski cap with withered petunias sitting snug on the crown of it. "I thought you had more sense than that."

Luke stood, extended his hand. "Miss Gertie. Good to see you. It's been a long time, hasn't it?"

Her head fell back as she gaped up at him. "You've grown since I last saw you. How tall are you, boy?"

"Six-three."

"All you McKenzie boys are tall." She sat and reached for her coffee cup. "You know I live out on Bear Camp Road. I know two of you were up there on that trail. Who was with you?"

Luke sat just as Sarah's wiggling fingers popped up. She smiled sheepishly. "Sarah Morgan, Miss Gertie."

"You look a dern sight smarter than you acted, young lady. Don't you Texans have sense enough not to hike a closed trail with a winter storm boldly staring you in the eye?"

Luke shrugged. "Well, no, ma'am, apparently not."

Jim choked on a biscuit as a few chuckles were being stifled around the table.

"Thank you, Penny." Miss Gertie took the plate of pancakes and set it down. "Maybe this breakfast will help with the sleepless nights I had worrying over you two."

Jim thought they all needed a smile or two this morning. As everyone ate, he glanced out the window. He didn't recognize the young man sitting on the bench across the street. That wasn't unusual this time of year, when tourists began to encroach upon their last two months of winter weather in what the rest of the world called spring. The young man's gaze darted around the area—

"Jim, how long until the trails are open?"

Sarah's question brought his attention back to their table. "Another two or three weeks. Usually around May fifteenth to the twentieth. We'll remove the signs around that time. 'Course, signs don't stop some people." Jim lifted his brows. "Do they, Luke?"

Luke grinned and lifted his brows at Sarah. "Do they, Sarah?"

"Oh, right. Put it off on me."

Everyone finished eating, stood, and thanked Penny for the meal.

A.J. headed for the door. "Let's walk to the station and get your official statements on paper."

They all stepped outside, turned left, and walked past Gally's Hardware, cattycornered to Jodee's Salon and the bank. Miss Gertie left them to go to the drugstore.

*Uh-oh.* Jim ducked his head and tried to hurry everyone along. He'd spotted the small, skinny frame of Miss Gertie's sister, Miss Winnie Sue Jansen, shoveling her porch. When her keen gaze spotted the group standing at the red light, she stopped shoveling, leaned her shovel against her porch wall, and moved carefully down her steps and across her yard to the hedgerow.

Thankfully, they wouldn't actually pass in front of her 1894 Victorian house, one of the first homes built here. Her property was due south of the police station. She waited for them to cross the street. *Like a hawk.*

They'd be stuck for an hour if they stopped to visit. Out of the corner of his eye, he saw her clean her hands on her apron, lean over her hedgerow, and cup her mouth to engage anyone she could catch.

He quickly checked his watch and then waved at her. Since he was bringing up the rear, he felt obliged to speak before she could open her mouth. "We can't stop today, Miss Winnie Sue. Got police business to take care of inside. Miss Gertie said to tell you she went to the drugstore and would be by your place in a little bit."

"What business?" she asked, shielding her eyes with a hand.

The group reached the front door of the police station. Seeing as how they were inches from going inside, Jim figured she might consider raising her voice, which would not be entirely acceptable to Miss Winnie Sue Jansen.

"Is it Lulu, Mr. Banks?" she asked in as genteel a voice as possible without coming anywhere remotely near a screech.

"We have to run now, Miss Winnie Sue. You take care, ma'am."

"Well, forevermore," she said just before the station door closed behind him.

Sarah sat at the table against the back wall while Luke headed for the coffee pot and poured a cup. He lifted the pot to the others.

A.J. pulled out a chair. "I'll take a cup. How long you folks expecting to be here in Little Texas?"

Luke handed A.J. a cup. "I still have almost four weeks' vacation coming so I'll stick around a bit to see what happens."

Sarah glanced at A.J. "I took six weeks off from my store, and I've been here less than a week, so I'll be here, too."

Jim straddled a chair when A.J. called the meeting to order and said, "We need to find out what's in that crevice."

"Did you learn anything, Miss Gertie? Did the Banks brothers say anything important about Lulu?"

Gertie's younger sister, Winnie Sue, sat with crossed ankles, blended knees, erect back, and a white handkerchief fisted in her thin veined hands. She wondered how her little sister could be so prim and proper every minute of every day. Winnie Sue's gaze roamed the lace-covered windows for anyone walking by before they rested on her older sister.

"They said absolutely nothing. I couldn't be too obvious, Winnie Sue. Those boys are sharp."

"Not too sharp, with three murders already, and they haven't caught on yet!" She picked up a folded fan, spread it, and quickly flapped its wings in front of her face.

Gertie put up with her prissy younger sister because she was, after all, only sixty-three and not well versed in the ways of any society other than the well-mannered kind. She watched her uncross her ankles, position them the other way, and pull on her skirt to make sure it was properly covering her ankles.

Mercy, mercy, but the woman was as tight as a purse string. "What are you saying? That I should give them a hint or two?"

"Good gracious me, no. What a preposterous thing to say. It took the third murder for us to figure it out or at least *think* we've figured it out. I'm saying if *we* can, why haven't they?"

Laws, the woman would test a saint. Did she think a pea roosted in the hollow between Gertie's ears? "I know what you're saying, and I'll try to find out what's what and let you know." *Or better yet, keep your trap shut, Gertie Jansen, because Lord knows, and most of this town, too, that Winnie Sue Jansen is a yapper of the first order.*

"And the letters. You've carefully hidden the letters, of course."

Gertie forced her eyes not to roll. "Of course."

"Where?"

"In my attic, under a loose board in the northeast corner."

"The anonymous note that said, 'You know, don't you, Rosie?'"

"It's there, too. I don't think anyone could find them even if they went up there. What are you having for supper tonight?"

"You're trying to get around me, Sister, and I won't have it."

*What a trial.* With the age difference, Gertie had been more of a mother to her baby sister than a sister, and the fact that her sister was sorely lacking in a sense of humor made things much more tense than they need be.

"I was just wondering if you were going to fix fried chicken." She wanted to add, *It's Friday, y'know,* because Winnie Sue Jansen *always* had fried chicken on Fridays. But Gertie didn't let her know she'd figured that out because Winnie Sue hated being considered predictable, as if it were a sin. Orderly, sensible, even prepared, but certainly not *predictable*.

"Why, yes, I am, as a matter of fact. Would you like to join me? And bring a salad. Not the green things you brought last time. Bring sweet carrot salad with raisins in it."

Ugh. Gertie hated that salad with a passion, but to get to Winnie Sue's fried chicken, she'd do it and be cheerful about it. "Consider it done. Six o'clock?" Written in stone, her time for dinner.

"As good a time as any, I'd say."

And she'd been saying that for forty years. Truth be told, Gertie was sick and tired of hearing it. It was a shame she'd never been able to marry her little sister off. Then, maybe she could endure a quiet week by herself. But her little sister demanded time together out of sheer loneliness.

"I'll pick you up at five-forty, then, Miss Gertie."

*And not a minute sooner.* She kissed her little sister's cheek and headed outside where most things were disorderly and illogical, and only sometimes predictable—like Lulu Baines' death.

It was no surprise at all to Gertie that someone else died. She just wished it hadn't been Lulu.

Jim needed to concentrate on his job and not on the picture of Lulu staring up at him from today's newspaper.

A.J. folded the paper. "That man down to Willow Falls, Jim. What's his name? The caver who's also a forensic investigator? He'd be our best bet to find out if Lulu's alone at the bottom of that hole." A.J. tossed the newspaper onto Jim's desk and looked out the window.

"Name's Josh Daniels."

"That's it." A.J. nodded. "I'll give him a call."

Luke sat on the corner of A.J.'s desk and cleared his throat. "The man in the cave was roughly five-foot-two or three. How tall is Daniels?"

The obvious question. "About five-eight or so." Jim picked up the newspaper and turned it over as Tommy and Buddy came into the police station. Jim had given them the day off from Search & Rescue because of Lulu's death. "You two couldn't stay away, I see."

Tommy slipped his hands into his coat pockets. His cowboy hat covered his face as he looked down. "Lulu was my friend, too."

*She was everybody's friend.*

"Either of y'all know Josh Daniels down Willow Falls way?"

"The caver." This, from Tommy.

"His sister married my cousin." Buddy picked up a donut, plopped it into his mouth, and chomped on it as if he hadn't eaten in three days.

"Does he still live in Willow Falls?"

"Yep," Buddy said with his mouth full. "We got his number down at the office."

"Elva Lee's gone to lunch. Would you mind getting that number for me, Buddy?"

"Sure, Jim. So long as I can take reinforcements." He stacked three donuts on a thumb. Tommy opened the door for him.

Just before the door closed on them, Jim said, "Don't get sugar gunk on that address card, Buddy." To A.J., he said, "If we call Josh and he's able to get into that crevice, we might end up tipping off the killer that we found his dumping spot. If he's still here, that is."

"He could be someone we've known all our lives."

"Yeah. I thought of that. I'd have a hard time believing that someone I know could've hurt Lulu."

A.J. crumbled the newspaper into a ball and threw it into a wastebasket.

Jim had seen his brother's temper plenty of times, but grief was driving it at the moment. Any other time, he would have engaged him in a little verbal wrestling. "But if he is local, why does he start killing our women? What would make a man do that?" Jim's phone beeped. "Buddy texted Josh's number to me."

He gave it to A.J., who called him. He put the phone on speaker.

"Josh Daniels."

"Yeah, Josh, this is A.J. Banks, police chief here in Little Texas. We have something we'd like you to investigate for us if you would."

"A cave?"

"A crevice in a cave wall that we think goes down a ways. One opening to this system is there on Bear Camp Trail. The crevice isn't too far from Gem's Peak Park."

"Heard of that cave, years ago, but I've never been down."

"We think there's a body in the crevice. Wondered if you could go down and take some pictures for us."

"A human body?"

"A murdered human body. Do you think you could meet us there and have a look-see as soon as possible?"

"I can meet you there at one o'clock today. Anyone going in with me?"

"Not with you into the crevice but, yeah, I got one. Luke McKenzie."

"A caver?"

"You could say he is."

"Are you going in, Chief?"

"No, sirree. I get claustrophobic stepping inside my shower."

# NINE

Luke, Josh Daniels, and Moe Wiggins, a crime scene investigator on Josh's staff, headed across the grass toward the parking lot. Luke glanced over his shoulder. It had been grueling in the cave. He never wanted to go down there again.

The purpose of this trip had been to get away from the murder of his father, the sadness that still enveloped the ranch, and here, he'd walked into three murders and an entire town that was grieving. He'd get past this in the next few days and try to enjoy the rest of his trip.

The three men walked away from the entrance to the crime scene toward A.J. and Jim who were standing in the shade of a pine tree. Jim frowned at them as if he searched for news on their faces. They'd come out after two long hours with nothing good to tell anyone.

Holding baggie-wrapped camera equipment, Josh and Moe set their gear on the back seat of Josh's vehicle and slammed the door.

Luke had nothing but respect for both men, investigating the scene and then Josh going inside the crevice alone to face the horrors he'd found.

"Chief."

A.J. nodded at Josh. "What you got for me?"

"It's a long, tunnel-like cave. Goes down about thirty feet at a twenty-five-degree angle. Pretty steep. Then it splits into two passageways but at that point, the three bodies stopped their slide."

"Three?"

"All women, all dressed up, very well preserved, like he'd just put them in there. That's the norm in deep caves, being preserved so well. I got some good pics for you. Do you want me to email them to you or do you want to see them now?"

"Was Lulu one of them?"

"From the photos you gave me of her, yes. Two other women, small, dressed up. I didn't try to move them to get better pictures. I just left them *in situ* in case you call in the FBI."

"No need for that at this point. Any other evidence collected where the killer walked, moved around? Shoe size, hair samples?"

Luke looked at Moe, who didn't say anything, so Luke nodded and said, "Small tennis shoes, like a child's, a size six or seven. Got a cast of a really good one. Didn't kick up much dirt. No fingerprints, no hairs, nothing left behind."

A.J. blew out a long breath. "Got good pics of that, too?"

Josh nodded.

"Why don't y'all get yourselves cleaned up and eat some supper, and we'll meet back at the station." He looked at his watch. "Somewhere around seven-thirty. Let's keep this information hush-hush. We don't need everybody in Little Texas getting anxious until we have more information to give them. In the meantime, I'll check the photos and see what we've got."

Jim glanced at Luke. "It might be a good idea for Sarah to stay with you. There's safety in numbers."

He'd already thought of it. "She's there now, staying with my chef, Eduardo, and his wife, Yolanda, my housekeeper. I'll drive her to her cabin, get her things."

Jim turned to Josh and Moe. "Y'all can come to my house to get cleaned up and go with me to Penny's to grab some supper. Then we can head over to the meeting together."

At McKenzie Cabin, Sarah followed Luke outside as he headed toward his truck. "I don't recall anyone giving me the *option* of staying at my cabin or yours."

"It's safer for you in our cabin," he said as he opened the driver's door and slid in just as Sarah did.

"You and Jim decide something, thwack people over the head, and then expect them to just fall in line."

"Thwack? Is that a word?" He grinned, backed up the truck, and drove toward the road. "Your seatbelt."

She grunted and fastened it. "You don't *ask* if people want to do something. You just decide for them and expect them to go right along with you."

"I'm not trying to thwack you or decide for you, but when the right course of action is obvious, no discussion is necessary. You can't honestly think you'd be safer in your cabin. Three bodies, Sarah. Three. And he was so close to getting *you*. Do you really think you'd be just as safe at your cabin as at mine?"

"I didn't say that."

"That's exactly what you said." He turned onto the road to her cabin. "Thwacking, you said."

"I didn't disagree with what you wanted me to do, only with how you handled it. I need my independence. That's why I'm here, to find it and myself again. To live without looking over my shoulder every step I take. I have to do this. I don't need your help."

In silence, he turned into her driveway, parked, turned off the engine. "I'm adaptable."

She sent him a sidelong glance as she got out and shut the door. "Meaning?" The conversation wasn't moving in the direction she'd intended. Maybe his only tactic wasn't thwacking.

Luke met her at the front door. "I won't help unless you ask for help."

"Good." She looked at him as she unlocked the door. With his hands in his pockets, Luke raised his brows and smiled as she withdrew the key. "Or make decisions for me."

"Or make decisions for you," he said amiably as the door opened.

She headed for her bedroom and shut the door. Even as irritating as Luke was at times, he cared about her safety. Now that she'd rebuked him, the shield of protection he'd placed around her had crumbled. She wasn't at all sure she wanted it gone. Not *completely* gone.

Maybe that was one of his other tactics, to make her regret her rash statements and eat her words. She scooped her things out of a drawer and tossed them into a suitcase.

Well, it worked. She already regretted scolding him.

But she wouldn't take back the words.

He walked to her doorway just as her phone rang.

"Hey, Mom." She turned away from Luke and looked out the window. "I'll be staying at the McKenzie's cabin for a few days. Yes, I'm fine. What?" She couldn't speak, couldn't think. "A-are they sure?" A quick glance at Luke. "I will. I will, Mom. I love you, too. 'Bye."

"What it is? You're as white as a sheet."

"They, uh." She dropped to the edge of her bed. "Another two girls were killed in the last week. Same M.O. as the man who went after me. The Darkslayer."

"Where?"

"The first one was near Goodland in western Kansas, not fifty miles from where I live. The second, in Limon, Colorado. A man was seen leaving the scene of the crime on a motorcycle. The motorcycle is a new clue."

"Do the police think he's on his way here? That he's following you?"

Sarah's face drained of color. "I don't know. She mentioned that the FBI will probably want to interview me."

"The one who got away."

"And the one who saw absolutely nothing."


Jim's phone rang. His brother, A.J. "Yeah, A.J."

"Can you come down to the station? I'll meet you out front."

"Right now? Josh, Moe and I are about to head to Penny's for supper."

"Now, if you can. You can eat later. I'll go with you."

"All right. I'll be there in five minutes."


Jim saw A.J. sitting on top of his patrol car. He turned off his headlights as he parked. Opening the truck's door, he stood on the running board and placed his arm on top of the door as if it could somehow shield him against what A.J. had to tell him.

"Jim."

Nodding, Jim calmly said, "You found Renee."

A.J. sighed. "You always could figure things out faster than me." He touched the hood of his car. "Come on over here and sit with me."

When Jim didn't move, A.J. slid off the car and headed toward him. "Shut that door. Let's walk."

"I don't want to walk."

"Then let's drive and talk about it."

In silence, Jim regarded his brother. It was obvious he was hurting for Jim. At this moment, facing the horrible truth of Renee's death, he didn't want to feel anything for anybody but himself. But he couldn't do that to his brother. For A.J.—to help his brother deal with this—Jim would go with him. He walked to the passenger side and got in.

A.J. slid inside the car, started it, and backed up.

"I've hated her for a year for leaving me, but she didn't run off."

"Yeah." A.J. took a deep breath and let it out. "Jim, I gotta tell you something else."

"Bonnie's down there, too."

"Yeah. And Lulu."

"I gotta get out."

"I know."

"We're at City Park. Let me out."

When A.J. slowed down, Jim bolted out of the car and ran down the concrete path, away from the memories of that last night before she left—the night she died. Her eyes had filled with tears when she told him she was pregnant. They had tried for five years, and she was finally pregnant. After she disappeared, Jim thought the baby was someone else's, that he couldn't have gotten her pregnant, that she'd run off, that she'd needed another man to fulfill her dreams.

But none of it was true.

All of his accusations and blame and hate had been misplaced. She *hadn't* left him. There *was* no other man. The baby *was* his.

What kind of love had he had for Renee that he would think the worst of her so quickly? At the first sign of trouble, he'd come up with every theory on why she'd left him and all of them attacked her character. None of them involved *murder.* None of them had someone else at fault.

Bending over, he gasped for air. The cold air made his chest hurt, but he deserved it. *Did she die quickly? Did he torture her? Was she alive when he put her in that hole?*

"I don't want to do this, Lord." He stood, walked off the last of his run, and made a vow, right there and then: he would hunt down the man killing their women, and when he found him, he'd hurt him until he screamed for mercy—and then he'd make it worse.

The man took one step back behind a tree as the chief's brother ran past him. So, they had found Rosie.

He could feel the rage already boiling inside him. Red colors spiked with bright oranges and yellows swirling in front of his eyes. He ground his teeth until his jaw throbbed, and then he slammed a fist into the trunk of a tree. He whined and gasped at the pain.

He'd earned the pain.

She was getting out.

It was his fault.

It was always his fault.

He had to get her back in there.

His heart raced as he tried to think through the desperate haze.

No, not back in the hole. Somewhere else. Somewhere no one would find her.

She had to be stopped. He couldn't bear the beatings anymore, the screams, the pain.

She had to be stopped.

He stepped out from behind the tree and walked toward the lights on Edgar Drive.

"You all right, buddy?"

He jumped at the words coming from behind a tree, left of him.

The chief's brother again. Jim Banks. He was probably one of the men down in the hole today. "Sure am, sir. Just enjoying this night. It's perfect for walking, isn't it?"

Jim headed down the long driveway to his parent's ranch home, but instead of going to the main house and scaring his mother half to death at this hour, he drove to the garage. The light was on. Dad was probably inside, working on a figurine. Good memories in that garage when he was growing up, watching his father's hands work magic on a piece of wood. Jim stopped the car and got out, his steps crunching on the gravel.

He gripped the shop's door handle and opened the door. "Dad? You in here?"

His father sneezed and came out from behind some shelving. "'Course I am, son. Where else would I be at eleven-thirty at night? Come in. Come in." Tucking his handkerchief in his back pocket, he stretched out his other hand and pulled Jim into a quick hug, then held his shoulders as he looked into blue eyes mirroring his own. "What are you doing out here at this time of night? Trouble at the job?"

Jim rubbed his eyes but not before tears welled up.

Dad nodded at the refrigerator. "Grab us a soda."

Jeb—an acronym for James E. Banks—cleaned his tools and set them in a neat row on the table, then tugged on the towel in his back pocket, wiped his hands, and flapped it at the two lawn chairs sitting by the garage door. "Have a seat while I open this door."

He leaned over the miter saw workbench and felt behind the wood stack for the light switch. The double-wide garage door opened to a cool moonlit night with stars glittering in a coal-black cloudless sky. Jim handed him a soda can. They both sat, drank, and looked out at the night.

"Dad? They found Renee's body today."

With his head back, Jeb had drawn in a breath to take a swallow, but he stilled and stared at his son. "S-Say what?"

"They found Renee's body today."

"Found?" His hand was frozen mid-air.

"She was killed in our home and taken to a cave and thrown into a crevice with Bonnie Washburn."

His dad blinked at him as if he couldn't understand the words. Slowly, he lowered his hand to his lap.

"And Dad? Lulu's in there with Renee and Bonnie."

"L-Lulu?"

Jim knew this one hurt the most. Dad's sister, Melody, had only one daughter—Lulu.

Jeb sat in the darkness, obviously shaken. He glanced over at Jim. Tears filled their eyes. Jim had no idea in the world how to comfort Dad or himself. They had never been a touchy-feely kind of family, but he sure wouldn't mind a good hug about now.

"Son, I was wrong about Renee. I was wrong about her, and I'm sorry for it."

"I was wrong, too."

The night grew cold. The crisp, chilly air settled around them like an icy blanket. "And Lulu. Dear, sweet Lulu. What is going on here? Someone... someone you arrested in Denver or... or something?"

"Maybe. Maybe not."

Silence enveloped them. Jim knew this was Jeb's favorite time of the day when he could come out to his workshop to design and create his figures. His time to relax and think about his day, to plan tomorrow.

Jeb would remember this night forever, and it saddened Jim.

Gravel crunched again.

Debra appeared around the corner, smiling, carrying two small plates and two cups of steaming coffee on a tray. "Well, I thought that was you." Her smile wilted as she looked at her husband, then her son. "What is it? Something's wrong. Jim, what is it?"

Jim sighed and took the tray from his mother as he stood. "Apple pie. My favorite." He sniffed deeply. "Sure not a night for cold drinks, is it?"

He motioned Debra toward his chair and took the two cups, handed one to Jeb. "Sit down, Mama. I've got some news that won't wait on these pies."

By five o'clock the next afternoon, Police Chief A.J. Banks had rounded up a team tasked with going down in the morning and bringing up the three bodies of the women murdered in Little Texas, Colorado. Despite his best efforts to keep this news quiet, media began to arrive in the area. He held a press conference with his brother, Jim, and the staff at S&R, along with Officers Larry Traylor and Roland Graves. Briefly, he advised the press of what authorities knew up to this point and kindly asked them to respect the privacy of grieving family members.

## TEN

Luke was dreading going back down in the cave this morning. He got up long before the sun rose. His routine involved jogging two to three miles at least four times a week. If he didn't run, he pumped iron and did sit-ups or followed a kick-boxing video. He looked forward to the run more than anything. Running had helped him this last year with the stress of losing his dad and the stress of his job as foreman of his family's large working ranch.

After his run and shower, he got dressed and was about to leave when a quick knock on the adjoining door was followed by the door opening. Sarah stood in her robe with her hands in its pockets, her sad expression telling him she wished he didn't have to do this.

"You're headed out?"

He grimly nodded and walked over to her.

"I've felt so useless the last couple of days. I want to help, but I don't know how."

"Your number one priority is keeping yourself safe. I ordered a security system for the cabin. It should be here tomorrow."

"You didn't have to do that."

"Yes, I did. If I thwacked you into coming here, then you need to know you're protected." Good. It brought a little smile, but it didn't last very long. "I have to go."

"Be safe."

"I will."

Fifteen minutes later, he parked at Gem's Peak Park, got out, and stood with A.J. and Jim. Reporters were standing behind the yellow tape. Every little movement made by the three men sent cameras clicking. Some of the people of Little Texas were there, too, holding up cell phones, snapping pictures, or making videos as the recovery team tasked with bringing up the bodies parked and exited their vehicles. Officer Larry Traylor drove up and joined A.J. and Jim.

Conversations ended as Luke stood with the recovery team members and then ducked under the yellow tape surrounding the area. They all headed for the hole under the tree. The crowd stood in silence as they hovered near the opening of the cave and then, one by one, disappeared underground.

Three hours later, the bodies of Lulu Baines, Bonnie Washburn, and Renee Banks were brought up. They lay side by side in bags as the recovery team stood around, making notes, talking on cell phones. Then the bodies were loaded into vehicles and driven off-site.

A.J. instructed the recovery team to clean up and meet him at the station in about an hour. Everyone but A.J. left without saying a word to those waiting around for any morsel of information. "We'll have something for you soon, folks." With that, he told them to leave the area.

They dispersed, he knew, to worry, to wait, to whisper to neighbors and friends and family about what had happened out at Gem's Peak Park.

And to wonder what kind of monster could have done this to three of their own.


Winnie Sue had her back up.

On top of all the news about the murders, the press intruding everywhere, her sister Miss Gertie too busy to come over, and no one out and about to talk to her over her fence, she had forgotten to get her library books back on time.

*And, oh, won't Miss Tiger Claws like that!*

Winnie Sue hugged her bag of books close to her chest as she walked across Main Street and up the sidewalk to the double doors of the library. She gritted her teeth and tugged with all her might on the right side of the double doors. She had informed the town council for years that the library door was much too large and too heavy for the ladies of Little Texas and when it got a little suction to it, when the wind kicked up, why, it was nigh onto impossible to open.

But nothing had ever been done about it.

She hated being in a cantankerous mood when she went into the library, but she was and deserved to be. She loved reading and was determined to continue to read regardless of the fact that Laura Langston sat behind the reservation desk, primed and ready to give Winnie Sue an ungraciously hard time. Most of the time, her complaints had nothing to do with Winnie Sue. "I hate the rain, Jansen. Did you do something evil to bring us this wretched rain?" or "The Simpsons' house burned down. Did you do it, Jansen?" or "Mrs. Claremore is sick, Jansen. Did you put a spell on her?"

Oh, Laura Langston was a burr in Winnie Sue's side! And she had no idea why Laura was so rude to her. She'd never once been unkind to the woman.

Not bothering to lift her eyes in any semblance of a well-mannered greeting, Winnie Sue approached the reservation desk.

She could sense Laura Langston watching her, waiting like a hawk ready to swoop. If the town council was going to do anything at all for the library, it should remove Laura Langston as librarian. The intelligent people of Little Texas who read and broadened their small worlds with the creative minds of people who wrote deserved a reprieve from the likes of Miss Sour Puss.

Very primly and very properly, eyes down, Winnie Sue quietly set her bag of books on the reservation counter and turned.

"You're one day late, Jansen."

*Because of that monster,* she wanted to retort, but Winnie Sue ignored her. She'd learned a long time ago that Laura Langston hated for her barbs to be dismissed. So, Winnie Sue started toward the romance section with the tip of her tongue between her clamped teeth and a deep breath easing out of her lungs. One of these days that tongue was going to jump right out of that clamp and give Laura Langston a piece of Winnie Sue's cultured and well-read mind.

"One day late, five books. A quarter, Jansen. No more books until you pay up." Her voice got louder as Winnie Sue walked away.

Heads turned. Activity stopped. Flushed, Winnie Sue hummed "Amazing Grace" ever so quietly under her breath as she walked toward the sweet haven of romance.

"This isn't a choir loft, Jansen."

Reverently, Winnie Sue slid her fingers across her favorite books. She pulled out the book she'd read many times and clutched it tightly against her bosom. She could see Bart Carpenter's large hands grabbing Lilly Tarentino's blazing bronze hair, pulling her head back as he said, "You're mine, Lilly! Now and always, you are mine!" And then his mouth devoured her.

Wistfully, Winnie Sue smoothed the cover of the book as she imagined what 'devoured' meant. She had been respectfully kissed in her younger days, once, but she didn't consider it a 'devouring' act, had no concept of *being* devoured. Certainly, if one was experiencing a 'devouring' kiss, one would know it.

She blushed as she remembered where she was and looked around, grateful no one was watching her. Then her gaze connected with Miss Grumpy Guts' quick glance as she waltzed past the end of the aisle. She rolled her eyes at Winnie Sue and shook her head.

"Never you mind," Winnie Sue whispered as she lifted her chin and walked down another row of books. She picked out four more paperbacks and, like a soldier gearing up for war, set her teeth and her feet toward the enemy and the librarian's bitter attitude.

An extended stiff hand waited for her when she set her books down. Calmly, she opened her purse, drew out a quarter, and placed it gently in the woman's claw.

Out of the corner of her eye, Winnie Sue saw a white head move. She turned and looked into the eyes of a handsome gentleman near her age. He was staring at her. She lowered her eyes, picked up her newly reserved books, pressed them close to her heart and, as she walked through the front door, she glanced at him.

The gentleman sent her smile and a wink.

Why, of all the nerve! Did he think she was some...some *trollop* who expected such...such...why the words weren't even in Winnie Sue's vocabulary! Embarrassed beyond measure, she huffed across the street and into the sanctuary of her own home where she could wonder in private if the gentleman she'd seen had ever devoured a woman and was quite certain he had, by his manners!


Laura Langston waited a mere three minutes. Without preamble, she strolled back to her library office, which occupied the enviable location of being directly across the street from Miss Winnie Sue's parlor. Laura locked the door behind her, opened her window, sat down, and smiled as the piano music began.

So, it was "Onward Christian Soldiers" first. Miss Winnie Sue absolutely tore up a piano and every time she endured a visit to the library, she waltzed home and played for a good hour. Maybe it was time to just *ask* her to play songs when she got home instead of riling her up. But riling her up was so much fun, and it produced what Laura wanted: the music.

With her elbows resting on the windowsill, she placed her chin in the palm of her hand, closed her eyes, and allowed the music to glide over her.

She sighed. Miss Winnie Sue's music was beautiful.

Ah, now. "Amazing Grace." So wonderfully played.

Perhaps by now, Miss Winnie Sue had forgiven her. Next, "Oh, For a Thousand Tongues to Sing," her absolute favorite. Laura would love to hear this song in church one day. But that would never happen.

The deaths of three innocent women lay squarely at her door. She'd been expecting him to come here. After the second death, she knew he had. Listening to this music was the only thing that assuaged some of her guilt.

But it simply wasn't enough.

A knock on the adjoining door startled Sarah, even though she'd heard Luke coming up the stairs. She'd seen him drive up and walk toward the cabin with his head down.

She opened the door. He looked so weary. "Are you okay?"

"Yeah. It was grisly, to say the least."

"What did they find?"

"The three women Josh discovered. Did you talk to the FBI today?"

"Yes. They came by and asked me a lot of questions about the Darkslayer."

Luke didn't come into her room. His gaze settled somewhere on the floor, and he rubbed his chin. "I kept thinking all day that you could have been down there with them."

Impulsively, she took his hand. "But I'm not—because of you. I haven't thanked you enough for saving my life. No telling what would have happened to me if you hadn't come along."

"If Molly hadn't."

"If you hadn't listened to your dog. If you both hadn't come to my rescue. You saved me from him."

He looked down at their joined hands. "I'm glad I met you that day, Sarah Ann Morgan," he said without looking into her eyes. It was a moment she would never forget. This hurting man gave comfort to *her*. It lasted only an instant, and he let go of her hand.

He crossed to her window, moved the curtain aside, and looked around the yard. "Have you watched any TV today?"

"No. Why?"

"The media is all over this story. A.J. wants the recovery team, S&R, his staff, and me down at his office." He checked his watch. "Listen, Sarah. We don't have any neighbors. We're secluded here. Don't open the door to anyone. Call me on my cell if you need me. Call our caretaker, Angus, if you need him. Here's his number." He gave it to her. "My chef, Eduardo, and his wife, Yolanda, are here. Let him know when you're ready for supper. He'll have it ready for you. I'm sure you've figured out that they live here year 'round. They have an apartment in the back."

"I suspected it, but I haven't actually had a tour of the house yet. Hint, hint."

"I'll give you that tour when I get back this afternoon." He headed for the door to his bedroom and stopped. "We'll try to slip in a picnic soon if we can stay out of the way of the press. Would you like that?"

"I'd love it. We both need to get outdoors and away from here."


The meeting with the recovery team, police staff, and S&R started later than Luke thought it would and ended earlier than he could have hoped for. Everyone left shortly before four. Only Luke was left, with A.J. who was writing in a notebook.

Looking out of the window blinds, Luke dreaded walking out with the chief of police to face the tall microphones swaying above reporters' heads and all the camera equipment aimed right at the station's front door. The reporters stared at the door, too, waiting for the chief of police to make a move.

"A.J., you need to get outside. They're waiting for you."

"I know. You still coming with me?"

"I am."

The door opened. Everyone shouted at once. Cameras clicked.

Microphones extended toward Luke and A.J. Someone tugged on the sleeve of Luke's shirt and almost pulled him down. He jerked away and watched A.J. hold up his hands for quiet.

"Chief, Chief, do you—"

"Chief Banks, how long do you think the bodies—"

"Hey, A.J.! Do you have any idea—?"

"How were they—?"

"Were the women sexually assaulted, Chief?"

A.J. patted the air again and again for quiet. "We'll give the press a statement at six-thirty. No comment until then." Despite his words, questions continued to be thrown at him. He ducked under a flying microphone and shimmied through the mass of cameras and bodies, and both he and Luke slipped into his truck.

A.J. pulled out his cell phone, dialed Search & Rescue, and put it on speaker phone. "Elva Lee, let me speak to Jim, please."

"He's not here. He said he needed to be with Renee's sister and her family, that he'd be gone the rest of the day. You might catch him there."

He backed up his truck. "The media over at S&R?"

"Oh, yeah. They're camped out all over the parking lot, although I told them Jim wouldn't be back. They captured Tommy, and you know how Tommy likes attention, but he didn't tell them anything you didn't want told. Are you giving them a statement?"

"Yeah. You might wanna stick your head out and let them know the chief of police is giving a statement at six-thirty at the station house. That'll get 'em off your back. And lock your door. They're a pushy bunch." He shut down the phone. "Let's head over there. Maybe Jim's ready for supper, too."

"Did y'all ever consider these women might have been murdered, A.J.?"

"No, not really. Rachelle mentioned to me not two months ago that Renee would've contacted her by then, that she wouldn't have run off with someone and left Rachelle to wonder and worry. She thought Renee was too embarrassed to call her family because she'd been stupid to leave in the first place. We never really considered that she had been murdered. Not seriously considered, at any rate. Not *out loud* considered. There was absolutely no evidence to suggest it, and nothing like that had ever happened in Little Texas. She had simply driven away from her husband in her own car, which had never been found."

A.J. slowed down and leaned over just as the front door of a house opened. Jim stood with a man and a woman, hugged the woman, shook the man's hand, and walked toward his truck with his head down as he wiped his face.

A.J. pulled over to the curb and rolled down the window. "Where you headed?"

"Thought I'd stop by Penny's for supper."

"We'll meet you there."

Five o'clock was Laura Langston's favorite time of the day. It meant she could lock up the library and go home and leave all the nitwits in Little Texas behind her for an evening. She hated dealing with them all day long, listening to their stupid questions. "Could you tell me where the children's section is?" She would point up at the sign across the room that said, "Children." Some were worse than that. "What time do you close?" She'd point right in front of the patron at the sign on the counter that showed the library's hours. "Excuse me, do you have a restroom?" She'd point at the sign down the hall that said, "RESTROOMS."

But more than that, she was exhausted from the worry and stress eating away at her nerves. She crossed the street and walked by the police station with more interest than usual. The curtains were wide open. A.J. and his brother were inside.

Laura couldn't help but wonder if they'd discovered anything of importance on the murders by now.

She headed north the half-block to her home, went around to her back door, opened it, and froze.

A standard white sheet of paper sat in the middle of her kitchen table. The vase of artificial flowers that had been on the table was now sitting on the counter.

Leaning over without touching the paper, she read, "You know, don't you, Laura?" And it was signed, "Rosie." Written in simple childlike letters.

"Well, well, well. So, you found me, Rosie."

The wooden slat-backed chair she'd picked up in a garage sale scraped on the tiled floor as she tugged it away from the table. How had Rosie connected Laura to the murders? She'd changed her name and moved far away. She worked in a library, for heaven's sake, not a biochemical lab anymore.

She sat and glanced at the note again. Yes, Laura had figured it out. She was sure she had no reason to be frightened for herself.

But she shuddered anyway.

Across town, Luke returned to his family's cabin around six-thirty. As he approached the front door, a crude cut-out of a red rose was stuck to the front door. He plucked it off. A piece of rolled-up tape was on the back. "Weird," he muttered. Eduardo and his wife, Yolanda, were always making crazy love-things for each other. Probably something of theirs.

He was about to go inside when he noticed his mountain bike wasn't leaning against the garage. Had Sarah taken it somewhere?

"Eduardo?"

As much as Luke wanted to be alone at the cabin, it was nice that he didn't have to cook and clean while he was here. Eduardo and Yolanda were very adept at making themselves scarce so Luke could have privacy. "Eduardo?"

The chef came out of the kitchen wiping his hands.

"Is Sarah here?"

"She insisted on going into town. I told her not to leave, but she said she needed some things, that it was a good time for her to go shopping."

On an oath, Luke grabbed his cell phone. "When did she leave?"

"About two hours ago."

"Two hours!" His heart raced as he punched in her number and tried not to glower at Eduardo for not hog-tying her to the nearest banister. Luke listened—and counted—the rings. On the fifth one, she answered.

"Where *are* you?" he bellowed as he turned his back to Eduardo.

"Luke? I'm, uh, about a half mile from your cabin."

"How can you be so stupid?" He scooped a pillow off the sofa, threw it at the curtains, and tried to shove the day's horrendous discoveries out of his mind. And here Sarah was, outside and alone! *Here, let me hand myself to you on a silver platter!*

"I wasn't being stupid. I needed some things. I'm out in broad daylight."

"And being an idiot. It's almost *dark!*" He set his teeth and paced. He knew how he sounded, but he was so angry, he could hardly restrain the need to lash out at her. But he did, although it cost him. "I want you to stay on the phone until you get here."

"I'm coming up on the turnoff."

Luke couldn't say another word. What if the killer had seen her leave? What if he had followed her, had, had—

"I'm here," she said and disconnected the phone.

Luke stalked across the room. He jerked the front door open and made sure it slammed shut behind him.

Frowning at him, Sarah slipped off his bike.

He stepped back as she bounded up the steps. "Your room," he said as she breezed past him.

"Maybe I want some privacy."

"Not this time."

Luke followed her up the stairs, opened her door, and shut it behind them. "Don't you realize the danger you're in?"

"I was in no danger. I was careful. No, hear me out." She set her backpack on a table. "I thought about the shooter. He didn't have a car or a bicycle at the trailhead. I think he was on foot. I felt relatively safe riding a bike. Also, the killer murdered his victims inside their homes. I was outside." She held up her hand. "*Also*... the man stalking us here at the cabin is on foot; no bike or car has ever been seen. And, finally, I don't appreciate your calling me stupid or an idiot."

"You forgot one. The man who almost raped and killed you in Kansas. A motorcycle can easily overtake a bike!" Luke leaned over, nose-to-nose with her. She stared wide-eyed at him. "I'll tell you this, Sarah," he said in a low, controlled voice. "You were being stupid, idiotic, and you *were* in danger. Next time you want to go on a bike ride, let me know, and I'll go with you. Use your head, and you just might stay alive."

He stormed out of the room.

"Well!" Sarah took a deep breath and stared at the door. The room throbbed with his angry words.

She sat on the bed and fell back against her pillow.

He had it all wrong. She wasn't being stupid. She was being brave.

After chastising herself for being so afraid, she'd made herself go outside and face the fear, had ridden into town, constantly looking over her shoulder as if the killer was hot on her trail. She had her pepper spray with her, with one finger on the trigger in case she had to use it quickly.

She was so proud of herself. She had faced the agonizing fear and trampled on it. Yes, she could see Luke's side. Maybe she had been a bit reckless. But she hadn't come to the mountains to sit in a cabin all day and be afraid. She loved the outdoors and desperately wanted her life back.

After stopping at the market, she'd driven to an area where the views were incredible, the wildlife abundant, and the sounds of a gushing stream all but swallowing up any man-made sounds. She'd sat on a boulder and enjoyed the peace of it all. She hadn't been followed; she'd been very careful about that.

She was determined not to let the fear win again.

She started toward the bathroom. She needed a shower.

But first, she owed Luke an explanation and maybe an apology for frightening him. She called him.

He didn't answer.

So, her shower would come first after all.

With her hair still damp, Sarah slipped into her pajamas. Her shower had turned into a bubble bath, and she'd allowed herself the luxury of taking her time. Maybe Luke was in his room now and had cooled off since his outburst. She understood his anger. He'd lost his father. She knew a little about feeling utterly helpless in the face of evil. He must have felt the same way, but more so. It was no wonder he went over the top in his reaction to her leaving. He was afraid for her.

She knocked on the door separating their rooms.

"Come in."

She did and clasped her hands.

"What do you want, Sarah?" In his tee-shirt and pajama bottoms, Luke walked across the room to his bed, tossed the covers to the side, and sat on the bed as he grabbed his cell phone.

"I want to say I'm sorry you were afraid for me. My intent was to get back a part of the life I gave up months ago. But I hurt you in the process, and I'm sorry for that."

"Apology accepted."

"And the forgiveness?"

"Given."

"I was actually proud of myself for going out alone. Yes, I was afraid, but I didn't want to let him win."

Luke finally looked at her. "He wins when you're dead."

She didn't know what to say.

"Good night, Sarah," he said and turned off the bedside lamp.

Thoroughly dismissed, she swallowed hard and groped for the doorknob.

He giggled. Rosie was back! He was so excited, he couldn't stand still. He'd seen her leave, of course, but he couldn't follow her on his bike. He had waited for her to return.

And now she was in the house, feeling safe and secure, like she had nothing to worry about with four walls around her.

"Morons," he whispered into the night. Did they think he'd just let them take Rosie out and do nothing about it? She had to go back in. The beatings had to stop. *She* had to be stopped.

He'd wait for a place and a time when she'd be alone, with no one around to help her. At the thought, he giggled, clapped his hands excitedly, and then slammed his head into a tree and whimpered.

"Not again." Sarah turned on the light. Her digital clock read *2:21*. She was exhausted. But every time she closed her eyes, she saw the little man laughing and singing and dragging a bag with a green shoe sticking out the bottom. It didn't help that Molly was wide awake, too, staring at the windows, whining occasionally.

If Sarah called the police, the man would be gone before they'd get here.

She crawled out of bed and headed for the bathroom. When she came back out, a floorboard creaked under her foot. She looked toward the adjoining door and listened, afraid she'd awakened Luke, but no lights came on under the door.

It was just the wind scaring her—the branches scraping across the glass, the storm howling like a persistent wolf. She slipped back into bed and pulled the covers up to her chin.

The heater came on, startling her.

A branch stabbed at the window.

Molly whined.

Spooked, Sarah flew out of her bed. She quietly opened the adjoining door and rushed into Luke's dark room. Molly followed her and stopped when she stopped. Now what?

Closing her eyes, Sarah crossed her ankles and sank to the floor near Luke's bed. *Oh, God, I don't know what to do. I'm so tired.* Molly sat beside her and nudged her hand. Needing the contact, Sarah curled her arms around her neck and tugged her close.

The branch still scraped against her window.

Molly still stared at her room with worried eyes.

Sarah didn't want to go back in there.

"Oh, Father," she whispered, clutching her hands. With her head bowed, she prayed for several moments. Nestled against Molly, she curled up on the floor, placed her arm around her, and fell promptly to sleep.

Luke woke up at his usual time, four o'clock. He'd had a peaceful night despite the stresses of yesterday. A good run this morning would help him start the day off right. He rolled over and saw Sarah snuggled with Molly on the floor. Molly lifted her head. Luke held out his hand like a traffic cop, and she lowered her head again.

God bless her, Sarah must have been terrified if she'd sleep on the floor. He accepted some of the blame for her restless night, the way he'd treated her after her trip into town.

He'd have to apologize.

He leaned over, gently picked her up, and placed her in his bed. He tugged the covers up to her chin. She didn't wake up.

He snapped his fingers at Molly and pointed to the end of his bed. She jumped up and settled at Sarah's feet. "Good girl," he whispered and patted her head.

He walked into Sarah's room and headed for the windows. Nudging the curtain aside, he noticed that from the ridge, there was a clear line of vision into this room. She'd have to keep her curtains closed all the time. But for tonight, they were switching rooms.

# ELEVEN

Winnie Sue had never been so uncomfortable. As she turned off Main Street and walked the half-block to Mountain View Church, a woman in a short skirt with matching jacket and heels raced up to her, stuck a microphone in her face, and signaled a cameraman right beside her.

"Ma'am, did you know the ladies who were murdered here?"

Just past the lady reporter, cameras were positioned up and down the sidewalk leading up to the doors of Mountain View. Winnie Sue wanted to point her white-gloved finger at them and ask them why they weren't in church this fine Sunday morning instead of harassing people who chose to be.

She mumbled, "Excuse me," sidestepped the woman, and marched up the sidewalk. Pastor Clay lent her a helping hand up the steps and gently tugged her inside the door.

She sat next to her sister and considered taking off her white gloves because the air conditioner hadn't been turned on and there were so many people in church that the air was too warm and they actually had to sit close enough to smell each other's mouthwash which was entirely too snug to suit Winnie Sue considering Alvin James was sitting right next to her and he apparently hadn't used any.

She edged closer to her sister.

Miss Gertie glared at her. "Get off my lap."

"Did they accost you, Sister?"

"They who? Oh, you mean the media."

Her eyes widened. "Why, who else would I mean?" Winnie Sue touched Miss Gertie's arm and nodded toward the front. Pastor Clay had stepped up to the podium.

Shocked at having three of their own murdered, the people of Little Texas had turned out in droves at Mountain View this morning. Winnie Sue sat back to enjoy Pastor Clay's sermon, "The Total Depravity of Man," which seemed to coincide poignantly with the recent goings-on in their town.

Most of the people in church probably had no idea what 'depravity' meant, but it sure seemed like Pastor Clay was talking about their murderer having an extra dose or two of it. He ended the service with an admonition to pray for the families of Bonnie, Renee and Lulu. And as an afterthought—it seemed to Winnie Sue—Pastor Clay mentioned praying for the killer.

As the first one outside, Gertie was happy to see that the nosy reporters and all their equipment had moved on. Mountain mornings were always crisp and clear and cool. She couldn't wait to get out in it and as far away from the church crowd as possible, except, of course, for Luke McKenzie.

"Do you see him, Sister?"

"You know I don't, Winnie Sue. You've been glued to me ever since we got out here." She smiled at Harriet and Henry Flagstone inching by. "Oh, there they are."

She tracked Luke following Sarah through the crowd toward his truck. As he reached for the door, Gertie, breathing a little heavily from running, boomed, "Well, there you two are! Trying to sneak out of here, are you?"

Luke turned around and frowned at her. "We're not sneaking out, Miss Gertie. We're just headed home."

Sarah elbowed him. "Good morning, Miss Gertie. Where's your sister?"

Gertie looked around. Well, for heaven's sake. Where had Winnie Sue gone off to? "Oh, visiting, I expect. We don't get out much or invited to people's homes like we used to. So many of our friends are dead now, y'know, with me being seventy-six and my little sister being sixty-three." It grated to act like such a dimwit but, hopefully, it would get them what they wanted.

"You're welcome to come to my cabin for Sunday dinner today if you think you could stand some Mexican food. We'll be serving around one or you could come home with us now and relax a little before we eat."

Trying not to appear smug, Gertie said, "Why, Luke, that would be wonderful. Been awhile since I've had Mexican food. It's good, is it?"

"The best. You can ride with me and Sarah. Where's your sister?"

She thought she'd throttle the lot of them if anyone else asked her where Winnie Sue was again. "I'll go get her," she smiled sweetly and stalked off to where her sister was yapping away with Floyd Watson.

"Excuse me, Floyd, Winnie Sue and I have an invitation to Sunday dinner. If you'll excuse us now." She took her sister's arm and yanked her toward Luke's truck.

"Why, Miss Gertie, he was just getting to the part about—if you wouldn't *run,* I might be able to keep up with you—oh! Did you say we've been invited?"

Gertie smiled. "Mission accomplished. We're riding with Luke and Sarah. Try not to be a complete bore, Winnie Sue."

She gasped. "What's gotten into you today, Sister?"

"Nothing's—"

"My manners are nothing but proper and pleasing."

"I'm not talking about manners. I'm talking about *interesting.* Either appear intelligent and interesting or keep your trap shut. Oh, what a nice red truck, Luke. Is it this year's model?"


A few paces from the steps of Mountain View Church, Allison shielded her eyes with a flattened hand and watched the two elderly women get inside the red truck and drive away. She was sure one of the Jansen women could help her find her long-lost grandmother.

"I don't believe we've met." A tall, blonde, older woman extended her hand to Allison. "I'm Debra Banks."

"Allison McIntosh." Her stomach clenched. Anonymity was vital, and she'd given her real name to the first person who'd asked. Dolt!

"Do you live around here, Allison?"

She kept her eyes down. "No. I'm here for the funeral of my cousin, Lulu Baines."

"Your cousin! Which side of the family—?"

"The Jansens."

"Well." Debra patted her hand. "It's a small world. We lost our Renee because of that monster so I know what you're going through, dear. I'm sorry for your loss."

She wanted to mutter, "There was no loss," but she managed a smile she didn't feel, lifted her chin, and withdrew her hand.

"If you need anything while you're here, please feel free to call the church office. Chelsea will direct you to the Women's Auxiliary."

"Thank you." Allison lifted a disdainful brow as the woman left. She had no intentions of feeling free to call anyone but the elderly Jansen women.

At McKenzie Cabin, a lull in the conversation made Gertie think that now was a good time to bring up the murders of the three women. "It's strange, I suppose, for two sisters in one family to remain unmarried," she generously surmised over a pile of spicy refried beans smothered with cheese sauce, jalapenos, and black olives. "But we were never lookers, Winnie Sue and I, and never turned a man's head."

"Why, Miss Gertie." Winnie Sue leaned forward. "Don't you remember my Owen?"

Gertie glared at her sister. They weren't here to talk about their non-existent love lives; they were here to find out what Luke knew about the murders. "Well, like I said, it's unusual, I suppose, but there you are."

Winnie Sue closed her trap and stuffed it with a small bite of beef burrito.

"Where did Little Texas get its name, Miss Gertie?" Sarah asked. "It seems unusual for a mountain town in Colorado."

"Oh, it is, that. Four friends and their wives and children left Texas in early 1890 and made their way to Colorado. They happened upon the valley just below here and fell in love with it but one of the friends, Cooper Banks, wanted them to go up a mite more. He found this valley and dubbed it 'Little Texas.' Natural borders prevented the town from growing overmuch. Within a year, six or seven family friends from Texas, with their wives and children, settled here, too.

"Through the years, other Texans came to stay. We're just a little hole in the wall, actually—a well-hidden secret and we'd like to keep it that way. Almost everybody in Little Texas is kin in some way to everybody else. That's why we're all so upset about the three women who were murdered." She hoped it didn't seem suspicious to bring the conversation around to Renee, Bonnie and Lulu.

"Yes," Sarah answered. "What were the four friends' names?"

"Banks, Jansen, Washburn, and Baines. All of us kin somehow." Gertie laughed and hoped it sounded sincere, hoped someone would jump right in and start talking about the murders.

"I see. So, Jim and A.J. Banks' great-grandfather—"

"Great-great-grandfather. He was only twenty and newly married when he came here. Cooper Banks."

"Have you always lived here, Miss Gertie? You and Miss Winnie Sue?"

Frustrated, Gertie almost slammed her fork down but caught herself and managed a smile. "All our lives. In fact, your property, Luke, was originally Jansen owned." Her thumb jabbed the air behind her shoulder. "Back of there a ways was the original home site built by our grandfather, Hiram Jansen. His wife's parents owned the twenty-acre plot and culled ten acres off for Hiram and their daughter. Two homesteads on the twenty acres. Hiram's eldest son, our uncle, died without an heir. With the death of her parents, the properties were then joined into one again and passed to my father who sold it about fifty years ago to Kenneth McKenzie."

Luke nodded. "My grandfather."

"Yes, I remember him and his family visiting here, but most of his children were grown then with kids of their own. His sister, your great-aunt Doris, lived in Denver and had two sons and an adopted boy and girl. She was a nurse, and her husband, Edmond, was in real estate. They were killed in a plane crash, as I recall."

"Well, I'll be. It's a small world." Luke leaned back in his chair, patted his stomach, and grinned at Sarah, who playfully rolled her eyes at him. "That was a great dinner. Eduardo, come out here and take a bow."

The right side of the swinging doors opened, and Eduardo poked his head out.

"That meal was great. You outdid yourself."

"I'm glad you enjoyed it. Everybody ready for dessert?"

"We are. Bring it on in."

"Oh, Mr. McKenzie, I don't think I could eat another bite, sweet or not."

"Why, Miss Winnie Sue, where are your manners?" Gertie slid her practiced smile toward Luke, took the cup of coffee Yolanda offered, and kindly said, "Of course, we would love some dessert."

Eduardo reappeared with a tray. "Chocolate cake and ice cream."

Gertie muttered, "Oh, how nice." And then she smiled. Winnie Sue was allergic to chocolate and lactose intolerant. She captured the panicked look her sister sent her and nudged her knee.

"I am just too stuffed, Mr. McKenzie," Winnie Sue ventured, patted her chest, and moved her knee out of Gertie's range.

After Miss Winnie Sue stifled a second yawn, Luke offered to take the ladies home. He turned to Sarah. "Would you like to go with me, maybe take a ride?"

Surprise was in her eyes. "I'd love to get out. Let me get my sweater and my big purse. We might end up in a tourist town." She ran upstairs and was back in a couple of minutes.

"Ladies, shall we go?"

It was a quiet drive to first Miss Gertie's cabin and then Miss Winnie Sue's Victorian home. As Luke backed out of her drive, he said, "If you like tourist towns, we could drive to Estes Park and show off the mountains, maybe shop downtown."

He preferred the country with its quiet, the raw appeal of the land, the spiritual awareness he had when he was alone in it. But Estes Park had enough of nature around it that he could survive an afternoon of crowds, shoulder-to-shoulder shopping, and waiting in lines to buy a memento. "It's not uncommon for elk to cross the streets and stop traffic. We can act like tourists for a day, take a bunch of pictures, buy a few things. Estes actually has some world-class shops."

"Sounds wonderful. I miss being outdoors. Luke, thank you for putting me in your bed this morning. I just couldn't stay in that room."

"You're welcome. My windows are completely covered by trees. So, we're switching rooms permanently."

"I appreciate it." She glanced around at the beautiful scenery. "Oh, look. It's just so magnificent."

"It is. I'm sorry you have to stay inside, Sarah. I know you didn't come up here to sit in my cabin all the time."

"No, but it's necessary right now. I've enjoyed the indoor pool. I'm used to running most days or walking long distances but swimming works, too."

"We have a gym in the basement. You're welcome to use it any time. Plus, you and I could go for another hike away from Little Texas."

"That would be nice. I've thought, too, about going back home, but I just can't bring myself to leave, to admit defeat."

He slowed for a cop who'd pulled over a motorcyclist.

She gasped as they passed them.

"What is it?"

"That man. Oh, never mind. I didn't get a good look at him that night but—"

"I'll turn around."

He did, but just as they drove up, the man's helmet slipped over his face. "Could you tell if it was him?"

"Not really. Something about him... his body shape, his height. Maybe it's just the fact that he's on a motorcycle."

"Did it have a Kansas license plate?"

"I didn't see."

He made another U-turn. They drove slowly past the man and his bike. *Kansas plates.* He looked up, appeared to be tracking the truck. Luke glanced in the rearview mirror. He hadn't moved and was still turned toward them. "Let's go back to Little Texas."

"No, Luke. I don't even know if that man's the Darkslayer. He might have stared at us because he thought I was flirting with him. Oh, look." She picked up her cell phone. "That view is absolutely stunning. Let's get out."

They stood beside a rock with the mountains behind them. A woman standing near them said, "Would you like me to take your picture?"

"Oh, uh. Sure." Sarah handed her the phone.

Luke placed his arm around Sarah and rested his hand on her shoulder. *Comfortable fit.* He looked down at her, which caused her to look up at him. He smiled. She smiled. He reflexively tightened his hold. And the woman captured the shot.

"Oh, it turned out beautifully!" she gushed and handed Sarah her phone with the picture still showing.

"Thank you," she said to the woman who turned back to the man with her. Sarah turned off the camera and opened her purse.

"I didn't see it."

She dismissed him with a shrug. "It's not a very good shot."

"Let me see." He held out his hand, amused at her wary expression. What was she afraid he'd see?

With a grimace, she handed it to him.

He found the picture. Anyone looking at it would think the couple smiling at each other was deeply in love. He shook his head at his foolishness. "You have a nice smile."

She lifted a shoulder and took her phone. Just as it slipped into her purse, a motorcycle approached them. The same man! He slowed down, revved his engine twice, and nodded once at them. Then he sped up toward the next curve, taking it dangerously fast.

"He must like blondes." Luke knew it was a flippant response, but what were the chances that the killer of those women was right here, at this same spot, the day Sarah was here? "Come on. The elk might not wait around for us to get there."

They drove into congestion. The green lights no longer meant 'go.' Traffic cops at every corner tried to regulate all the people on foot and the long line of cars on every roadway. Luke found a spot near the library building and parked. As he rounded the truck, Sarah got out and faced the other direction. She shut the door, turned, and bumped into him. He placed a hand on her arm to settle her.

For just a moment, they stood still, frowning at each other.

"Oh, I, uh, I didn't see you." Her laugh was spontaneous, and he found himself laughing with her.

He stepped back, but a group of teens converged on them, two walking right through them. He grabbed Sarah's arm, slid his hand down to hers, and headed toward the sidewalk and the crowds.

He was pleased that she didn't resist. Maybe she felt the same way he felt, that holding hands seemed natural between them.

He wouldn't dwell on that right now. He wanted to keep her safe and try to keep his sanity as the noise of conversations, squealing kids, shuffling feet, horns honking, and traffic cop whistles ushered them into the Estes Park shopping area. To some, this was exciting. He could understand that. But to him, it was suffocating.

The snow-capped mountains stood above the fray, reminding him to get into nature as soon as he could. When he needed it, he'd look up. "Shops are this way."


"Oh, look at these!" Sarah clutched a rock cut in half with beautiful, polished colors in the middle. "Agate Bookends," according to the sign above them. "My sister, Elizabeth, is a book worm. She'll love this set."

Luke was tired of shopping. He'd picked up some gifts for the women at the ranch: a girl named Emma; his sister-in-law, Marianne; his brother's secretary, Helen; and Stella, a ranch hand's wife. He could admit he missed the ranch and its simplicities. This busy, busy, push-and-shove, wait-and-wait-some-more world wasn't for him. "How about some taffy? There's none better anywhere, and the store's just down the street."

"I'd like that." She paid for her purchase and placed the bag in her oversized purse.

He took her hand and weaved through the people when Sarah squeezed his hand suddenly and leaned into him. "I heard him, Luke. He's here." He felt her hand trembling.

"Who?"

"The man in my home," she frantically whispered and looked around.

He searched the crowd, too, to see if someone was watching them. Was it possible he was here? It seemed too coincidental, but Sarah thought he was, and that was good enough for him.

"Let's leave, okay?"

Holding hands, they stepped outside. Crossed the street. Walked toward his truck. The same motorcycle zoomed past them. Luke still couldn't make out the numbers on the license plate. Sarah squeezed his hand as they both hurried to his truck.

Myra Simms had racked her brain every day, trying to remember anything she might've forgotten to tell A.J. and Jim about the day she and Lulu were planning to go shopping in Estes Park. That had been one of the most trying days of her life. Sometimes—rarely, really—a person found a soul mate as a best friend; Lulu was hers, despite their age difference of twenty years. She'd missed her every second of the past few days.

Myra's husband, Fred, settled into the rocking chair beside hers on their front porch. They sipped hot chocolate as night approached. "Not a soul's been by." Myra glanced over her cup at the street, blew on the still-too-hot drink, and sipped again.

"Naw, honey, they's too scared to come out now. Them murders is scaring everybody off the streets at night."

"Casey Pollard 'll be by. She never misses her exercising. I'm telling you what, that girl can fast walk."

"I don't reckon she'll be by, mother." Fred glanced at his watch. "She's fifteen minutes late already."

The familiar, steady rhythm of their rockers crunching on the wood porch was soothing. Myra leaned forward and looked past Fred, two doors on the right. "Harriet and Henry aren't sitting out either."

"I seen that." He cleaned his teeth with his tongue, smacked his lips. "It's a mite cool."

"It's not the cool that's keeping them in and you know it, Fred. Now here comes a brave soul." Myra stopped rocking and squinted into the night as she leaned forward. "Who's there?" she laughed.

"Just me, Aunt Myra."

"Joy? Honey, come on up here." Myra pursed her lips and whispered, "Something's wrong, Fred." To Joy, she said, "Come on now, honey. We got plenty of room." She lifted her brows at her husband and tilted her head. "Fred."

"I'm getting up, mother. You come on up here now and sit a spell with Myra, Joy. That supper's working its way through me already. I 'spect I need to go inside for a bit."

"You want some hot chocolate, child? I've got more in the kitchen."

Joy sat in the rocking chair. "No, no, Aunt Myra. I'm fine."

"What are you doing out and about tonight? Didn't you hear about the bodies they found at Gem's Peak Park?"

"I did, but Sonny and I had a fight. I needed to cool off and give him some time to cool off. I figured I'd make it to your house alive and well."

"With that killer loose, he shoulda come with you and not let you walk out here by yourself."

"The killer won't look in my direction. I've heard those other women were pretty and wore fancy clothes. I'm not pretty, and I don't wear fancy clothes."

"Oh, tosh."

Harriet and Henry's porch light flicked on. With her gaze on their screen door, Myra said, "What'd you and Sonny fight about?"

Joy's legs were too short for her feet to touch the floor. "Oh, same ol' thing. Leaving Texas to come up here."

Harriet's screen door opened a crack. Myra leaned forward, ever watching. "Sometimes we gotta accept the things we can't change, honey."

Harriet stuck her head out and looked at her and Joy. Myra waved. "Y'all coming out tonight, Mrs. Harriet?"

The frail woman shook her head, flapped her hand at Myra, and closed her door.

"You said some things can't change. But I could change it if I wanted to press it. I could make Sonny go back. But then he'd be hard to live with like I am now, and I don't think anything would be accomplished by it. Sonny likes having y'all close by to spoil him, so I think we'll probably stay. I'll straighten out my attitude and everything will be all right."

Myra patted her hand. "Let me tell ya something, child. Being a woman is tough. We give and give and then give s'more. It's in our nature. But in the long run, I don't think you'll regret the giving."

"I totally agree." Joy eased her head back against the slats and rocked awhile.

Myra enjoyed the peace of the cool night, the rustle of the leaves. A screen door slammed, and Myra looked toward Joy's home. Sonny stood on the porch, hands in his pockets. "Probably worried about you."

"Uh-huh." Joy stood and kissed her aunt's cheek. "I better get on back. Thanks for listening. See you tomorrow."

She waved as Joy turned right out of her driveway and headed down three doors and waved again when she reached her front door and Sonny. They both disappeared inside.

The door opened behind Myra. "Better get on in here, mother. You don't know where that killer might strike next." He held the screen door open for her.

Myra frowned and stood. "Laws, Fred, get your thinking cap on. That man's not interested in the likes of me."

# TWELVE

The next morning, Jim placed his hat and coat on the elk rack. Elva Lee stood by her desk staring at him, the concern in her eyes for him obvious. It touched him deeply. "'Morning, Elva Lee."

The emerald sweater she wore made her eyes appear bottle green. "'Morning, Jim. You doing all right?"

"Getting there." She stood and poured him a cup of coffee from his clean cup—she always cleaned his cup for him—and set it on his desk.

He glanced up and smiled and took a swig of coffee and almost choked. Her fingernails were gone! Every last one of them. "What happened to your nails?"

She tucked her fingers into her palms and shrugged. "Got tired of them. Felt kinda pretentious and silly, what with everything going on. Just not important anymore."

"Looks nice. More natural."

A.J. walked in. "'Morning," he muttered and headed for the coffee pot. Jim knew his brother's brain misfired a little until he'd had several cups of caffeine in the morning. Jim joined him in the kitchen area and leaned against the counter.

"I wanted to talk to you—" A.J. grimaced as his phone rang. "Gonna be a heck of a week," he muttered just as Luke walked inside S&R and greeted them with a single nod.

"Hello?" A.J. listened for a long time without saying anything, muttered, "Thanks," and hung up. He glanced at Elva Lee, then said to Jim and Luke, "Let's go outside a minute and talk."

The three men crossed the street to a little corner park and sat on the concrete picnic table that faced S&R. Just down two blocks was the City Park. The town council was big on little resting spots for its citizens. These corner parks were at several intersections in the downtown area.

Jim took a swig of his coffee and figured Elva Lee was glued to the window, watching them.

"Jim, you know anyone named Rosie?"

He slowly shook his head. "Can't say I do. Rosemary Atkins, but everybody knows she hates to be called Rosie."

A.J. glanced at Luke. "Did this man in the cave mention 'Rosie'? Did he call Lulu 'Rosie'?"

"No, not that I—wait. Yes, he did. When Lulu's shoe came off, he threw it into the crevice and said, 'Oh, Rosie. You're such a kidder.'"

"The coroner says all three women had something written on their stomachs. 'Rosie is dead.' That's what was written on them. 'Rosie is dead'."

Jim frowned. "R-O-S-I-E?"

"Yep."

"Was Renee—were they—?" Jim couldn't get the words out.

"None of them were molested; all were fully clothed. Just the hit on the head and some bruising under their arms."

"How?"

"Crowbar. All three exactly the same area of the head. 'Rosie is dead' written on their stomachs."

Jim nodded. "He validated her death by clearly writing 'Rosie is dead' on their stomachs just in case the authorities didn't get it."

"Serials are predictable. The patterns are there."

"So, Renee was killed by someone who *thought* she was someone else." Frustrated, Jim threw out his coffee. "Rosie must be small. Miss Gertie's small. Miss Winnie Sue's small. Shoot, the whole Jansen clan is small. Let's start with them and see if they know anyone in their family, or in this area, named Rosie."

"First, let's get to my office and run a check on Rosemarys or Rosies or Roseannes or Roses around here. Heck, maybe this guy's middle name is Roseman and he's killing his mother over and over for doing that to him."

The curtain fell back as Jim stepped off the picnic table. "Elva Lee knows everybody, too."

"Computer first, then we're talking to Miss Gertie. If Rosie lived around here in the last seventy years, Miss Gertie will know."

Jim nodded at Luke. "And if this idiot is focused on Sarah because he thinks she's Rosie, then she's in more trouble than we thought."

Luke cleared his throat. "I'm about to add more to the story." He told them about Sarah's attack, the killer's return that night, the two murders that seemed to suggest the killer was on his way up here, and Sarah's thinking she saw and heard him yesterday. "Sarah doesn't want any of this to get out in case she really didn't see or hear him."

A.J. nodded. "We appreciate you telling us about this. Two men after Sarah. No wonder I haven't seen much of her the past few days. I'll contact local PD in Riadon. See what I can find out."

"And I've got to get back to the cabin and check on her. Call me if you need me for anything."

"What's this?" Sarah plucked a paper rose off the gazebo post and turned it over. Rolled-up tape was on the back.

"Probably some game Eduardo and Yolanda are playing. They're always doing something like that with each other. They haven't been married long. Still in the gooey stage."

"Gooey stage?" Sarah chuckled.

"Sticky sweet."

"The expression on your face said 'yucky'."

"Yeah, that works." Luke shook his head at her. "I've seen my brother and his wife do this stuff, too." He playfully shivered.

Smiling, Sarah leaned against a rail and crossed her arms. She really loved the quiet and beauty of this place. It was a two-story home with enough perks that the word 'cabin' fit only because of the rustic furnishings inside. "When I think of Texas, I think of cattle and oil. Is there oil on your land?"

"You're talking about McKenzie Ranch, right? Yes, there is. Lots of it. I have oil, too. Those are two separate entities, though. One is my family's ranch that my great-great-grandfather founded in the early 1880s. My ranch is brand new. I bought two-thousand acres from my brother last year."

"Oh, okay. When I think of Texas, I think of cowboys and horses."

"Yep. We have those, especially on a ranch."

Nodding thoughtfully, she shrugged, enjoying this game. "When I think of Texas, I think of big, really big."

"Yep. Everything's big in Texas. Big dreams. Big opportunities."

"When I think of Texas, I think of southern gentlemen and beautiful ladies."

He grinned. "You'll find both at McKenzie Ranch. But not on my ranch. There's only me."

She knew she was flirting with him, but it was harmless fun, something she didn't usually do. "Are you a southern gentleman?"

He took a step toward her. "You'll have to answer that one."

"Then I will. Yes, you are." Before he could react, she changed directions. "What's the name of your ranch?"

"I haven't settled on one yet."

"Hmmm. When I think of Texas, I think of miserable heat. Maybe you could name it 'The Sweating Like a Pig Ranch'."

He laughed. "I'm not sure I could get a woman to marry me and live there with a name like that."

"You won't know until you ask her." She turned toward the trees. Neither said anything for a few minutes. Luke seemed as content as she was to be quiet. "Nothing has gone as I'd planned on this trip."

"I know."

"I thought I'd be out on a trail every day, exhausted from hiking, at peace with nature, no mental stress. Instead, I'm stuck in a cabin, *not* outside, and have more stress than I've ever had."

"Then let's go for a hike, Sarah. Back of the ridge. Plenty of miles to hike."

"Oh, I'd love that!" For the first time since coming to the cabin, she was excited. "Now?"

"Sure. We'll head out when you're ready."

"I'll meet you at the back door in fifteen minutes."

They headed up the ridge with Sarah in front of Luke. In shorts, her legs showed off well-toned muscles. Her foot was sure. He'd never had a female friend that thrived on being outdoors for exercise. Working cattle or horses, sure, but not just to enjoy nature.

"This trail heads up at a pretty tough grade. Then it tees into a trail that goes on forever, connecting to other trails, so we could be out here for a month if we wanted. Once it tees, we go left. Then it's a pretty easy hike, but we'll want easy after the grade up. From there, it's mostly hiking around a mountain in a circle."

"I am so ready for this."

They hiked in silence for about thirty minutes. It was simply too difficult to hike up and talk. Grouse appeared. A ground squirrel or two popped up. A black squirrel watched them. At the tree line in a small pasture, a couple of elk rested in grass.

They finally reached the trail circling the mountain and headed left. Sarah pointed to a fallen tree nearby. "Let's sit and rest for a minute. I'm thirsty."

"There's an overlook about five minutes away. How 'bout we stop there while I take a bio break?"

She drank and put away her water. "Sounds great."

Very little dirt was kicked up by either of them; there were enough small rocks on the path to prevent that. Coming around a wide corner, a red fox scampered across the path on its way down. Sarah stopped to admire it and then continued on. "Are there any caves in this area?"

"Not that I know of."

The trail moved away from the drop-off they'd contended with since turning left. The path headed into trees. "There's the lookout." Luke pointed toward boulders above them. "If you want to wait for me, I'll go with you."

"That's okay. I'll head on up and take a look."

"Keep me in your sights. We don't know if anyone followed us."

"Okay." She headed off. After a few steps, she turned around and focused on Luke. He glanced back at her at the same time and waved, laughing. She waved back and continued up.

She was almost to the top when she stopped again and looked for him. She didn't see him, and her skin tingled.

"Come on, Luke." She took a few steps back down and looked again. He was nowhere. "Behind a tree maybe?" She moved to the right, then the left. Nowhere. She stood still, searching the trail, the area. She shivered. Something was wrong.

Then she saw him, lying face-down on the other side of the trail. "Oh, no!" She started down but realized that someone had hurt him. Someone was out here.

She froze, too scared to move.

The pepper spray!

She scrambled to get it out of her shorts pocket and turned it to the 'on' position. By now, her hands were shaking so much, she didn't know if she could press the button if her life depended on it.

She hid behind a tree. Quick breaths and her pounding heart kept her from hearing anything else. She tried to breathe deeply but couldn't. She needed to get to Luke. *Please let him be alive! Please!* Easing her head from behind her cover, she searched for any movement anywhere.

Quietly, she ran down to the next tree.

A gun cocked. She gasped and turned toward the sound, due east of her position, mid-way between the trail and the lookout.

"Put the pepper spray down."

He was hiding in thick bushes about thirty feet away. Could she make it to the next tree?

"Now."

She knew one thing for certain. If she put the spray down, she would be defenseless. It took her a moment to garner the courage to speak and when she did, she used a forceful voice. "No. If you want me, you have to come and get me." Such brave words for someone shaking like a leaf.

"I said drop the pepper spray."

"No."

He fired at her but missed. A warning shot.

Another gunshot went off, but it wasn't from this man's weapon!

Sarah looked at where she'd last seen Luke. He wasn't there.

Another gunshot from below her. Another.

Rustling in the bushes. Then a 'pop, pop, pop' from them.

Another shot, closer to her but still south of her position. Another. Another.

"Run, Sarah! Run!"

With continuous gunfire coming from below her, she raced down the mountain. She reached the trail and slipped behind a tree. Luke was now above her, scampering up the mountain, hiding behind trees as he did. He circled to the east side of the bushes with his weapon aimed right at the center of it.

He slipped in back of a tree and looked around. Using a tree as cover, too, Sarah couldn't see anything moving.

Luke started down toward her, stopping behind trees as he did.

"He's gone. For now." Luke rushed toward her, and she stepped out.

"We don't have time for anything but running. Back the way we came."

He led the way. "Watch above us. He could be anywhere."

Close behind him, she huffed, "How did he get you?"

"He popped me in the back of my knees with something hard. When I fell back, he hit me on the head. I think he knocked me out for a few seconds."

"Was it a crowbar?"

"No, some sort of piping, I think."

"When I saw you face-down on the ground, I thought you were dead. I don't think I've ever been that scared in my life, including the night of the attack."

"I'm sorry for that." They reached the trail to McKenzie Cabin. "He could be anywhere by now. I'm sure he knows where we live. Now move as if your life depended on it."

Ten minutes later, they raced inside the back door. Luke slammed it and locked it. "That was stupid of us, hiking so close to the house. Next time, we'll—"

"Next time? Are you kidding? We're lucky to be alive."

"You're not thinking of leaving again, are you?"

"Of course not. I leave; he wins."

"You're a brave woman, Sarah. I admire your tenacity."

She strolled away from him to the other side of the room. This morning, her first thought was of Luke. *Feelings* for someone she hadn't known but a very short time. She'd lain in bed, excited about seeing him again after their afternoon of shopping together yesterday. Her mind told her to stop this nonsense; her heart welcomed it.

A little over a week. That's it. She'd only known him a little over a week. "Was that a line?"

He was silent for a long time. "A line?"

"Yeah, you know, what guys give girls to, you know, gain some ground." She closed her eyes. She had to put a stop to any ideas he may have about any kind of relationship with her.

"You really think—?"

When he faltered, she turned around. "No, I don't. I don't know what I think. I do know I'm going home to Kansas in a couple weeks, maybe sooner. And you're headed to Texas."

"And never the two shall meet?"

"Something like that."

"You're right."

Her breath caught as she looked up at him.

"You have roots. I have roots. They don't grow in the same area."

He was hurt and trying it hide it, but she could see it in his eyes. *Explain, Sarah.* "Luke. I'm trying so hard to regain some measure of who I am, who I was."

"So you attack my character to help you do that?"

"It was stupid. I thought I was putting distance between us, to stop anything that might be happening here. I'm sorry. I don't know what to do about anything."

He grabbed her shoulders. "Yes, you do. You just did it. You survived another attack. If you're trying to find out who you are, then start from here. Right now. You can't go back—that's gone. But he doesn't own your 'today.' He doesn't own your 'tomorrow' unless you give them to him. Don't let him steal *you*, the strong woman who's a survivor, a fighter. I see her. She's beautiful and strong."

He dropped his hands. "But whatever you decide, you're welcome to stay. I believe you're safer in this house with me. It's still not wise for you to be out and about alone."

"Thank you for making this easier for me." She touched his arm. "I need to go to my room. I'll talk to you in a little bit."

Luke watched her walk away. After everything they'd been through, she'd accused him of manipulation. The one thing he'd prided himself on his entire adult life was being genuine and treating others the way he wanted to be treated. His parents had drilled that into their boys. *Be truthful. Be kind. Do what's right.* And here the first woman he'd been drawn to in a long time was calling him a fake.

"Her problem, not mine." After a few seconds, he added, "Not true, buddy, and you know it." To get his mind off her, he called A.J. to tell him about what happened on the trail.

"Did you see him?"

"I saw a glimpse of something. He was small. That's probably why he kneed me; I'm too tall for him to hit."

"I'd like to see where this took place."

"I'll take you up there whenever you're ready." They hung up.

Luke's phone rang. "Yes, Sarah?"

"I thought you might be too angry with me to answer my call, but I had to tell you again that I'm sorry. I don't know why I said such a callous thing. I've never once thought of you as being deceptive or disingenuous. Please forgive me?"

"I already have. How 'bout a game of checkers or cards or dominoes to prove it?"

"I'd love that. We'll stay holed up here and relax a bit."

"Until A.J. calls me. He wants to see where the killer shot at us today."

Later that morning, Dr. Vince Graham, the coroner, released the bodies of the three women to the funeral home. *Cause of death: blow to the head with a blunt instrument, possibly a crowbar.* Not complicated.

"We got no murder weapon, no fingerprints, no hair samples, no body fluids, no eyewitnesses to the murder, and the only blood sample belongs to a victim."

Jim looked over at his brother.

"How are we supposed to find a murder suspect who's a male, short, wears size seven shoes, has a fondness for peanuts, and is killing 'Rosie' over and over again? No Rose of any kind in our area but Rosemary Atkins. You were right about asking Miss Gertie and Miss Winnie Sue. We'll start there and see where it takes us. Also, Luke and I hiked to the shooting site and found absolutely nothing."

"Story of our lives lately."

"Absolutely nothing to go on, and we're supposed to find a killer."

Jim listened as A.J. called Miss Winnie Sue and put the call on speaker.

"Hello?"

"Hey, Miss Winnie Sue. This is A.J. Banks."

"Why, Officer Banks. I trust you're doing well today, sir?"

Jim smiled. Miss Winnie Sue was a treasure, for sure.

"I'm fine, Miss Winnie Sue. Wondered if Jim and I could come over and ask you a few questions related to the three women."

Jim heard a gasp and thought she could very possibly be in a dead faint. She was known for her fainting spells.

"Miss Winnie Sue?"

No answer. *Great!* A.J. had gone and scared the living daylights out of her.

"Miss Winnie Sue? Are you there?"

"Oh. Yes." She swallowed hard. "Officer Banks."

Jim could just see her patting her chest and fanning herself with her white, lacy handkerchief.

"I'm sorry," she muttered. "Such a dreadful thing."

"Yes, miss. Would you feel better if we took you out to Miss Gertie's and talked to y'all together?"

"Oh my, yes. That would be much better. When may I expect you?"

"About five minutes, if that'll give you enough time."

"That would be fine. I'll expect you then."

With her white gloves on, Jim was sure. And all gussied up in her Sunday best. Miss Winnie Sue was never seen in pants or anything other than a nice dress and white gloves.

Sure enough, when they drove up, she walked down the steps, all prim and proper, tugging on her gloves with her purse dangling from her right elbow.

Jim hopped out and opened the front door for her.

"Oh, Mr. Banks. Would you mind if I sat in the back, sir? I have always wanted to sit in the back of a police car."

"Not at all, miss." Jim gallantly opened the back door for her.

"Thank you, sir. It's a lovely day today, isn't it?"

She didn't say another word. It took only a matter of minutes to drive up to Miss Gertie's.

Her older sister was hanging some towels on the clothesline when they drove in. Jim thought it peculiar when Miss Gertie spotted Miss Winnie Sue in the back seat of A.J.'s patrol car that she didn't even blink an eye. It wasn't every day Miss Winnie Sue Jansen rode in the back seat of a patrol car.

"Winnie Sue," Miss Gertie said with a straight face as she leaned over and picked up another towel. "You been drinking again?"

Miss Winnie Sue slipped around Jim and shook her gloved finger at Miss Gertie. "That is not funny. Not funny in the least." She touched the back of her head and patted her perfectly placed hair. "You know I never touch any alcoholic spirits."

"Not what I heard," Miss Gertie teased as she pushed a pin over the folded corner of a wet towel and slid her fingers down the towel toward the basket.

"Officer Banks has come to ask you some questions about the three murdered women."

Color slid out of Miss Gertie's face when she turned around and squinted at her sister.

"Actually, we have a lead and wanted to pick your brains, both of you. Would you like to go inside or sit out here?"

Miss Gertie flicked her gaze around the yard, then up to her porch. "I think inside would be better where we can all be comfortable."

With a lift of her chin, Miss Winnie Sue floated past Miss Gertie, through the screen door A.J. held open for her and into her sister's small cabin. Jim raised his brows at A.J. as he walked inside, too.

Jim could count on one hand the number of times he'd been in this house. The living room seemed exactly the same as his last visit. Two double-paned, over-large windows sat opposite one another. The one on the right, the north window, showcased one of the best views of snow-capped mountains he'd ever seen out a window. It had a short-backed sofa under it that didn't block any of that spectacular view. Beside it was a large fireplace. The south window showed off mostly thick trees; in front of it sat a lounge chair with a small table beside it.

To the left of the front door sat a green floral sofa with a coffee table in front it. Anyone sitting on that sofa had a perfect view of the grandeur out the north window. Above the green sofa, a rectangular window afforded a view of Miss Gertie's porch and front yard. She had a pretty good view of most of her property.

"Have a seat, A.J., Jim, and I'll get us some iced tea."

"I'll help you, Miss Gertie." Miss Winnie Sue quietly followed her sister into the kitchen.

A.J. sat on the sofa while Jim parked himself in the lounge chair.

"Man, that's one fine view." Jim took himself to the north window and looked out over the greening up of Colorado, with snow caps above all that green. Sure, they'd have more snow, but it was the wet kind that disappeared at the stroke of a sun's ray.

Gertie glared at her little sister and lugged the big container of sun tea out of her refrigerator and onto the counter.

"It's not my fault," Winnie Sue whispered as she opened the freezer top and pulled out an ice tray and twisted it. "If you'd get a telephone—"

"I don't *want* a stupid telephone!" With one hand, she grabbed three glasses and shut the cabinet door.

"Well, *if* you had one, I could have warned you."

Gertie put ice in and poured the tea. "I don't have anything to hide."

"Why, you most certainly do, Miss Gertie. We both do."

Gertie picked up the serving tray with three iced tea drinks and glared at Winnie Sue. "While we're in there, Winnie Sue Jansen, keep—"

"Your trap shut. I know, Sister. I know."

They walked into the living room. "Here we are, Jim, A.J." Smiling, Miss Gertie held the tray while each chose a glass.

"You have a great view here. I could stand here all day."

She paused in her ministrations and glanced out the window as if she'd never seen it before. "That's what everybody says, Jim."

They all moved to the small living. The two women perched on the sofa some distance apart, sipped their teas, and then rested their glasses in the palms of their hands. Both looked expectantly at A.J., who was in charge. Jim was just an observer.

"We've got a clue. Wondered if y'all have ever heard of a Rosie in these parts?"

Miss Gertie never moved a muscle.

Not so with her sister. She gasped, drew her free gloved hand to her mouth, stared wide-eyed at Miss Gertie, and sank back against the sofa.

"I take it that's a yes, Miss Winnie Sue?"

Miss Gertie recovered first. "Well, now, A.J., I don't recall ever having met a Rosie before. I've known a Rosemary, and—"

He held up a hand to stop her. "Miss Winnie Sue," he said softly and set his glass on a coaster. "Have you ever known a woman named Rosie?"

She looked sideways at her sister and frowned. "I—Officer Banks, I have never known a woman named Rosie."

He sat in the wood chair opposite her. "You sure?"

She didn't meet his gaze. "I was merely reacting to what I thought you'd said, that a woman named Rosie was the killer."

"I didn't say that."

Her hand fluttered over her chest, and then rested on her cheek. "I know, Officer Banks. I'm sorry. I don't know a woman named Rosie."

"Anyone named Roseanne—"

Both shook their heads and said, "No" and "No, sir."

"Or Rosemary."

All color drained from Miss Winnie Sue's face. But she resolutely shook it 'no,' with fingers cradling her chin as if she needed them to keep her head still so it wouldn't nod a 'yes.'

A.J. slapped his knees, which caused Miss Winnie Sue to jump and utter, "Oh, my!" He stood, Jim stood, and waited for the ladies to rise.

"That's all I had today, so I'll be on my way. If you *do* think of a Rosie, would you mind letting me know? I was hoping you two could help us out."

"We sure will, A.J., Jim, and thanks for coming by."

"Keep us posted if you hear anything, Officer Banks."

"Will do, ladies. Oh, one other thing. Do you have any idea why a man would be after our three women? Why he'd be after these three *particular* women? Any idea at all?"

Miss Gertie raised her brows, looked at her sister. "I don't, A.J. Do you, Winnie Sue?" It seemed to Jim that she did her best to put a don't-you-dare-say-a-word-about-anything look in her eyes.

"I don't." Winnie Sue shook her head. "No, Officer Banks, I don't." She lowered her gaze and then sent a sidelong glance at Gertie.

"Well, appreciate your time." A.J. nodded once and left. Jim smiled at the ladies and followed his brother.

When they reached the patrol car, Jim muttered, "I would have never thought I'd witness either of those ladies telling a lie."

"Me, either. But they sure did today."

Gertie caught the door before it could slam. She and Winnie Sue stood on the porch as A.J. backed out, waved, and drove away.

"Well, you sure messed things up, Winnie Sue!" Gertie marched to her kitchen and set her iced tea glass on the counter with a clunk.

"Me?"

"Yes, you! Almost swooning when he mentions *Rosie*. What in the world were you thinking? Don't you have an acting bone in your body, Sister?"

"Don't you 'Sister' me, Sister! I did the best I could under the circumstances!"

Gertie smacked both fists on her hips. "What circumstances? A man asks a simple question, and you fall to pieces!"

"I most certainly did not! I-I... fluttered... a little—"

Gertie snorted. "Fluttered? A little?"

A knock on the door startled them both. They held their breaths and waited.

"Miss Gertie?"

Her eyes widened as she leaned over and whispered, "It's Jim!"

Winnie Sue slapped both hands on her cheeks and gasped, then lowered her head and whispered, "Do you think he heard us?"

Gertie picked up a towel and threw it on the table as she glared at her sister and stormed out of her kitchen. "Why, Jim, bless your heart, did you forget something?"

"Yes, miss, we did. Your sister."

"My sis—oh." She laughed. "You need to take her home. Winnie Sue, your ride is here. Mercy, Jim, I totally forgot A.J. brought her."

"Yes, miss. Too much on our minds, I expect."

Winnie Sue said a meek goodbye to her sister and walked out without so much as a glance in Jim's direction.

Gertie rolled her eyes behind her sister's back and wondered just what Jim had meant by his 'too much on our minds' remark. She wondered, too, if he'd heard anything she and Winnie Sue had said.

Officer Banks draped a hand over the steering wheel and eyed Winnie Sue in the back seat. She averted her gaze.

"Miss Winnie Sue, you sure seemed edgy when I said the name 'Rosie' back there."

Good gracious, what should she say? She *had* been edgy, but she couldn't let him know she knew that. If she did, the next victim in this town would be Winnie Sue Jansen at the hands of her big sister! "Well, Officer Banks, truth be told, I knew a Rosemary once over fifty years ago now."

"What happened to her?"

"Oh." She held up her hand and admired her gloves. "She's no longer with us. A tragedy befell her a-and she's no longer with us. The only other Rosemary I know is Rosemary Atkins, but she certainly doesn't seem like a killer to me. Why, she's the president of the Women's Auxiliary at church, and I can't imagine her being a part of anything like—"

"I didn't say the killer was Rosie."

"You didn't?" She blushed. Mercy, she was no good at deception! Unconsciously, she slipped the lace handkerchief out of the sleeve of her blouse and dabbed at her upper lip.

"No, miss. I said one of the clues was a woman named Rosie."

"Oh." Miss Winnie Sue glanced at the rearview mirror, then looked down at her hands. "I see."

"I'll be frank, miss. You seem to know more than you're saying."

She cleared her throat and touched it with a gloved hand.

"Am I right?"

"Well, Officer Banks, I-I... oh, there's my house. I'm anxious to check on my tomato plants. I'm sorry I couldn't be of more help to you. I will be praying for you to have wisdom and guidance in finding this perpetrator. Now, if you'll be kind enough to open this door, I'll thank you for the ride and wish you a good day, sir."

The Banks brothers watched Miss Winnie Sue walk at a fast clip down the sidewalk to her home. She opened her outside door, walked through her screened-in porch, and opened her front door, without a key. Jim jumped out. "Miss Winnie Sue!"

She turned around as he walked toward her.

"I'm advising you to lock your doors now, miss, until this man is found. It's not safe to leave 'em open." His gaze flicked to an unopened tomato seed package—not tomato plants—sitting inside an empty window box under her first large window.

Miss Winnie Sue followed his gaze and blushed when she looked back at him. "I'll do that, Mr. Banks. You can rest assured, sir, that I will do that."

Jim walked back to his car. The world must be coming to an end soon. This was the second time today that Miss Winnie Sue Jansen skimmed the edges of the truth and almost told an out-and-out lie.

# THIRTEEN

Tuesday morning brought cool showers and dreary skies, matching the mood of the people of Little Texas who opened their newspapers and found the headlines blaring that the funerals of the three women murdered in their own homes would be the next day, Wednesday, at Mountain View Church where all three women had attended. The funeral for Renee Banks would begin at nine in the morning with interment at ten-thirty. At Noon, Bonnie Washburn, with interment at one-thirty. And at three, Lulu Baines, interment at four-thirty. Mayor Terry Mason was quoted as saying, "It's going to be a long and sad day for the people of Little Texas."

Exhausted from crying, worrying over, and discussing the murders with every customer who came into her shop, Myra Simms locked the dress shop door. She'd lost her best friend, Lulu, and dear friends, the other two. She needed a break from the tears and decided a treat for lunch at Penny's restaurant next door was just the ticket.

Everyone knew A.J. came into Penny's on Tuesday. Myra wanted to see if those two birdbrains had the sense God gave a raccoon between them. Honestly. It was high time somebody did something to nudge those two back together. This separation of theirs was going on for too long now. Enough was enough.

The doorbell dinged as she walked into Penny's. Every head turned to look at her. Jim Banks' mother, Debra, sat at a small table for two. She immediately got up and pointed to a booth and waved Myra over.

"We can visit, catch up on everything," Debra said as she scooted in.

"How's Jim taking the news of Renee's death?" Myra moaned at getting off her feet for the first time that day and tried to relax.

"About as well as can be expected. You know he came to see Jeb the other night, to tell him about Renee. For the last year, he thought she had left him—we all did. That left a big hole in that boy. And now he's having to deal not only with the fact that she was murdered but with the fact that he's had some pretty awful thoughts about her."

The doorbell dinged again. Heather Ward walked in with her daughter, Elva Lee. The ladies in the booth smiled and waved them over. Debra moved closer to Myra. "Y'all come on. We'll scrunch up. How's everything at Search & Rescue today, Elva Lee?"

They slid in.

"Better yet," Myra said, "how's Jim doing this morning?"

The blush creeping clean up Elva Lee's face did not go unnoticed by Myra or anyone else at that table. She'd known for a long time—hadn't everybody?—that Elva Lee Ward was stuck on James Madison Banks. How long was it going to take that boy to sit up and notice how perfect Elva Lee was for him? Myra hoped Jim might finally find some peace and move on now that he knew the truth about Renee.

"I don't know, Debra. He's been at A.J.'s this morning. Tommy's at work, but Buddy won't be in. He's a little under the weather today."

"Under the bottle's more like it," Myra mumbled as the other women nodded, and then shook their heads in a moment of silence.

Francie came to the table, took their orders, and left. Myra was more than ready for Penny's hot chicken noodle soup—it was always Tuesday's special. She conspiratorially leaned toward the center of the table. "I heard there's a Rosie connected with the killings," she whispered as her gaze flitted around to each woman.

Everyone at that table slowly eased forward. Myra was pleased as a pear tree to be the one enlightening them. "Rosie is dead." She over-enunciated her quiet words. "Written right there on their tummies."

"Who's Rosie?" Debra rested her arms against the table. "I don't know any Rosie." The others shrugged and shook their heads.

Francie walked up with a pot of coffee and all four women sat upright. Myra turned her cup over and patted the back of her hair while Francie silently poured everyone a cup and left. Myra lifted her hot cup of coffee, looked over her glasses, and shook her head. "No one knows who Rosie is or what the name means."

Elva Lee unfolded her napkin and put it on her lap. "Jim thinks it's a woman the killer can't touch, like his mother or something, and he's killing people who look like her."

Debra set her cup down. "Why, Elva Lee, that just doesn't make sense." She picked up the sugar container and spooned in three heaping servings. "If he wants to kill someone, he should kill *her* and not other people."

"He *thinks* he's killing her."

"And he can't tell the difference?" Debra shook her head. "Seems to me if I had a mind to kill someone, I'd certainly make sure I killed the one I intended to kill and not some stranger!"

As if to chastise the women for gossiping, A.J. and Jim Banks walked by Penny's window and into the restaurant. Jim spoke to his mother, nodded at the other women, held Elva Lee's gaze for a moment—which tickled Myra no end—and perched on a stool beside his brother who sent a general wave to his mother's table.

A silence fell across the restaurant, a reverence of sorts—like being in church—as the brothers ordered their lunch and looked around at the guilty faces behind them. When Jim looked right into Myra's eyes, she blinked rapidly and glanced toward the ceiling.

All talk ended. Their presence forbade it. When words were spoken, they were whispered. Someone loudly slurped a hot sip of coffee, and everyone turned to frown at him. Forks nudged plates but did not clink against them. Gazes darted around the room.

And not a soul asked the chief of police or his brother about the women, or the killer, or about that woman Rosie and how she fit into all this.


At S&R, Tommy and Buddy were called out on the rescue of an eight-year-old boy who slid down a ten-foot embankment and was caught in shrubbery at the base of it. His parents were frantic and couldn't reach him. It was not a difficult rescue. They were expected to be back within an hour.

Elva Lee and Jim were left alone.

Elva Lee's desk sat by the north window, facing the front door.

Jim's desk rested under a small window, facing Elva Lee.

It was difficult at best to gauge his mood, but Debra had told her privately that he was struggling with finding Renee's body, dealing with the loss, the anger, the funeral coming up.

She poured him a cup of coffee and set it on his desk. "Jim?"

"Umm?" He crossed a 't' and looked up at her.

"I just wanted you to know that I have a great pair of ears."

He rested his cheek on his fist, his gaze squarely on her, and it unnerved her.

"And sometimes my mouth shuts down when my ears are in gear." He smiled at her.

"It's a good possibility that conditions are prime today for both to happen."

Jim leaned back in his chair. When he nodded, she wanted to touch his hand but knew she shouldn't.

"You're a good friend, Elva Lee, and I appreciate it. I'm all right, I think. Just need some time to process all this. Got a lot going on right now."

She nodded. "Well, I just wanted you to know that I'm here for you, if you need anything."

"Thank you. I appreciate it."

That night, Jim sat in the dark, alone, and stared at the picture of Renee he'd put on the mantel the day Josh Daniels had found her body. She was smiling, as usual, and her eyes, those big brown eyes, were focused right on him.

Her teeth had been perfect, her mouth small, her face heart shaped. Her long curly brown hair, hanging over her shoulders, had been full and bouncy.

He missed her. He'd missed her every second she'd been gone but he couldn't face what she'd done to him, couldn't believe their life together had been nothing but a lie.

A whole year, he'd longed to hear from her, longed to touch her, ached to find out why she'd left him. What had been the lack in him that had caused her to leave him? Had their baby been born? Was it being raised by another man?

He hadn't talked to anyone, not even A.J. or his parents, about any of that. They would have pitied him for being such a fool.

He *had* been a fool! He'd believed the worst of Renee and none of it was true. He jumped up and sent his iced tea flying.

Glass shattered all over the creeping ivy Rachelle had given Renee on her last birthday and the firewood Jim had brought in the night before. He growled and kicked the stack of firewood and when it didn't budge, he shoved it with his boot. The logs tumbled out in slow motion. Just like he felt, tumbling in slow motion and nowhere to go but down. He grabbed one and threw it into the fire. Angry sparks flew out at him.

He leaned against the fireplace, which put his face right in front of Renee's photo. He stared at her mouth, her eyes, her hair. A surge of longing hit him, and a whimper escaped his pinched lips. He gasped. Racking sobs erupted from deep within his soul.

"I'm sorry." His heart ached. His fist pounded the mantel as he gritted his teeth against the pain. "Oh, Renee. I'm. So. Sorry." He leaned on the mantel, buried his face in the crook of his arm, and shook his head, back and forth, back and forth. Then he stilled and let the grief wash over him. "I'm so sorry, honey. I'm so sorry."

Tears fell onto the brick landing where he stood. Wave after wave of sorrow and anger and regret swept over him. He cried for the loss of his love, the loss of their love, the loss of his only child.

A big hand slid across his shoulder. Lost in his anguish, Jim turned into the arms of his older brother. He and A.J. held on to each other unashamedly as Jim wept for the woman lost, the senselessness of her death, and the indescribable pain of being left behind.

Easing out of his brother's arms, Jim sniffed. With his head down, he walked into the hall, grabbed a couple of washcloths out of the linen closet, and handed one to his brother.

Wiping faces, they both stared at Renee's picture.

"Came to see how you were doing."

"You saw."

"Didn't expect anything less."

Jim took A.J.'s washcloth and put both on the mantel. "Want something to drink? Tea or juice."

"Tea. I'll turn the TV on. Game's started. Rangers are ahead."

Jim left, came back with two glasses of tea, and handed one to his brother. For the first time in a long time, Jim felt a measure of contentment. For some reason, he thought of Elva Lee. He wanted to tell her about tonight. He wanted to tell her that he was going to be okay now.

Easing into a chair opposite A.J., he took a good-sized guzzle as the commercial ended and the baseball game came back on.

"You let her go."

Several seconds ticked by as Jim stared unseeingly at the screen. "I did."

A.J. lifted his glass.

Jim leaned over, clicked his glass against A.J.'s, and turned up the volume on the TV.

Sarah was curled up on the sofa closest to the roaring fire in the den, grateful for the thick woolen socks that kept her feet warm. She tried to read a mystery book, but it was difficult to stay in it with the wind kicking up and noises creeping around the windows and the house creaking in the blustery weather. "I sure wish we could steal some warm May weather from Kansas and bring it up here, Luke. I'm ready for winter to become a distant memory."

"Won't be like that until the middle of June."

She groaned. "Are you going to any of the funerals?"

He looked up. "I thought I would. Are you?"

"I don't know these people. I'd feel like I was intruding."

"Then I won't go. It's going to be an all-day event." He popped the newspaper and folded it. "That's too long to leave you by yourself."

"Won't Eduardo and Yolanda be here?"

"No. They've lived here all their lives. They'll be at the funerals."

Through the dark trees, the lighted clock on the bank said *11:36* as Casey Pollard jogged down the empty town square, headed west. She crossed the street to the City Park. It had been horrible the last few days, what with losing her sister, Lulu, and dealing with everyone coming to the house, bringing food and hugs and tears and... she was just so very tired of it all. And she was angry. This man comes to their town and *kills* her sister! Tonight, when she'd thought about running, she remembered what A.J. had said earlier today at the grocery store: "No running, Casey. Not after dark."

It felt good to be running at night for a change, even with all this wind. Her husband, Will, had taken the day off, and they'd both worked hard on fixing some things around the house. When he fell asleep on the sofa watching the baseball game and all the kids were asleep, too, she figured she'd get in a short run.

Not once, in all the years she'd been running, had she ever experienced fear in Little Texas.

But tonight, she sure did.

But what were the chances that this lunatic would be in her path? Small town, sure, but he could be anywhere. She did think about turning around. A little farther and she would.

Her gaze darted into the row of trees along the sidewalk. Up ahead, around a corner, the brush was close to the sidewalk. She edged over to the right and avoided it and breathed a sigh of relief as she—

Her hair was caught! Something was pulling her back, dragging her into the dark shrubs!

Pain gripped her temples. She grabbed her head to stop the agony, but she couldn't.

"Stop it, Rosie." Next to her ear, smelly breath hissed.

Rosie! The killer! "I'm not... Rosie." Her face contorted as she gritted her teeth against the ripping pain. "I'm. Not. Rosie!"

He yanked on her hair. Casey almost fainted.

"Shut up, Rosie. You got out, didn't you? You got out *again!*" He yanked her hair. Casey barely hung on to consciousness. "You're going right back in there, y'hear me? Right back in there!"

Casey knew she was dead if she didn't do something. "Let me go."

The killer stopped, and the screeching pain yielded. "What'd ju say, Rosie?"

"I said, let me go." She didn't have the strength to grab her hair. "I'm not Rosie, you fool. I'm Casey. You can't kill the wrong person, can you?" She looked up and couldn't see anything in the dark surrounding them.

The man jerked her to her feet and what she could only describe as a scuffle occurred behind her.

"Let her go." A deeper voice, more mature.

"No, it's Rosie. I have to—"

"It's not Rosie! Rosie's dead!"

"No, she isn't. She got out!"

"Let her go. NOW!"

"No!"

Casey tried to see who was behind her, but a crushing weight slammed into her head, and she knew nothing.

*"And it's a home run!"*

Will Pollard stirred enough to watch through narrowed eyes as the batter ran around the bases. "Honey? Could you get me a beer?"

*"With the score four to two—"*

"Honey? Casey?" Will sat up, threw the pillow he was hugging onto the sofa, and looked over his shoulder toward the lighted kitchen. He clicked the TV off and listened. "Casey?"

He stumbled into the kitchen and pulled out a beer, popped the top, and drank. He took another swig and listened. She didn't go out running, did she, after A.J. told her not to?

He headed for the basement. "Casey?"

No answer.

He checked their bathroom. Ran out the back door. "Casey?"

Rushing back inside, he plucked the keys off the hook by the garage door and cursed. He grabbed his phone, punched in the numbers, and waited. "Mom, Casey's out running. I've got to go find her. Okay. Thanks."

Will hustled inside his truck and started it as the garage door lifted. He backed out. His mother was running down the sidewalk.

"Be right back," he yelled as she waved and walked inside the house.

He knew Casey's route. If she was out running, he was going to let her have it, in spades. Running in the dark with a killer on a murder spree!

He was frantic after twenty minutes. He drove by the police station, but no one was there. He headed over to Search & Rescue.

Lights were on. He ran inside. A.J. and Jim both jumped up when he crashed inside.

"Casey's missing!"


Larry's hands shook as he reached for his radio. He fumbled it. It crashed beside Casey's body, and he swiped it up as if he could take back the clattering sounds. "A.J.? Uh, I-I found her, A.J. In the shrubs, just north of the curve in the walking path on the west side of the park. We need an ambulance. She's in bad shape."

## FOURTEEN

The news spread like wildfire that the killer almost succeeded in snuffing out the life of Casey Pollard. Jim called Luke early in the morning to let him know to be alert, that the killer was spiraling out of control. He hadn't succeeded with Casey or with Sarah the day before on her hike, so he might be more desperate to get Sarah.

The funerals began at nine in the morning with Renee's. Surprisingly, Jim felt sadness, not torment, at seeing Renee's closed casket at the front of the church. She was at peace; he was at peace.

By the interment at ten-thirty, snow clouds hovered. A chilly breeze glided over and around the tombstones. Long winter coat hems lifted in the blustery air; scarves floated above shoulders as if they wanted to fly away from all the sadness while mourners' hands held hats securely on their heads.

Myra Simms was clinging to Jim's arm. Fred stood to the side, hands in his pockets, head down, his long black coat flapping in the wind. Myra pulled away from Jim and took Fred's hand. He led her away to their car.

All during the funeral and the interment, Jim had caught Penny looking at A.J. with something like regret in her eyes. He supposed that death made people re-evaluate their lives. That's what she seemed to be doing, standing by her car, watching A.J. again. Hopefully, something good with those two would come out of all this.

She got inside her car and slowly drove off.

Jim was alone now, standing over the grave of his wife with his head down. His new black suit felt awkward on him—it was tight in the wrong places and way too thick. The black tie he'd bought to go with it danced on his shoulder in the cool breeze.

Renee's family had left right after the graveside service ended.

A.J. came and stood beside him. He heaved a sigh. Neither said a word for several moments. "You know she's in a better place."

Jim tilted his head back and stared up at the gray-layered clouds. "I had nothing to do with her going away." He sent his brother a sidelong glance and lifted his brows. "'And the truth will set you free.'"

A.J. smiled at him. Like Jim, he was probably remembering Mrs. Musselman's scripture-of-the-week for the kids in Sunday school and how she'd have them stand up and quote it and put a star by the names of those who'd learned it. Jim memorized his scripture every week because he wanted those multi-colored stickers beside his name. Because he wanted to shine. Because he wanted Mrs. Musselman's praise for a job well done.

Looking around at the huge array of flowers surrounding Renee's grave and feeling peace right now, he'd like to tell Mrs. Musselman that her diligence had paid off. "Wasn't she something?"

"Mrs. Musselman. Man, she was tough. But also kind. Such a sweet woman."

Nodding thoughtfully, Jim said, "The truth," as he squatted, picked up a clod of dirt, and bounced it in his hand. He stared at it, then squeezed his hand and sprinkled the dirt on top of her shiny mahogany casket. "Goodbye, Renee. I will always love you."

The two of them walked back to A.J.'s patrol car.

A.J. slid in. "There's a community-wide dinner at eleven at Mountain View Church. It's for all three funerals. Plenty of food. Let's head over there and get something to eat."

Jim nodded. "Sounds good. I'm starving."


At Bonnie Washburn's funeral and interment, her husband Buddy was not among the mourners. He'd been too drunk to come to his own wife's funeral.

Miss Gertie and Miss Winnie Sue stood with the family. Howard Jansen, their brother, was Bonnie Washburn's grandfather.

"Hold on, Jim," A.J. said as he leaned over and studied a young woman he'd never seen. "Who's that?"

Jim's gaze swept the faces. "Where?"

"The small woman, right there beside Will Pollard, looking at us and making an effort not to. Who is she?"

"I don't know. Never seen her before."

"Sure seems interested in my patrol car. Maybe we need to take a closer look-see."

"Not at a funeral. We'll keep an eye on her when she leaves."

But she slipped away during the long prayer closing out the interment service.

Jim and A.J. went over to the station to check in.

Both dreaded the final funeral at three o'clock. It was packed. Everybody had loved Lulu. After the interment, A.J. and Jim, weary from this emotional day, headed to their offices to check in.

"Do you see any straight edges, Luke? I'm missing two pieces over here." Sarah checked the time. "The funerals should be over by now. I'm so sorry for all the hurt in this town." She was grateful Luke had stayed back with her. She looked outside. "What a beautiful snow. It's getting thicker."

She folded her arms on the card table holding their one-thousand-piece puzzle and leaned toward Luke as she scanned the pieces. "I saw that. You took my straight edge."

When he pulled his hand out of her reach, he said, with a nonchalant expression, "What do I get for finding this one?"

"Absolutely nothing. Now let me see it."

"For a price." He raised his brows and smiled.

"Extortion from such a fine, upstanding Texas cowboy?"

"Yes, ma'am."

"All right. What do you want?"

"Hot chocolate."

"Me, too."

She plucked the puzzle piece out of his hand and stood. "What's that?" Leaning over to see better, she pointed at something outside. "That red in the snow over there."

Frowning, Luke scooted around the card table and opened the sliding glass door. "A rose?" He picked it up, blew the snow off it, and sniffed it as he looked around. "In this weather? Why is a rose on my patio?"

"Maybe Eduardo gave some to Yolanda."

"And what? One of them got away?"

"Okay, smarty pants. You come up with an answer."

"I don't have one." He glanced up at Sarah's window and shook his head. "No footprints so it was here before the snow started about thirty minutes ago." One more quick look around. "Snow's not deep enough yet to cover anything up."

"Maybe someone dropped it from a window?"

"But that would mean someone was in the house. No one could have gotten in here without one of us hearing. Eduardo and Yolanda left before nine." Luke checked his watch. "Eight hours ago."

"So, it couldn't have been them. I'm cold. Let's go inside."

Luke followed her inside the house and shut the sliding door. "Why would someone walk to this cabin and place a perfectly beautiful rose on the patio in this cold? No one here has a family member who was killed."

"Maybe it's a custom in Mexico. Maybe it's for Eduardo and Yolanda. Are they related to anyone murdered?"

"Not that I know of." His gaze held Sarah's. "It might have something to do with the Rosie connected to the murders."

Sarah nodded slowly. She was surprised and pleased when her heart rate didn't spike. "He could have stood behind the garage and thrown it. No one sees him, and he leaves no footprints on this side. Let's check it out."

They both walked to the other side of the garage, but there were no prints anywhere. They searched around the corner of the house closest to the patio. Nothing. "So, what's the purpose of this rose?"

"It's for you, Sarah. To acknowledge that you're Rosie and that you're here." He checked the security system. It was set. Then he tugged out his phone. "I'm calling A.J."

Luke turned to the sliding glass door and watched the snow fall. "Hey, A.J. I hate to bother you today." He told him about the rose. "The security system is on at all times. Sarah and I checked it; it was on. I don't see how he could have gotten into this house. We have to disengage it to go outside the front door."

"Did you and Sarah go anywhere today?"

"To Alva's store, just down the road. But I'm sure I reset the system when we left."

"Does Sarah's bedroom overlook the patio?"

"Her old room did. We switched rooms."

"He could've slipped upstairs, dropped the rose, and left while you were gone. Have you checked her room?"

"No." Luke covered the mouthpiece. "Sarah, A.J. wants us to check your bedroom. Hold on, A.J." They walked upstairs and opened the door.

Sarah gasped. Red rose petals dotted the comforter covering her bed. "He was in here."

Luke nodded toward Sarah's bed. "He was inside this house, A.J. Rose petals are all over her bed. You need to come over here."

"On my way." He hung up.

Sarah hugged herself. "He knows that this is now my room, not yours, Luke."

Sarah couldn't sleep with Molly whining and staring at the open window. She looked out and saw only trees in the soft glow of the nightlight at the corner of the house. A chill crawled up her back. Something didn't feel right.

"It's your imagination," she whispered to herself.

She wanted to believe it, but she couldn't.

Something wasn't right.

Molly was still staring at the window.

Then she barked.

Sarah made herself walk calmly to her bed and fluffed the pillow. Then she quickly opened the drawer, tugged out the flashlight, and turned it on. She rushed to the window and searched the trees with the light.

She stopped.

Something...

Was that a pair of eyes surrounded by green?

They blinked.

"Oh, God!" Beside her, Molly barked several times. Sarah dropped the flashlight, lunged for the curtains, and drew them together. Her heart pounded. She had looked into his eyes!

The adjoining door opened. Luke rushed in. "What is it?"

"He was here!" She couldn't breathe. She was shaking so hard that when she picked up the flashlight, she fumbled it. Angry at herself, she plucked it off the carpet, opened the curtains, and shined it on the spot where he'd sat. He was gone, of course. "Right there. He'd completely covered himself in green and was sitting right there, staring at me."

"Then don't open the curtains."

"I thought, with the trees, that—"

"I know." He wrapped his arms around her. "I'm sorry, Sarah." He tightened his hold.

"*Did* you reset the system when we went to Alva's store?"

"I guess I didn't. I know I pushed the right buttons, but maybe I didn't hit ENTER or something."

She pulled out of his arms. "I prefer thinking that than thinking he was able to breach your system."

The next day, Thursday, promised to be beautiful. Snow glistened with the promise of spring in the sun's rays. Elva Lee opened the door to Search & Rescue, thumped her boots against the door jamb, and slammed the door shut. "I'm here to tell y'all, I am glad today's Thursday and yesterday's over with." She hung her coat on a fuzzy pink hangar and set it inside the coat closet.

She fluttered a hand at the room in general. "Now, don't get me wrong. I loved Lulu and I'm gonna miss her like crazy but I'm glad those funerals are over with. It gives all of us a chance to get on with living. Anybody know how Jim's doing? I haven't talked to him since before the funerals. Tommy, how's Buddy doing? Has he crawled out of that hole he dug Tuesday night?"

Without waiting for his answer, she picked up the empty coffee pot, filled it with water, and raised her brows at Tommy as she reached inside the cupboard and pulled out the red coffee can. She yanked off the lid and took out the scoop.

"He sure feels like a fool for missing the funeral."

"Well, he should. Two, three. Missing his own wife's funeral—four—because of his drinking. Five, six. Jim had the same thing—seven, eight—happen to him and—nine, ten—he was there *and* at the hospital with Casey and Will, *and*—"

The door swooshed open, and their boss stepped in.

"'Morning, Jim." Elva Lee dropped the scooper into the can and pressed the lid on it.

"'Morning. You losing some weight there, Miss Elva Lee?"

She felt her smile slide across two states. He noticed! "Yes, I am, Mr.

Jim Banks. I've lost twenty-five pounds already." She shrugged and turned on the coffee pot. "'Course, I'm sure some of that at first had to do with stress and water weight."

Water weight? What in the world was water weight? Jim sat and rifled through some of the papers on his desk.

Search & Rescue was gearing up for the summer months when people tried to pull foolish stunts against unyielding natural laws. Nature lived by the rules even if the tourists didn't. They unwittingly proved over and over again that nature held the upper hand when they didn't use the brains God gave them.

The sun slanted morning rays across his desk. His cell phone rang. "Hey, A.J."

"Our little miss's name is Allison McIntosh."

"How'd you find her?"

"At Penny's. Just waltzed in, spotted me, and clipped out of there as fast as her legs could carry her. But I caught up to her. Her brother has a rap sheet."

"Doing what?"

"Petty theft, twice. Jail time, less than a year."

"What's his name, and where does he live?" Jim's pen was poised to write.

"Brian McIntosh. Last known, Pueblo, Colorado. No permanent address. Her other brother is spotless. Name of Robert McIntosh, an accountant out Denver way. He's in Arizona this week as part of a team auditing a company in Phoenix."

"Interesting. What would Brian's connection be to our women?" Out of the corner of his eye, Jim saw Elva Lee's head turn toward him.

"Don't know that either. She didn't have anything else to tell me. And just for your information, I stopped by Luke's last night. Apparently, our killer dropped rose petals on Sarah's bed and then tossed a rose out her window. We didn't find a single print. A rose for Rosie. If he's the killer, he sure has a talent for B&E without making a sound."

"Any prints on the crowbar you found with Casey?"

"No. Lulu's blood was on it, though, as was Casey's."

Winnie Sue tentatively answered the phone because she didn't recognize the number on her caller ID. No one called her before nine in the morning, ever. "Hello?"

"Miss Winnie Sue Jansen?"

She hesitated, as she didn't recognize the voice either. "Yes, who's calling?"

"You don't know me. I'm looking for my grandmother, Rosie Jansen." *Rosie Jansen!* "I wondered if I could come by and talk to you and your sister Gertie for a little bit sometime today."

*The girl at the funeral.* Miss Gertie had noticed her and had pointed out that the little woman standing beside one of the Pollards was the spitting image of herself at twenty-five. "Were you at the funeral yesterday?"

"Yes, ma'am, I was."

"I saw you there." Winnie Sue edged toward the front window and regretted watching Trace Simms walk by without being able to visit with him. Owning Gally's Hardware afforded a wealth of information passing between Mr. Simms's ears and Winnie Sue liked to avail herself of that knowledge as much as possible.

"Would it be convenient for me to come by today or tonight? Maybe we could go to your sister's house and talk or go out to eat somewhere. Maybe dinner?"

Winnie Sue re-crossed her ankles and smoothed her skirt. What in the world would Miss Gertie want her to do? Since the subject had never come up, she simply didn't know. "And what is your name, miss?"

"Allison McIntosh. I'm looking forward to talking to you, Miss Jansen. I hope you can give me information on Rosie Jansen. What time shall I come by?"

*Mercy me.* "Seven would be fine." *That gives me all day to prepare myself.* "Do you know where I live, Miss McIntosh?"

"Yes, I do. I'll see you at seven." And then she hung up.

"Forevermore!" Winnie Sue cradled the phone and heard the dial tone buzzing. Carefully, as if her life depended on it, she set the phone down and wished her sister wasn't such a tightwad and would get herself a phone.

There was no way to warn her that a McIntosh granddaughter neither of them knew even existed was coming to visit.

Sarah and Luke stopped by the police station after lunch. A.J. was sitting at his desk, holding a bag with the rose inside, studying the contents as if a clue might squeeze through the bag's zipper and jump onto his desk.

"Afternoon, you two. Wanted to update you on what I found—or didn't find, in this case. No prints or any evidence of the killer being in your cabin, Luke, or in your room, Sarah." A.J. lifted the bag. "This rose isn't much help, but it might point us in the direction of our next victim."

*That would be me.* Sarah felt the blood drain from her face, leaving her cold. But she refused to be afraid. She would be a lion—strong and brave and wise and maybe even send out a growl or two. But she would not be afraid.

"Uh, possible victim." A.J. glanced at her, a little sheepishly.

"So, it *was* him in my room."

"I believe it was."

A phone rang behind A.J. and someone answered, "LTPD."

Sarah glanced outside as Molly barked from the bed of Luke's truck. A man was patting her and laughing with her. He walked off, turned, and waved at Molly when she barked at him. She watched him until he turned a corner.

Luke poured himself a cup of coffee. "A.J., why is this man so hard to find? He's small, has a fetish for peanuts, and must be strong, maybe a bodybuilder or an athlete."

"It's tough sometimes. We'll keep looking until he snags himself on a mistake. You have a gun, Sarah?"

"Yes."

"We also have guns at the cabin." Luke turned to her. "Do you know how to shoot?"

"I had lessons years ago. But shooting another human might be a little challenging for me."

"Not if your life is at stake."

# FIFTEEN

Allison pulled up to Winnie Sue Jansen's property and parked.

She considered herself a tough woman. She was mostly kind but tended toward quarrelsome and sometimes sulking when under pressure. It wasn't difficult to understand why. A messed-up father meant a messed-up daughter and a messed-up family.

As he'd explained—she groaned. Explained? Ha! As he'd *beat into them* so many times— his little witch of a mother was the source of all his troubles, and theirs. And there were many.

Marek Riley McIntosh had resented just about everything in his life. His parents had given him a strange name with no nickname in sight except 'Mary' so he called himself 'Butch' to compensate for the name.

At the top of his list of resentments—again, a mild word for virulent hate—were his two brothers who were both well over six feet tall. Marek, at five-foot-three, had never fit in. One of his brothers in particular teased and bullied him, pulling on his arms, and shouting, "Grow! Grow, little munchkin! Are you off to see the Wizard? You're not even tall enough to get on the rides at the fair!"

Both his parents died in an airplane crash when he was twenty-one. It was then, as he sifted through their papers, that he found his original birth certificate and his adoption papers.

His focus of hate now rested squarely on his birth mother.

And eventually on his oldest son.

Her father never let Brian forget that he was inadequate because of his short stature. He beat him senseless, pulled on his arms and legs, screaming, "Grow! Grow, you little toad! You're going to amount to nothing if you don't grow!"

Their useless mother had stood by, quietly fretting—as did Allison and Robbie—while Brian curled up into a ball and wept. They weren't even allowed to comfort him.

Allison had asked both her brothers if they knew their grandmother's address. Robbie said a definite no. Brian told her to look for someone in her seventies or eighties with the name Jansen or a maiden name of Jansen. After asking at the post office, Allison was told that "Miss Gertie will know who you're looking for."

A curtain moved at Winnie Sue Jansen's house. She was probably wondering why Allison was sitting in her car, staring at the front door. Allison squared her shoulders, walked up the steps, rang the doorbell, and listened to the melting snow dripping from the corners of the house.

The door opened.

"Winnie Sue Jansen?"

"Yes?"

"I'm Allison McIntosh. I believe I may be related to you." She extended her hand. Winnie Sue simply stared at her and turned white as a snowbank as she slowly melted toward the floor.

Allison caught her. "Miss Jansen? Are you all right? Miss Jansen?" She couldn't explain the genuine fear gripping her for this old woman she didn't know. She weighed almost nothing and was a good two or three inches shorter than Allison's five foot two.

She carried the woman to a sofa and sat beside her, stroking her arm. "Miss Jansen? Are you all right?"

The woman finally opened her eyes. "What happened?" she whispered.

"You fainted. Are you all right?"

"Oh, my goodness." She tried to sit up, fluttered a hand in front of her face, and smacked her lips in a very unladylike fashion.

Allison smiled. She didn't think she'd ever heard "Oh, my goodness" in her life. "May I get you some water?"

"Yes, please."

Allison patted her small spotted hand. "I'll be right back. Will you be okay while I'm gone?"

A weak smile, a flicker of a nod, and Allison scampered down a hallway.

The kitchen was delightful with colors of bright yellow and cherry-red. A low-sitting island in the center was perfect for Winnie Sue's height, with hanging pans above it that she could reach. Flowerpots stretched along the windowsills.

Allison opened a cabinet door and found a glass with cherries painted on them. Everything was pristine and in order. The woman who lived here must be very special. She smiled at the sentimental thought, filled the glass, and hurried back to her.

Winnie Sue was sitting up, pale as a ghost but wearing a wan smile. "I'm so sorry, dear one," she said as she took the offered glass and sipped.

Allison fell in love with her right then.

"You're so pale, ma'am. Is there any medicine or anything I can get you?"

"Miss."

"Excuse me?"

"It's 'miss' not 'ma'am'." The older woman patted her hand. "I'm fine. Coming out of a good spin takes a moment." She smiled. "You have the same height and coloring as Miss Gertie and me. Light brown hair, big brown eyes, thin lips, a heart-shaped face. You're very pretty."

"Thank you. Are you feeling all right?"

She touched Allison's hand again. "If I could sit here for a moment, dear, and catch my breath."

She took her time sipping water and taking deep breaths. "I am much better, Allison. Maybe we should go to my sister's home now."

Allison helped her up.

Winnie Sue straightened like a pin rod and slipped on the white gloves sitting on her white purse. "If you're ready, then, dear."

Resting on Allison's arm, she walked carefully out the door.

It was a cloudy evening, although it wasn't late—not even six o'clock. Snow was on the way again, and it was cold. Luke thought he and Sarah shouldn't be outside too much longer. A few more minutes on the porch swing, and they'd head inside.

"The news coverage about the murders has been constant back home. My mother's worried." Sarah welcomed Molly with open arms and scooted over to allow her room to sit between her and Luke.

"You've spoiled Molly rotten."

"And proud of it, I am. It's such a pretty night. I wish we could take a walk down your road and just enjoy it."

"Me, too." Holding hands while doing it would be nice, too.

Molly's head jerked up. Around the corner, the sliding glass door opened. She jumped up and raced toward it. *Eduardo or Yolanda.*

"My mom's worried. Thinks I should come home, get away from all this. She's probably right. Leaving would solve all my problems."

"The Darkslayer could be back in Kansas." Luke was a selfish man and wanted her here with him. He liked her. He didn't consider it unreasonable that he didn't want her to go home. He'd spent more time with her than with any other woman he'd ever dated.

She touched his arm. "Luke? Were you listening?"

He nodded. "You said your mother was worried sick and wanted you to come home."

"After that."

"Okay. You caught me. I was thinking I didn't want you to go."

She searched his eyes. "I'm not ready to leave. There's just too much I want to see, and no other place I'd rather be."

Darkness pressed in around them. A twig snapped. Sarah gasped and jerked back.

Luke spun around, searching behind them. He unsnapped his gun holster and tugged out his weapon. "Come on." He eased off the swing, his gaze circling around the front yard, the side yard. He nudged her in front of him, pushed her toward the front door, and opened it.

Hustling inside, they both breathed a sigh of relief when the lock clicked, and the security system was set.

The man watched her rush inside. "Now, Rosie, you know you can't run away from me." He gritted his teeth as he slammed his head against the smooth bark of an aspen and whimpered.

"He was out there." Anger sliced through Sarah. Breathless with it, she spun around and looked into Luke's eyes. "I was wrong. I've got to get out of here. He's waiting for me to make a mistake. I have to go home as soon as possible." She sidestepped Luke and ran toward the stairs.

Early evening was Gertie's favorite time of the day. She loved sitting on her porch, listening to her knitting needles clicking away as the cold crispness of night settled in. Snow was on the way. An elk strolled past the cabin, glanced at Gertie, and lay in the cushion of green grass in the same spot he'd chosen the night before.

"Hello, old friend," she muttered without looking up from her knitting and smiled at the easiness between them.

In the distance, a car came down her gravel lane and crept toward her cabin. The elk jumped up and bounded across the yard, head erect and rack simply magnificent.

Gertie set aside her knitting and stood, wrapped a hand around a gnarly post, and felt the blood drain from her face as the woman at the funeral and her sister exited the little blue car.

The young woman reached her steps. Gertie stepped back.

Neither of them spoke or took their gazes off the other.

Winnie Sue, being graced with all kinds of good manners, moved forward and waved a gloved hand first at her sister, then Allison. "Miss Gertie Jansen, Miss Allison McIntosh."

Gertie had never been speechless a day in her life, unless it was the time a doctor had spoken the word 'pregnant' and 'home for unwed mothers' after the brutal rape. That news would have made a magpie speechless. But she wouldn't think of that time. She *never* thought of that time, over fifty years ago now. She'd buried it deep within her so that it wouldn't have the power to crush her.

And now she faced the offspring of that rape, with not a clue what should or should not be said in such a situation.

Winnie Sue ventured, "Allison's come all the way from Portland, Oregon, Miss Gertie."

Allison turned to her. "You call your sister 'Miss Gertie'?"

Winnie Sue patted Allison's upper arm. "Yes, dear one, out of respect. She's considerably older than me and helped raise me."

"I *did* raise you, Winnie Sue, and you know it." Laws, she didn't want to fight with Winnie Sue first thing after meeting Allison.

"You're nothing like your sister."

Winnie Sue gasped.

Gertie frowned.

"But what could I expect from a woman who gave my father away as if he were nothing? You're Rosie Jansen, aren't you?"

Gertie smirked. The best course of action would be to ignore the little whippersnapper's sarcasm. "Portland, you say?"

Allison looked as if she might scream, but she didn't. She glared up at Gertie. "Yes, my father moved from Denver when I was fifteen."

"Oh, dear," Winnie Sue patted again, "that must have been so difficult at such a young age. To lose all your friends and... and..." She floundered when she glanced up at her sister and connected with the fierce glare she was sending her way.

With her unyielding gaze on Gertie, Allison said, "You're quite right, Aunt Winnie Sue."

*Aunt Winnie Sue?* Gertie ground her teeth while Winnie Sue smiled and patted Allison's arm again.

"It was hard to leave everything I knew and move to a strange town."

*It was hard to give the baby away.* Gertie crossed her arms and pursed her lips.

"Well." Winnie Sue touched Allison's arm. "I'm sure you made friends very quickly, my dear."

Allison continued to pout and glare at Gertie.

Winnie Sue looked from one to the other. "I need to check on the roses I planted last year on the other side of Miss Gertie's cabin and see if there are any buds on them yet, for roses have to be tended to and my sister is not the tending-to-roses type."

"Turn on the outside lights."

"I know, Sister."

Winnie Sue stared at both of them for an uncomfortable moment, sidestepped Allison, and teetered along the thin path beside the cabin.

The roses were eager for attention, but she couldn't tend to them tonight, with snow coming in. She stepped into the basement, turned on the light, and looked for the pruning gloves she'd given her sister last year.

"You're never too old to learn to garden, Sister," she'd said to Miss Gertie who, quite disgusted, had rolled her eyes, shook her head, and stalked off. Winnie Sue slipped out of her white gloves, placed them in her purse, set her purse on a table. She yanked the work gloves from under a pair of metal thingies. They hadn't been cleaned since she'd used them.

"You're going to have roses whether you like it or not, Sister," she muttered as she brushed off the gloves. She'd be back in the next few days and tend to the roses. Right now, she needed to keep herself busy for a few more minutes to give the two on the porch enough time to settle in with each other.

She jumped when she heard it.

"Forevermore," she whispered. Then she heard it again.

Laughter.

Well, her plan had worked. Pleased as punch, she nodded once as she smiled rather smugly. She turned off the light, tugged on her white gloves, picked up her purse, marched around the house and found her sister and Allison sitting on the porch steps with smiles on their faces.

Allison flapped a hand at Miss Gertie. "And then the goat lunged for his suit jacket, grabbed a mouthful and yanked—"

Head back with laughter, Miss Gertie slapped her knee.

"He led my brother around the yard with him yelling, 'Stop it! Help!'"

Winnie Sue stood in front of the giggling pair, not sure what she should do, if anything. She wanted them to tell the story from the beginning, but it didn't look like the appropriate time to suggest it.

"Come on up, Sister. Sit with me and our kin." Miss Gertie nudged Allison's knee and grinned ear-to-ear at her.

"I believe I'll sit in a chair, Miss Gertie, if you don't mind."

"Suit yourself."

Allison and Miss Gertie looked at each other and burst out laughing again.

"And what, pray tell, is so funny?" Winnie Sue was on the verge of being miffed.

"The story she just told." Miss Gertie slapped her knees and stood. "Let's go inside and have some iced tea and visit for a spell."

Winnie Sue was beginning to feel a little left out. Then, Allison wrapped her hand around her arm and walked in with her.

"Your gloves are so pretty, Aunt Winnie Sue."

She smiled at Allison.

Having a new member of the family around was surely going to be a very pleasurable experience.

When Sarah passed him the bowl of mashed potatoes, Luke's fingers brushed the tips of her hand. He glanced at her, hoping for a playful response, but she lifted her chin slightly and kept her gaze on the bowl.

The thought of her leaving—even if it was for the best—left him unsettled. He thought something good was happening between them. Maybe she didn't think so. But he didn't want her to walk away from it or from him. Not yet. He could keep her safe if she'd just trust him to do it.

She picked up the bowl of bacon-laced green beans, scooped up a spoonful, dumped them next to the mashed potatoes on her plate, and passed them on to Luke.

He grinned and tried his best this time to completely cover her hand as he took the bowl.

Her golden eyes flashed. Man, she was a beautiful woman, even when she was annoyed. She probably didn't realize it, but her dimples deepened when she pursed her lips like that and glared at him.

She'd been doing plenty of that since they'd run inside the house an hour earlier.

He sat back.

He'd have to let her go.

But he wouldn't let their friendship go. Four hours wasn't a long drive, and he was willing to drive it. They could stay in contact through e-mail and phone calls and texts. It was workable.

"I need to pack so I'll be going back to my cabin in the mor—"

"The heck you will!" Luke threw the spoon back into the green beans and glared at her.

She set her roll down. "Heck has nothing to do with it. And yes, I will."

"You can't be that dense."

"I am *not* dense. I'm merely—"

"*Being* dense!"

She scooted her chair back. "Obviously, you're not in the frame of mind to discuss this civilly."

"And you're not in the frame of mind to listen to reason!"

She stood. *"Reason?* I've yet to hear *reason."*

He stood. "You want reason, then I'll give you reason. You just had the life scared out of you at *this...very...cabin,* and you expect me to let you go to your cabin *alone?* God didn't give you the sense He gave—"

"Apparent—"

"Exactly!" Point scored, Luke threw his napkin down and stormed out of the room.

Sarah sat in a huff, not sure what to do with the napkin she found in her hands. "Well."

"For what it's worth, Sarah, I think Luke's right."

She looked at Yolanda and then Eduardo. "Of course, he is. He gets my dander up in the worst way when all he has to do is *ask* me but, no, he has to lay down the law as if I'm a nitwit."

"Not a nitwit. As if you're someone he cares for deeply." When she looked up at Eduardo, he raised his brows, pursed his lips, and nodded.

Sarah pushed back her chair and stood. "Thank you for the—" She burst into tears and sank into the chair again. "I'm so tired of being afraid to do *anything,* even admitting to liking Luke. I know it's too fast, and I don't know what to do. I don't even know him."

Yolanda put her arm around Sarah as Eduardo left the room.

"You can't help who you love, Sarah. If it's your time and the man is right, then go for it and enjoy it. I've known this family for years. You couldn't have picked a finer man than Luke McKenzie, and I think you know it."

"My parents will think I'm absolutely nuts when I announce I have feelings for someone I haven't even known two weeks."

"Maybe not. They were there once, caught up in new love. You've spent time with Luke in difficult situations. You've gotten to know him quickly and well."

Sarah nodded. "It's too early to talk about *love.*" She searched Yolanda's eyes. "Isn't it? I don't want to go back to Kansas and lose what we're discovering here, but I don't want to leave my life in Kansas either. It just seems hopeless."

"If you care for each other, you'll find a way."

"I don't know if Luke even likes me. He's bossy and domineering and—so gentle and kind and giving. Oh, I'm so confused."

Yolanda smiled and lifted a brow. "I think it's safe to say he feels the same way about you. Maybe you two should talk and get everything out in the open."

Nodding, Sarah stood. "Please don't say anything to Luke about this. I'm sorry about ruining dinner. Please make my apologies to Eduardo. I don't—maybe if—I'm sorry." She ran from the room.

Sarah found the quiet and solitude of her room oppressive. She was afraid to turn on the lights. The killer had been in this room, so he knew it was hers.

She dressed for bed and slipped under the covers. She heard the twig snap again and again. The killer had stood within inches of her, watching her, watching Luke, waiting. What if Luke had gone inside for just a minute? What would have happened?

Thinking about the killer took her to that night in her apartment. She shuddered as she remembered the power in the man's hands. If her roommates hadn't come back—but they had.

Sarah would never forget how small and weak and impotent she'd felt against the utter dominance of that man.

She never wanted a man to have that kind of power over her ever again, even if her heart gave its permission.

Even if that man was Luke McKenzie with all his wonderful attributes and good intentions.


Luke simmered for another thirty minutes. He'd never once had a temper problem. Even with Dad's murder, he'd held it together. Cried, of course. Threw things. Worked extra hours until he was exhausted. Rode hard with his horse, Pepper, until they were both ready to head for home. But none of his frustration and anger had involved another person. What was he doing with Sarah? His temper frightened *him,* so he couldn't imagine how it affected her. He was just so afraid her carelessness would end up with the killer getting what he wanted.

He sighed.

He loved her. He knew it now.

God help him, he loved a woman he hadn't known two weeks.

He'd always figured that when love hit him, it would be quick and hard. And, man, it was.

He loved her.

And he'd do whatever it took to keep her safe.

When all was quiet in Sarah's room, he opened the adjoining door and found her asleep with a book on her chest and the lamp still on. He set the book on the table, left the light on, and gently touched her cheek. "I love you, Sarah."

She mumbled, "Luke," and turned on her side.

He left the adjoining door open and prayed they'd have a chance to talk first thing in the morning.

Sitting alone at his desk at eleven o'clock on Thursday night, one day after the funerals, Jim's phone rang. *A.J.*

"Casey's awake."

"I'll meet you at the hospital." Jim grabbed his coat and hat.

A few minutes later, they stood at the foot of Casey's bed with Will on one side and Dr. Vern on the other. A beeping monitor, two hovering nurses, and soft lights surrounded them.

"Casey?"

Her bandaged head rolled toward Jim's voice. Her eyes fluttered open.

"Hey, Casey. Glad you're back." Her lips moved and her mouth twitched, but Jim couldn't make out what she said. "Casey, we need some information. Can you answer a couple of questions for us?"

"Yessss." Her eyes drooped closed, and she stilled.

Jim waited, looked at A.J., at Will, back at Casey. Her eyes trembled open.

"Can you describe him?"

She tried to shake her head, and her frown deepened. Drool had accumulated in the corner of her mouth. Her eyes seemed sunken and dark. "No. Behin' me."

Jim leaned closer. "He was behind you?"

"Yes. Two." She winced, sucked in a breath.

Jim waited until the lines between her brows eased a little. He took her hand. "Two, Casey?"

"Men."

A.J. bent over. "Honey, there were *two* of them?"

"Two."

A.J. sent Jim a so-you-were-right look. "Any details about them you can tell me?"

"Strong. Pulled my hair. Called me Rosie." She swallowed and flinched, and her face softened so much that Jim thought she had fallen back to sleep.

Will turned to Dr. Vern. "Can she have ice?"

He nodded. One of the nurses left and came back with a cup of shaved ice and a spoon. Will thanked her. "Casey, honey, would you like some ice to wet your whistle?"

She opened her eyes and her mouth. Will spooned in some ice. She moved it around, swallowed.

"Anything else you can remember that might help us catch these men?"

"One voice deep, one voice young." Will slipped more ice into her mouth. "He stopped him."

"Who?"

Her eyes wilted closed. "Deep stopped... young."

"Anything else?"

She coughed, gritted her teeth. "He said I got out. Rosie got out."

Jim nodded. "Did he say he was going to take you back?"

"Yessss. He was mad, so mad."

"Did anything about these men seem familiar to you? Their voices?"

Casey tried to shake her head and cringed.

"Okay, Casey, we're going to let you rest now. If you remember anything else, tell Will to call us, all right?"

She blinked a couple times as she pinched her lips and tried to swallow. "K."

Jim and A.J. thanked Will and the doctor and left. Walking across the parking lot, A.J. pulled up the collar of his coat. "Why didn't Sarah and Luke see two men, Jim?" His breath frosted and disappeared as he spoke.

"Maybe they did. One was the shooter. The second was in the cave. I'm not sure I go with that theory, though. The shooter had plenty of time to leave, find Lulu, and get her to the cave."

"Only one set of prints at Lulu's, too." They stopped at A.J.'s patrol car. "Although it's hard to tell in that amount of snow."

Jim nodded.

"Could be Allison McIntosh's two brothers. Whoever the killers are, they're as clean as polished grits. Haven't left behind any prints or anything. No mistakes. We even have an eyewitness, and she can't tell us a blasted thing about either of them. Oh. And, uh." A.J. cleared his throat. "Penny and I are back together."

"Yeah?" It didn't surprise Jim. He'd seen Penny looking over her shoulder at A.J. at every funeral with a look that said she was sorry. "So, you're out of the doghouse and back in the house? About time." His keys jingled as he pulled them out of his jeans. The night was cold, hazy, and starless. Jim stuffed his hands in his coat pockets. Probably more snow on the way in. He could smell it in the air.

"She called me this afternoon and asked me over. We talked. Everything's good, for now." He reached for the handle of his truck.

"That's great, buddy." Jim's vehicle beeped. "Have a good one."

"Oh, I intend to." A.J. laughed and got in his truck.

"Yeah," Jim muttered as he walked toward his empty pickup on his way to his empty house.

# SIXTEEN

Jim swatted at his ringing cell phone and groaned as it fell to the floor next to the digital clock reading *3:10* on Friday morning. He rolled over and groped on the floor until he found it.

"Jim? You there?"

"Yeah, A.J." He thought about jettisoning himself back onto the bed, but he needed to be alert and slid to the floor. "Whatcha got?"

"Another body."

"Where?"

"That new family. The Martins. Just moved here about three weeks ago. The husband came home from partying and found his wife Joy on the living room floor. M.O.'s changed. The killer left the body and didn't pack anything or take a car."

"Versatile guy. We found his dumping place so no reason for him to do that other stuff." Jim rubbed his eyes. "Joy Martin's small, isn't she, Larry?"

"Little over five foot. Kin to Myra Simms. Her niece. I'm headed over now."

"I'll meet you there."


With gloved hands, Jim lifted Joy Martin's blouse. Red letters spilled out of the band of her pants. He knew what was written there, but he tugged them down to expose all the letters. *Rosie is dead.*

"What kind of monster are we dealing with here, Jim?"

"Only one set of prints outside."

"Maybe his friend didn't come along this time, or maybe he was the lookout."

"But why choose Joy Martin?"

A.J. squatted beside him. "Other than her size, I don't know. We'll run all the vics through the computer and try to find something they had in common, other than their height. We'll keep trying to find Brian McIntosh and see if he has an alibi. He's the only person of interest we have in this case. And not much of one."

"And bring Allison McIntosh in. See what she knows about her brother."

"Her door was unlocked." A.J. leaned against a cold flagless pole concreted into the Martins' front yard and crossed his arms. "Sonny Martin said she always left the door open for him."

"Not anymore." *Stupid, stupid, stupid!* Sometimes people invited trouble to waltz right in and have its way with them. Jim shoved his cup toward A.J., pivoted, and walked inside the house where he found the husband sitting spread-legged on his bedroom floor, his back against his bed, and his blood-shot eyes focused on absolutely nothing.

"She didn't want to come." It was more a dazed mumble than speaking to anyone in particular.

Sonny Martin's calm appearance belied the horror Jim had seen in his eyes when they'd first arrived.

Moments after finding his wife murdered on their salmon-colored carpet, he'd collapsed into incoherent sobbing. The 9-1-1 operator had trouble understanding him. When he said "Myra Simms," they put it all together. He'd been able to confirm his address.

Jim had heard the man's wailing, but the halo-like pool of black blood around Joy Martin's head had stopped him from seeking out the husband. Her petite hands were neatly folded over her stomach, legs tied together, and eyes taped shut.

Jim prayed recognizable prints would be on the tape. "She didn't want to go to the party, Mr. Martin?"

"Colorado. She didn't want to come to Colorado."

Jim could certainly relate to the backwash of guilt the man would carry with him the rest of his life. Why had he dragged his wife to Colorado? Why hadn't he stayed home tonight? Why hadn't he come home earlier? Why hadn't he taken her with him? She'd still be alive if he had—or so they always thought.

Jim joined A.J. outside. "He scrawled 'Rosie is dead' on her stomach in much larger letters. He tried to make her look suitably dead this time. He expected her husband and the police to verify for him, to make it official, that Rosie was absolutely dead this time."

A door slammed behind them. The coroner, Vince Graham, exited a burgundy van.

"Good. Vince is here. I'm headed home." Jim shook Vince's hand and headed for his truck. He searched the horizon for any sign of Friday morning, but it was still too early. He might sneak in an hour or so of sleep before he had to be at work—if he could get these visions of Renee lying in blood, too, out of his mind.

Sarah opened her eyes to sunlight shining around her curtains—the best way to wake up. She remembered her last thought before she fell asleep: it's time to leave Little Texas.

A litany of other thoughts bombarded her. A killer was after her. She was making herself too available to him. Being here was not fun. She was too stressed. Too afraid. And, most importantly, she had to get off this man's radar.

She needed to get out while she still could.

Come tomorrow morning, she would leave Little Texas. That meant, of course, that she would be leaving Luke, too. She didn't know how to process that part of her plans. She didn't want to leave him. She wanted to know if these feelings she had for him were real. The best way to find out was to spend time with each other.

Time, unfortunately, was running out.

She glanced at the clock on her phone. She needed to get up. After not eating dinner last night, she was starving. She showered, dressed, and went downstairs.

Luke sat at the dining table. When Sarah walked into the room, he studied her for a moment and then plucked a coffee mug off the serving tray. "'Morning."

"'Morning." She poured her coffee and his.

"Thanks. I'm sorry for yelling at you last night."

"I understand why you did, Luke. You're afraid for me."

He nodded. "Were you able to sleep?"

"A little."

"I know I said I'd wait for you to ask me to help you, but I'm going back on that. I'm *asking* you to let me go with you to your cabin."

"Of course, you can. I want you to go with me. I'm leaving in the morning for home."

"I know."

"I am so ready to get this behind me. But not you. Just this stuff."

"Not me?"

When she shook her head, he was grateful that something shone in her eyes when he stood and walked toward her. *Friendship? Maybe the beginnings of love?*

"No, not you."

His arms went around her. He held her gently and caressed her back. It felt so good to feel her in his arms. "I'll look forward to making the trip to Kansas if I know you're at the end of it."

"I will be."

"Maybe Mac will let me borrow his plane. Make the trip about forty-five minutes."

She pulled back and grinned up at him. "He owns a plane?"

Nodding, Luke looked into her eyes, then down at her mouth. He needed the kiss he saw in her eyes. Gently, he lowered his head and touched her lips with his. "Is this a good memory?" he whispered against her mouth.

"Yes, but I need a little more than that to—"

He tightened his arms and deepened the kiss until she finally relaxed and let them both savor this moment.

On her way to Search & Rescue, Elva Lee slowed down as she approached the town square on Ridge Road. The trees in the middle of the square obscured the words of the sign hanging from the courthouse until she turned left onto Edgar Drive.

TOWN MEETING FRIDAY (TONIGHT) 7:00
*Concerning Our Women*

On her left, Norman Poindexter shuffled with his walker to the corner of Edgar Drive and Ridge Road and lifted a hand at Elva Lee.

She slowed down. "Lookin' good there, Mr. Norman! How's that new hip?"

"Needs a little oil this morning. You hear about that Martin woman?"

Elva Lee slammed on her brakes, looked in her rearview mirror, found no one behind her, and stuck her head out the window. "Joy Martin?"

"Yep. Found her dead this morning around three."

Elva Lee gasped. "Oh, no. Myra." She covered her mouth. Luke and Sarah stopped behind Mr. Norman just as he finished talking.

Huffing and puffing, they jogged in place, and then stopped. Luke touched his shoulder. "Excuse me, sir, what did you say?"

Norman pointed a gnarly finger toward the road. "I was telling Elva Lee there that that Martin woman—"

"Joy, Mr. Norman," Elva Lee said. "Did y'all hear about Joy Martin?"

Sarah and Luke high-stepped to loosen any muscles tempted to tighten up on them. Elva Lee had run track in high school and understood that need not to seize.

"Not until this second," Sarah answered and turned back to Mr. Norman.

"Yep. This morning around three. A.J., Larry, Roland, and Jim were there at the crime scene, looking things over."

"Joy was at home?" Elva Lee leaned further out her window. "He left her body there?"

"Yep. Apparently same fella who killed our other three women." Mr. Norman looked longingly at his bench which was another four feet in front of him. "Better watch your step there, Elva Lee. He likes his women short." He glanced at Sarah. "You, too, missy."

"I will," Elva Lee said. "Have you heard how Myra's doing?"

"I don't know but Imogene's over there with her right now."

"I'll give her a call when I get to work. You take care now, Mr. Norman. Luke, Sarah, I'll probably see y'all later." She waved and continued on around the town square until she hit Ridge again.

She slowed down. A sign on Myra's shop door said: CLOSED DUE TO DEATH IN FAMILY. Elva Lee headed north to Barrett's Auto Repair. When she parked around back, she pulled out her cell phone and dialed Jim's number.

"Banks."

"Jim, it's me, Elva Lee. I just heard about Joy Martin. What happened?"

"Found her at her home. Crowbar again. Same perp. The mayor's called a town meeting tonight at seven."

"I just saw the sign on my way to Barrett's."

"What are you doing there?"

"My car's missing a little. Barrett's going to look at it."

"How're you getting to work?"

"Well, that's why I'm calling you." She laughed. "I may be a little late. I might see someone here who could take me, or I can wait around until they get it fixed. Or, if you need me right now, I can start walking. It's not far."

"I'll come and get you. Are you there right now?"

"Yes."

"I'll see you in a few minutes." He hung up.

Elva Lee looked at the phone, a little confused. Jim had never offered to do anything for her. Why, she'd never even ridden in his truck. She dropped her phone in her purse. Just at the thought of riding with him, her heart jumped. Giddiness swept over her. "It's just a ride," she mumbled, chastising her crazy heart.

"Elva Lee?"

Oh. "Hmmm?" She internally shook herself. "Uh, yes, Barrett?"

"We'll have your car ready for you during lunch."

She thanked him and turned back around.

Jim was getting out of his truck. Oh! She didn't know how to act! *Like this is an every-day situation. Be cool.* Her heart laughed at her silly thoughts and beat harder.

Walking quickly, Jim reached them, nodded once at Barrett. "How's that baby doing?"

Barrett grinned from ear-to-ear. "She's the prettiest thing God ever made, plain and simple. You ought to come by and see her. Katherine would love to show her off to you."

"Just might do that." He turned to Elva Lee. He stared at her a moment. "You ready to go?"

"Yes," she murmured. He stepped back and ushered her to lead the way with a sweep of his arm. It was a strange feeling walking with Jim Banks to his truck, knowing she'd be sitting near him, watching him do something as simple as driving. Her heart fluttered at the thought.

"You take care of that baby now, Barrett. Say hey to Katherine for me."

"Will do."

Jim's arm brushed Elva Lee's when he grabbed the door handle. She smiled up at him and slipped inside the truck. No way could the words "Thank you" get past her tight throat. The door slammed. In the driver's side mirror, she watched him and wondered why he was grinning like a possum as he walked up to his door.

They rode in silence. But what did she expect? This wasn't a date. It was an expression of friendship. Hmmm. Friendship? Were she and Jim friends now because he'd offered her a ride?

"I appreciate everything you do at S&R to keep things going."

She glowed all over. "It's my job. I love helping people."

"It shows." He nodded several times thoughtfully, and then he looked out the window. He slowed down as he approached the stop sign in the town square. "Sarah and Luke are up early today."

Elva Lee nodded. "I saw them a few minutes ago at the square when Mr. Norman told me about Joy Martin. How awful for Sonny and for Myra. Bless their hearts. Lulu and now Joy."


Luke ran in place, waiting for the white "WALK" sign to appear so he and Sarah could run across Ridge Road on their way back to the cabin. A casually dressed man put a key in the glass door of Gally's Hardware store, opened it, flipped over the "CLOSED" sign, and turned on the lights.

Sarah paced behind Luke and waved at Jim and Elva Lee as they drove by. "I'd fly home if I could, but I can't leave my car here and you know it!"

Luke turned around. "You expect me to just let you go, on a road trip, by yourself, all the way to Kansas? Why don't you just put a blinking sign in your back window and have it say, 'Okay, here I am. Come and get me'?"

She followed him across the street. "Now, that's just brilliant, Luke." She sidestepped an open manhole and bumped into him. "I need some room here."

Luke ran ahead, jumped the curb, turned right, took another left, and ran in place until a scowling Sarah caught up with him. "My legs are shorter than yours!"

She'd been grumpy all morning. He didn't know why. He'd like to think it had something to do with leaving him tomorrow.

Waiting for her, he jogged a circle and smiled at her. At the lift of her chin as she jogged past him, he figured it was going to be a long day. "We need to talk, Sarah."

She ignored him and kept running.

Another fifteen minutes, they jogged up the driveway to McKenzie Cabin. Luke stopped at the back door, but Sarah kept running, right up the rise behind the cabin to the top. She jogged in place, then high stepped, and walked up and down the backbone of the ridge. She picked a flower, sniffed it, threw it to the wind, and disappeared down the other side.

Luke raced up and over the ridge and caught up with her. "What are you *doing?*"

Sarah jerked around and glared. *"Now* what's wrong?"

Luke flapped his hand at her. "Four women—count 'em—four." Dramatically, he swatted at his fingers as he ticked off the numbers. "Dead. And you're up here, *alone,* picking wildflowers where no one can see you. You can't be so careless!"

"I'll be as careless as I want." She frowned at him and then started laughing.

Luke threw up his hands. "It's not funny. You *have* to be more careful."

"I was just thinking how pretty these Indian paintbrushes are up here and how much I'd like to pick them."

"He was at the cabin. Maybe *up here* is his favorite place to hide. No one can see him *up here* which means no one can see you *up here*. You only have one more day to endure this."

"I know. I'll try to be more careful."

"Good." He scooped up a flower and handed it to her.

Smiling, she sniffed it and tucked it behind her ear.

"You have a beautiful smile." And with those words, he took her arm and guided her down the rise.


A white sheet fluttered on a clothesline as Allison parked her car under a nice shade tree. When she opened the door, she smelled bacon—crispy bacon—and bread baking. She couldn't remember the last time she'd smelled fresh bread.

"Wuh, hey there." Her smiling grandmother came out on the porch, wiping her hands on a smudged apron swatting the tops of her boots.

Gram held the screen door open for her. Allison decided this morning to call her 'Gram.'

"This is a nice surprise. Come on in and make yourself at home. Biscuits and gravy and bacon sound all right to you for breakfast?"

Allison walked inside the small cabin. "Throw in a cup of coffee, and I'll help you wash the dishes." She followed her grandmother past the living room/dining room and into the small kitchen. Everything was small.

"What brings you out here so early this morning?"

The oven door wheezed as it opened. Gram pulled out a pan of big fluffy biscuits and slammed the door shut with her knee. "Have a seat there, girl. I'll get you that coffee. Black?"

"Is it strong?"

"Not for me."

"Then black." Allison opened her purse and drew out a yellow packet of pictures. "I wanted you to see your son, Gram."

"That's what I called my grandmother." She set the bacon on the table next to the biscuits, a bowl of gravy, two canning jars of jelly, and a bottle of honey. She set a cup of black coffee beside each plate and sat down.

Before Allison could blink, Gram bowed her head and said, "For these and all other blessings, I thank thee, Lord Jesus." She looked at Allison and patted her hand. "I consider you one of those blessings."

"Thank you, Gram."

She waved a hand at her. "Help yourself, child."

Allison buttered a biscuit. "Have you ever seen a photo of your son?" She took a bite of heaven. "Mmm, this is great."

Gram took her time buttering a biscuit. "No, I haven't. In those days, over fifty years ago now, we weren't allowed to even look at the baby at the place we stayed."

"We?"

"Winnie Sue and I. We went together. She was only thirteen, and by then, our parents were dead." She set the knife on her plate. "At the girls' home, they thought it best for the mother not to see the baby so she wouldn't get attached—or be hurt. But the hurt came anyway. It came with a vengeance."

"I'm sorry, Gram." Her father had been so wrong about his mother. "Would you like to see his picture?"

Gram's hand shook as she held an almost-burnt piece of bacon halfway to her mouth. "Maybe after we eat."

When Allison frowned, her grandmother patted her hand. "After we eat, okay, honey?"

Allison crunched on bacon, sipped her coffee, and jellied her biscuit. As she watched her grandmother in her comfortable little world, she couldn't forget the horrors her son had brought on their family.

Anger, warm at first, hummed. "He hated you."

Her grandmother jerked and slowly put down her biscuit.

"He hated my brother, Brian." Her hands fisted as she gritted her teeth against the shakes. "Hate was everywhere."

"I know." Her grandmother whispered the words.

But they reached Allison. She sat up straight and took a deep breath.

"Allison."

Gray eyes the color of melted steel gazed into Allison's eyes.

"Let's look at your pictures, if you've a mind to show me."

"How do you know about everything, Gram?"

"Your father wrote to me many years ago. There was no return address. I couldn't answer any of his accusations, but I wanted to. Lord knows, I wanted to. I read and wept over that letter so many times. I never told anyone about it, not even Winnie Sue. He told me he hated me. He asked me why I didn't want him. Did I give him to such a tall family because I hated him? And *why* had I hated him? All those questions went unanswered because he didn't give me a chance to answer them. They've haunted me for years."

Allison looked at the ring on her right hand. "This was my father's. I've worn it to remind me how much I hated him." She slipped it off and handed it to Gram. "I don't want it anymore. I want you to have it, to remind you of what I'm about to tell you.

"My father found out he was adopted when he was twenty-one. He'd been adopted into a family of tall brothers and at five-three, he never fit in. His second oldest brother teased him, called him 'Runt,' beat him any chance he could, taunted and bullied him. None of my father's family ever checked his brother's behavior."

She shook her head. "My father hated being short. He could see the disparity between how people treated him and how they treated his taller siblings. He hated himself for it.

"When he found his birth certificate, Rosie Jansen was identified as his birth mother. No father was listed. A picture was paperclipped to it. On the back of it was written: 'Baby's mother, Rosie Jansen, Little Texas, Colorado.' Rosie was standing beside a car. It was obvious she was very tiny. The next year, my father married my mother, who was five two. They had two sons and a daughter, me."

"I remember the nurse at the girls' home taking that photo."

Nodding, Allison clasped her hands around her knees and rocked. "Something happened to my father when my oldest brother, Brian, was six. Brian was small for his age. My father started beating him, screaming things like, 'Rosie did it, Rosie did it,' and 'It's Rosie's fault. It's Rosie's fault.'

"He'd yank on Brian's arms and say, 'I'm gonna pull Rosie right out of you, boy'." Allison rubbed a spot on her forehead until it hurt. "The beatings, Gram. They never stopped until Brian was almost unconscious. No one stopped my father. No one.

"When I was in middle school, we had a project to do. We were to talk to one of our grandparents about their history, like an interview. My father threw that picture of you at me like a Frisbee and yelled, "There's your grandmother. Go find *her!*" But I didn't. I sent the picture to Brian, who was on the streets at that time in Pueblo, Colorado." She abruptly stood. "Can we walk, Gram?"

The old woman took her hand, and they walked outside and down the steps. "Brian is the sweetest man I know. But he's confused. He fights the demons like I do, but I don't think he can control what he does when the demons get too big."

"What demons?"

"Anger. Ugly anger. I'm in baby steps on how to control it and deal with my father's intense hate—along with my feelings of helplessness growing up. Abandonment. Low self esteem. You name it; we all experienced it."

"God help me, I tried to do the best thing for the baby."

Absently, Allison picked up a stick and threw it. "I wish someone had told my father he was okay, no matter how tall or short, that he could do or be anything he wanted. But because no one told *him*, no one told Brian or Robbie or me.

"My mother stood by and let my father destroy her. She died when I was eleven. By then, the damage had been done. Brian had already run away from home. Robbie was withdrawn but did well in school—learning was his escape. My father was a bitter, vicious man. He died of a heart attack three years ago when I was twenty."

"Hate kills." Gram took his ring and studied it, then clutched it tightly. "I don't want this."

Allison grabbed the ring and threw it as hard as she could. "My brother Robbie would say 'good riddance' and I will, too."

"Tell me about Robbie."

Allison's face softened. "Robbie's my lifeline. He's gentle, like Brian. He's been there for me so many times, especially after our father's death. He's a salesman for a pharmaceutical company. He defied the odds and became a success, despite my father."

"And you, Allison?"

"I'm a writer. Romance, believe it or not. I haven't been published, but I'm working on it. It's therapeutic for me to have two people come together against all odds and make it."

Gram patted her hand. "You'll be all right, Allison. I know you will. I have one question for you. Why are you here in Little Texas?"

Allison looked past her to the mountains beyond. "I've always wanted to meet you. I thought the time was right to do it. Plus, I needed to tell you about Brian."

Their gazes met. "And now you have. Let's go inside and finish our breakfasts."

# SEVENTEEN

"Would you come to Texas with me?" Luke pulled up to and parked at the high school gym about six-forty-five and lifted a hand in greeting as Jim, Elva Lee, and Myra walked by. He'd come up with the idea of introducing Sarah to Texas as he was dressing for tonight's town meeting here at the gym.

"Something's between us. I don't want us to walk away from it. Come to my ranch and stay for the rest of your vacation."

Luke framed her face with both hands. He held her eyes another moment, then lowered his mouth to gently kiss her. "I want you to see where I live, where I work, get to know my family, me. We have two more weeks to spend time together. I'd prefer doing it where no wackos are trying to kill us."

She smiled at him as his thumbs rubbed her cheeks. "Luke. I would love to go to Texas—"

He kissed her quickly.

Something hit the hood of the truck, and they both jumped. A.J. shook his finger at them. "Better get out of that vehicle, son, before I cite you for taking liberties with that young woman."

Luke grinned and waved as A.J. walked on. "If it's okay with you, Sarah, let's skip this town meeting. No reason for us to be here. We can leave early in the morning as planned."

"Sure. I need to pack. I want to see your Texas, Luke, but, uh, this doesn't mean that, you know, I mean, I feel strongly that we need to wait for, y'know, for anything that might be, uh." She blinked at his frowning eyes. Surely, she didn't have to spell it out for him.

He laughed and pulled her closer to his side. "I feel the same way. Not until marriage."

"Well, I'm certainly not suggesting that we get married."

"Let's not worry about the future, Sarah. Plenty going on in the here and now. Let's go to your cabin and get your things."

Five minutes later, when Luke slipped the key into the lock of Sarah's cabin, something crunched under foot. He yanked the key out of the door, turned on the key-ring flashlight, stepped back, and shined it on the landing. "Peanuts. He was here. Get behind me."

She did.

His skin tingled with anticipation as he tugged his weapon out of his holster. "Do you have something that I can cover the doorknob with?"

She pulled her hand up into her sleeve and opened the door.

Leading with his gun, Luke flicked on the light, swept the room.

Surprisingly, nothing was out of place in the living room or kitchen. But in the hallway in front of Sarah's bedroom, a single rose lay on the floor.

Sarah backed up to the front door, locked it, and hugged herself.

Luke walked over to the rose. "Looks like he placed it in front of the room I was using." He grabbed a washcloth from the bathroom, covered the knob, and opened it. Nothing was out of place. On the bed was an outfit—a blouse, pants, shoes, socks, underwear, a winter hat, all lined up as if someone lay there. As if Sarah lay there.

Gingerly, he lifted the blouse. "She is dead" was written on a white sheet of paper. Luke ground his teeth, so angry. He picked up a shoe and threw it as hard as he could against the wall.

"Luke?"

When he reached Sarah, he grabbed her in a tight hug. "We're out of here now, before daylight."

She nodded against his chest as he called Jim.

"Jim, Sarah had a break-in at her cabin."

"Is she okay?"

"Shaken up, but okay." Luke told Jim about the rose and the clothes.

"He's escalating. He wants her. I'll call A.J., then we're on our way over."

Luke hung up. It was freezing in the cabin. He unzipped his jacket and held it open as Sarah walked into his arms. He held her tightly without saying anything. He wanted to grab her and leave. Drive to where this jerk couldn't find her. *My ranch.* He owned two thousand acres. No way this psycho would get close to Sarah with the fortress he'd build against him.

His phone rang. "Yeah, A.J."

"Just got word that a man attempted to rape a woman in Estes Park. An eyewitness saw him leave the victim's home, jump on a motorcycle with a Kansas license plate, and roar out of town. The police haven't been able to find him. Because of the string of murders from Riadon, Kansas toward Estes Park, they believe there might be a connection with the Darkslayer."

Luke could hardly breathe.

"Luke?"

"I heard you. Do they have him in custody?"

"No. As to Sarah's break in, I'm on my way. Stay there."

Luke became aware of cold penetrating one spot on his shirt. Sarah was crying, quietly. "Did you hear A.J.?"

"Yes."

Still hugging her, he noticed the curtains were open. He wondered if the killer was standing in the trees, watching them, wanting her, calculating when he could get his hands on her and kill 'Rosie.' "We're leaving tonight," he mumbled to the man outside, daring him to come close to her again. "As soon as we can get packed and the cabins closed up."

She nodded as pink touched the trees just before swirling red lights pulled into her driveway.


A.J. approached Luke, patting the air with both hands as if he was trying to calm Luke before he said something. "I know you don't want to hear this, but I'm asking you and Sarah to stick around one more day. We might be able to catch this guy if she'd be willing to—"

"She's not going to be your bait."

"Yeah, 'bait' is a strong word. I wasn't thinking of her walking in cold somewhere. We'd have the place staked out, inside and out."

"No." Luke leaned into Sarah's bedroom. "Are you about ready, Sarah? We need to be going."

"I have to question her again, Luke."

"Fine. Then do it here and forget this other."

Sarah stepped out of the bedroom, her face pale, her eyes red.

"Sarah." She turned toward Luke. "A.J. wants to ask you something." Her gaze moved to A.J.

"I need to question you again, early tomorrow morning. Will you be available then?"

"We're planning to leave tonight. You can ask me whatever you'd like right now."

"Would you—?" A.J. glanced at Luke and then placed his attention back on Sarah. "Would you stay another day—"

"No. I said no." Luke held out his hand to Sarah.

She took it. "No to what?"

"You being the killer's bait."

Her eyes widened. "Bait?"

A.J. shook his head. "I wouldn't say 'bait.' You wouldn't be in any danger. We'd have every inch of you protected."

"No." Luke drew her against his side. "Question her now. Then we're packing and leaving as soon as we can get everything done."

The chief huffed out a long sigh. "Let's sit at the table."

For the next hour, A.J. interviewed her. Then he stood and pushed in his chair. "All right. We're finished. I appreciate your time. Y'all are free to leave. Be careful on your trip out of here." He shook both their hands. "Hopefully, your next visit to Little Texas will be a lot less eventful."

"Thanks, A.J. I'm sorry we have to leave like this." Luke lifted his brows at Sarah. She nodded. "We need to go."

As they drove off, Luke glanced in the rearview mirror. A.J. stood on the porch and watched them leave.

"We really aren't going to stick around and help A.J. catch him?"

Luke grunted. "Absolutely not. We're leaving as soon as possible. He'll have to figure out another way to get him."

Although the doors and windows were locked, Luke acted on the uneasy feeling he had and hurried down the hallway to the kitchen. It was dark. He almost turned around to go to the den when he heard a whimper.

His heart stopped. "Sarah?"

He found her curled up in a shivering ball under the table. He tensed, scanned the huge kitchen, found nothing out of place, and squatted beside her.

"Sarah?" She twitched when he touched her shoulder.

"The w-windows."

Luke looked over his shoulder. Open windows spanned the walls around the kitchen. A small night light shined above the sink.

"He's out there, Luke. I saw him."

He quickly turned off the night light. The kitchen was suddenly dark. "The moon's bright tonight. He's not there now. Look."

She did. "He won't show himself again."

"I won't let him hurt you."

She rested her head against his shoulder. "I know you won't."

As they walked out of the kitchen, the man stepped to the sliding glass doors, hands in his pockets.

"Rosie," he whispered, his face ragged with grief and despair, his breath fogging the door.

Shoulders slumped, he turned and climbed up to the ridge above the house where he had a clear view of her bedroom.

# EIGHTEEN

Saturday morning's overcast skies couldn't deter Gertie from her mission. She had to talk to A.J. Banks and his brother Jim if he had a mind to listen, too.

Dressed for the cold, she sipped one last gulp of coffee and headed out the front door.

And there sat Miss Allison McIntosh for the second day in a row, looking pleased as a pea hen. "Well now, another good morning to you, Allison. What brings you by so early?" Her breath frosted on this cold, sunless May morning.

"I need to tell you the truth about Brian."

Gertie locked her front door, pulled on the knob, and slipped the key in her coat pocket. "And what would that truth be?" She slipped into her gloves as she walked down the steps toward Allison.

The young woman stepped in front of her. "Gram, I think Brian is killing these women."

"Do you, Allison? That's quite an accusation from a sister to a brother and just yesterday you telling me how sweet he is." Gertie edged around her and continued walking. "I have to get on into town. You're welcome to walk with me."

"Gram, wait up. I know how this sounds."

"Accusing a brother of murder?"

She shrugged. "I mean, I know it sounds terrible."

"That it does." Gertie sniffed as she tugged on the ends of her cap and stuffed some rebellious hair back under it.

"But what if it's true and I *don't* tell anyone? What if he's out there killing these women he thinks is Rosie? My father told him to kill you, to rid us of you." Allison brushed her hair over her shoulder. "Because of the picture of you, we all knew Rosie Jansen lived in Little Texas. After I read the news accounts of the bodies with "Rosie" on their stomachs, I came here to warn you that Brian would be after you. To kill you."

"Then I've been warned, and I thank you for coming to tell me. Brian can come on and kill me if he wants to. I'm ready to meet my Maker. Not too anxious, mind you, but ready. Now, I've got to get into town. You'd best be talking to our police chief about what you've told me. So, I'll leave you now and wish you a happy day."

"I can drive you into town."

"I like to walk. But thank you for the offer." With that, Gertie headed up the long driveway to Bear Camp Road. Allison slowly drove by and waved at her.

A quiet stretch of the road gave her a chance to watch ten or twelve elk lying in the grass, eyeing her. When she reached the highway, the blare of a horn announced Tommy Blakesly passing by. He lifted his hand and waved through the gun rack across the back of his truck window.

It had taken her years to train her friends not to stop to pick her up. They had learned that she needed to walk and enjoyed it, no matter the weather. She'd told them many times that she lived a quiet life out in the country because she wanted to. The perks that went with it included these nice long walks into town.

In the brittle cold, a squirrel scampered part way down a pine tree, spotted Gertie, flicked his head and tail a time or two, and ran right back up. Circling overhead, a blue bird landed on a branch and studied Gertie as she crossed a small bridge.

She looked up as a truck took the curve ahead of her.

A chill arrowed up her spine.

The truck slowed down, let out a young man, and drove off. The young man carried a backpack on his shoulder. He scaled a rock embankment opposite her. High above her, he sat and looked down at her. He didn't just look. He stared with an expression of wonder and sadness and yearning.

He looked like her brother when he was in his mid-twenties. He neither smiled nor frowned but stared at her with big brown eyes.

Slowly, deliberately, Gertie nodded once. The man's eyes filled with tears, and he rubbed them with the heels of his hand. Still, he stared as if he expected her to offer him something. He abruptly stood and turned to leave but he pivoted and faced Gertie again. Then, he disappeared into the trees.

Flushed with wonder, Gertie stared at the last spot she'd seen him. Who was he? Was he one of Allison's brothers? Robbie or Brian? Or a cousin? Was he the killer?

Absently, she waved as another car honked at her. She decided in a split-hair's second that that young man was no killer. Not the man who had gazed into her eyes as if she could answer all the questions he had.

Besides, if he was the killer, why didn't he kill her right then and there?

A vehicle honked and pulled up beside her.

"Miss Gertie, you're up and at 'em early this morning." Jim Banks leaned over and opened the passenger door. "Can I haul you some place this morning?"

Gertie obliged the man and hoisted herself up onto the seat. "You're just the man I'm walking to see, you and your brother. Take me to his office, would you now? I have business with you and the chief of police this morning."

"Sounds serious."

"It is, that. How's your daddy doing these days? Don't see much of him and Debra. They doing all right?"

"Staying busy. Saw them a few days ago and then, of course, at the funerals."

"I'm sorry for your loss, Jim."

"Thank you, Miss Gertie. Here we are." He pulled up to the police station. Gertie helped herself out and walked inside. A.J. was talking to the dispatcher.

"A.J. Banks, I'd like to talk to you this morning, sir, if I may."

His face radiated with the smile he gave her, and she assumed the rumors were true that Penny had opened their door and said he could come home.

"How are you doing today, Miss Gertie, and up and into town so early, too?"

"It's not so early. I need a private place I can visit with you and Jim for a spell."

"All right." He led her into his office and pulled out a chair for her. Yep, a might cheerful today he was, so he and Penny must be getting along all right.

She yanked off her wool cap and pulled off her gloves. "Is there a coffee pot on somewhere?"

"Yes, ma'am. Black?"

When she nodded, Jim said, "I'll get it." He came back with two and handed one to her.

"All you need's an apron, Jim."

He shoved a cup at his brother. "You wanna wear this, A.J.?"

"A might touchy today, little brother." A.J. grinned at Gertie. "Do you want me to take notes or is this a social visit?"

"You know me better than that. I wouldn't bother you at your work if it was social. This is about the murders."

His grin disappeared. "I'll record this, Miss Gertie." His gaze flicked to Jim's as he opened the throw-up-green metal cabinet and took a recorder out, plugged it in, and searched for the record button.

He pushed it. "All right. You can begin. Identify yourself, please."

"I'm Gertrude Jansen. Years ago, I was the victim of a rape and went to a home for unwed mothers. One of the nurses wanted to adopt the baby. I used the name 'Rosie Jansen' there and that's the name that was put on the birth certificate." She let the words take root.

"Rosie. You're Rosie," A.J. whispered.

With rapt attention, A.J. and Jim listened to the story of a woman giving up her son for adoption and hearing not a word from that child until the letter she'd received years ago.

"I'd like to see that letter, Miss Gertie."

She took it out of her pocket, unfolded it, and handed it to A.J. She gave the chief and Jim a moment to read it. When they finished it and looked up, she told them of Allison's visit, her accusations against her father and her brother Brian. Of seeing one of the boys this very morning.

"Do you know where Allison McIntosh is staying?"

"I do." She told him. "She's been to my house a couple times."

"Miss Gertie, that day I visited with you and Miss Winnie Sue, why didn't you tell me then?"

She shook her head. "I don't know exactly. The name 'Rosie' brought back terrible memories. We—Winnie Sue and I—went to a home, lived there for seven months, had the baby, and left. Allison told me her brother Brian was behind the killings. I thought you ought to know."

"We appreciate you coming in and letting us in on this." A.J. looked at Jim. "We'll get a psychological profile drawn up on Brian, Robert, and Allison McIntosh. Their father died a while back?"

"Yes. A heart attack."

"And the, uh, the baby's father?"

"I never knew him or his name." She let that information sink in, too. After the attack, she and her sister were a little fearful of men and dating or socializing with them.

"I need to speak with Allison. Hopefully, she'll have a picture of her brother, Brian." A.J. threw out his hand. "Thank you for this, Miss Gertie. We'll work up a plan to get this young man, alive. I know it took a lot for you to come in and talk to us."

She put her hand in his. "Not as much as you think, once I decided to do it."

"Can I take you somewhere?"

"Thank you, Jim. I can walk to my sister's house. She'll be surprised to see me. But a little surprise at her age is a welcome thing," she chuckled, "so long as it doesn't kill her."


Twenty-eight pounds in three months!

Elva Lee grinned like a cat waiting to pounce on a mouse as she stepped out of Jodee's Salon, itching to tell someone her good news, that she had reached her goal!

Her Lighter and Brighter weight loss group met at seven-thirty in the morning on Saturdays at Jodee's before she opened at nine. Elva Lee had won the prize, a gift certificate to Myra's Dress Shop, for losing the most in the past three months. She thought she'd walk over to Myra's but remembered she was closed because of Joy's death. Would her sister Irma have it open for Myra?

Elva Lee had an hour before she had to be at work at ten. Search & Rescue closed at two on Saturdays until the season opened. Elva Lee wouldn't have time to shop today after work because she planned to see Myra and Fred and that visit would take a while.

"Girl, just look at you!" Irma fluttered a hand at Elva Lee as the door dinged behind her and shut. "How *much* have you lost?"

Beaming, Elva Lee answered, "My goal was twenty-eight pounds, and I met that goal today." She hugged Irma as they both laughed.

"Well, twenty-eight pounds on your little frame is a lot! If you're gonna get that man to sit up and take notice, you're gonna have to get out of those baggy clothes. They don't show you off. Haven't you treated yourself to any new clothes yet, hon?"

'That man' being Jim, of course.

Elva Lee shook her head. "I wanted to keep wearing big clothes, so nobody would know until my big reveal."

"Your *little* reveal, right?" Irma laughed at her joke as did Elva Lee. "Well, an eight's way too big for you now. Come on." Irma set off toward the petites and pulled out a dress. "This is *you*, girl. Come back here and try this on. Let's work on knocking Jim's socks off the next time he sees you."

Irma pulled the curtain across the dressing room doorway. "I saw you two at the high school gym. Did he take you?"

"Yes, but it's only because my car's in the shop. Barrett found something wrong with it and told me he'd have it ready for me some time today. Jim was just being a gentleman."

"Well, it don't matter *how* you get him alone, just so you make hay while the sun shines."

Elva Lee stepped out, shy and self-conscious. The dress fit her perfectly and showed off the curves that had been hidden under the fat she'd thrown away. She tugged at the waist. "Do you think it's too long?"

"It's just a couple inches below your knees. It's stunning on you. Turn around. You just have to treat Jim to that dress. Here, let me clip those tags. You keep it on and wear it back to work."

"That'd be a little obvious, wouldn't it?"

"Now you're getting the picture. Obvious is good!" She laughed as she took the tags to the cash register. "How about some chocolate boots? Go over there and check out a pair. And since you met your goal, I'm gonna give that dress and the boots to you for half price, kind of as a celebration."

"Oh, that's so sweet, Irma, but I have a gift certificate for losing the most weight."

"Then you keep that for another time. This purchase is on me."

"Thank you. How are Myra and Fred doing?"

A little bit of the sunshine fell from Irma's face. "As well as can be expected. Myra loved Joy and so did Fred. It's a crying shame what happened to her. Sonny's like a ship without a rudder, just drifting on through. You pray for him, Elva Lee, and keep yourself safe, y'hear? You being so little now, you'd better be careful."

"I will. Have arrangements been made for Joy?"

"When her body's released, they're flying her home to Texas for burial. Myra and Fred will be going. Sometime next week, I think."

"I'm so sorry for them."

"It's a tragedy, all around." Then Irma smiled at her and shooed her off to work. "I'll call you tonight. I just have to find out what Jim said about your dress."


Well, he couldn't say a single word, not a single word.

He could only stare.

What had Elva Lee been doing during her lunch hour? And where had all that weight gone? She was just a little thing now, and she'd come back looking like a Saturday-night date, all flushed and rosy and shy. And those green eyes. When did they get so big?

His gaze caught hers, and he couldn't seem to let her go. He hadn't been flustered by a woman since he was fourteen and Katie Washburn was sixteen and she'd pranced by him wearing a short skirt that barely covered her and a halter top fit to tongue-tie a gossip.

Elva Lee blushed and looked toward her computer screen while Jim threw his pen down, yanked his cap off his elk horn, announced, "I'll be back," and slammed the door behind him.

But Elva Lee only grinned as she scampered to the ladies restroom to the full-length mirror and stared at herself in her new dress. Jim Banks had noticed her, really noticed her, and by golly, that man was going to keep right on noticing her if she had to buy every petite dress Myra had.

With newfound confidence, Elva Lee pranced back to her desk and waited for Jim to come back. She'd be ready for him this time.

The phone rang. "Search & Rescue, this is Elva Lee."

"It's Jim. I'm leaving for the day but wanted to know if Barrett called yet about your car."

Disappointment ripped through her. "No, not yet. He said it'd be around two when it was ready."

"Well, when he calls, let me know, and I'll take you out there to get it."

She swallowed down the excitement of seeing him again and tried to sound normal. "All right, Jim, I will."

"I'll wait to hear from you then." And he hung up. The dial tone buzzed as Elva Lee hugged the phone for a moment before she hung it up.

A little before one, Barrett called to tell her the car was ready. Before she left to get it, she needed to check on supplies and went back to the storage room.

"Elva Lee?"

Jim! Why had he come back? "In here, boss. Did you forget something?"

Breezily, she walked out.

"Where, uh, where'd you get that dress?" Jim cleared the frog from his throat, but it jumped right back in. He felt like an absolute fool for standing and gawking and not knowing what to do with himself. It was only Elva Lee, after all.

In her pretty green and brown dress, she walked around her desk, reached under it, and pulled out her purse without even looking at him. "At Myra's."

"Umm." Was she doing that just to get under his skin? Prancing around like that? Ignoring him? Looking so good a man could forget to breathe? "Barrett just called me. Said your car was ready."

"Yes, he called me, too." Elva Lee turned toward him.

"He, uh, said he got your car done earlier than expected. Did you want to go ahead and get it?"

"That'd be fine, Jim." She picked up her purse.

Without a word, he opened the door for her.

Elva Lee turned off the lights as she walked outside to the passenger side of his truck. He opened the door for her, touched her elbow to help her up, and set his teeth against that dress flowing all over her legs. He slammed her door.

Then he slammed the driver's door, jabbed the key into the ignition, started the truck, and yanked it into gear. But he couldn't back up. Two women strolled by, behind his truck.

Elva Lee crossed her legs, turned around, and waved at them.

Jim tried to swallow and made himself concentrate on the ladies, too.

They waved at him. He waved at them and then glared into the rearview mirror.

Elva Lee watched them push their baby carriages, surrounded by their other kids, toward the City Park. "It's a pretty day for a stroll in the park," she said and turned those big green eyes on him.

Jim grunted. For some reason, he was mad at Elva Lee. He didn't want to notice her, didn't want to have these feelings come to the surface. He'd struggled with them for months and had prayed and prayed that God would take them away.

But He hadn't. So, what was he supposed to do now?

They drove down Deer Meadows to Ridge and hung a left. Two more blocks and she'd be out of his truck.

What was happening to him? This was Elva Lee. His good friend.

Barrett's shop. *Finally*.

He drove around back and stopped as Barrett ambled toward his truck and opened the door for her.

"Right on time." He winked at her. "Man, Elva Lee, that's a pretty dress. You been losing some weight there?" He turned to Jim. "Thanks for bringing her."

But before the door could even shut, Jim took off.

Across town, Luke was pumped to be on the road. He tossed in the last of his stuff and secured his truck's hard cover. He hadn't intended to sleep in so late. He and Sarah had eaten a late breakfast out, packed up everything, and were finally ready to go. Not exactly how he'd planned it.

"All right." He gave Sarah a quick kiss and glanced at his watch. "Just talked to my brother, Mac. Told him we were about on our way. Do you have everything?" He took one last glance around the yard, grabbed his shades out of the glove compartment, and shoved it closed.

Sarah looked under the front passenger seat, then the floorboard in back. "My purse. I thought I had it with me. It must be in the hall bathroom. Did you lock the front door?"

"Yeah." Luke yanked the keys out of the ignition and held them up. "Kiss."

She playfully lifted a brow. "And if I say no?"

"You won't." His hand snaked around her neck and drew her to his mouth. He took his time, his sweet, sweet time.

She laughed and held out a hand. "Keys."

Handing them to her, he said, "Let's hustle, Sarah. Time's a-wasting."

"Be right back." She jogged to the house, opened the door, and smiled over her shoulder at Luke before she disappeared inside.

Luke rolled down the back windows and turned on the radio. Reception was pitiful in the mountains, but Little Texas had its own FM station of Golden Oldies. Marty Robbins crooned out, "My woman, my woman, my wife."

Luke tapped his thumbs on the steering wheel to the beat as he gripped it with both hands and thought of his woman becoming his wife. *Rushing it a little bit, aren't you, buddy?* He smiled. *Absolutely not.* He checked his watch and stuck his head out the window. "Sarah, come *on!* Time's a-wasting!"

Molly barked at him from the truck bed. He tapped the window separating them and grinned at her. As he did, his gaze caught the vision behind him. He slid out of the truck, folded his arms on the cold wall of the truck bed, and admired the mountain splendor of white-topped peaks.

In the back of his mind, he was aware of Molly barking.

When Carrie Underwood started a song, he glanced toward the house. The door swayed a little in the gusty wind and he thought of saloon doors swinging in a deserted ghost town with tumbleweeds rolling down the middle of a dusty road.

Despite the fact it had only been five or six minutes, he stalked toward the house. Molly joined him. "Sarah, let's go."

He moved into the dark hallway. His heart pounded faster at the deafening silence. "Sarah?"

No movement. No answer. No sound.

"Sarah?"

He ran to the bathroom and flipped the light switch. Her purse was sitting on the lavatory. His heart hammered, and his breath hitched as he stepped into the hallway, glanced both ways, and raced toward the kitchen.

The back door slammed against the wall as he moved stealthily through the kitchen, jerking his head as he looked around the room. Molly barked at the back door.

"Sarah! Come *on*. We need... to..." The back door had been locked! He'd locked it himself and checked it. The only way it could have been opened was from the inside. "Sarah!"

He ran outside, his head snapping in every direction. "Sarah! Saraaaaah!"

A short piercing scream—or was it a bird screeching?—bounced off the mountain and splayed in an echo across the open air. Was it in front of him? Behind him?

*God, no, please!*

He had her! The killer had Sarah!

Blood raged like a madman through his body as he scanned the looming ridge, the gazebo area, the path down to the stream below the cabin, the pool house. He could have gone anywhere with her.

Luke darted down the path to the stream. Wild with fear, he pulled out his cell phone. Ran back up toward the house. Raced down the path past the gazebo. His gaze darted in every direction. His heart jerked his body with each pounding step as he punched in A.J.'s number. Desperately, he searched the trees where the killer had stood that night.

"A.J. Ban—"

"He's got her, A.J.! He's got her!" Almost delirious, Luke started up the ridge, stopped to catch his breath.

"Who's got who, Luke?"

"Sarah! The killer's got Sarah! At McKenzie Cabin. Hurry!"

Breathless, his head pounding like a jackhammer, Luke grunted as he reached the top of the ridge, bent over to catch his breath, and searched in every direction. Then he headed down to the house to scour the area below it where the path led to the pool house.

"God in heaven." A.J. spun around to face Larry and Roland on his way out the door. "The killer's got Sarah. McKenzie Cabin. Get out there." At their dazed looks, he shouted, "NOW!"

A.J. called his brother. "Jim. McKenzie Cabin. Killer's got Sarah."

"On my way. Call the mayor. Sound the alarm."

They'd just discussed it last night at the town meeting. A.J. punched the mayor's numbers. "Carol, sound the alarm. The killer's got Sarah Morgan, and we need *help!*"

"I'll... I... I'll let you talk to—"

"Then do it. We don't have time to chat!"

In two seconds, the mayor came on the phone. "A.J.?"

"Sound the alarm, Terry. The killer took Sarah Morgan out at the McKenzie's cabin. I'm on my way out there. Sound the alarm!"

"Okay. But who's gonna be there to talk to the people?"

"*You* are. We need help at McKenzie Cabin, at the cave site. Josh. Call Josh Daniels in Willow Falls, the caver. Terry, we picked out leaders for this kind of thing. We'll have something figured out by the time they get there."

He'd reached the driveway to the cabin and punched it.

A.J. slung gravel as he skidded to a stop and didn't wait to get his hat on or close his car door. He raced through the open door, into the cabin, weapon poised and ready to fire.

Jim swerved to miss a tree as he slammed on his brakes, barely missing his brother's patrol car. He ran toward a frantically waving Luke in back. "What happened, man?"

"He got her. W-we were in the truck, ready to leave, when she went back inside to get her purse. He must have been hiding inside. Maybe he took her purse, so she'd have to go back in and get it. I don't know. They went out the kitchen door and left before I realized she was taking too long. Five or six minutes. That's it. God help me, I should have gone with her."

Jim scanned the back yard. "Any sign of which way they went?"

"No." Luke pointed and walked toward a path. "This leads to the stream. They could have gone up, but I think that would have been too tough with him carrying her." Suddenly, Luke lowered his head, rubbed his eyes. "Oh, God, don't let her be hurt. Jim, we gotta *do* something!" Molly nudged his leg, and he patted her head.

"A.J.'s called the mayor. We have a system set up for such emergencies. This guy is probably close to the edge at this point." Out of the corner of his eye, Jim saw a movement in the house. "Wait." He stuck out his arm, hushed Luke, and pulled out his firearm. He backed around a tree just as A.J. walked out the glass door. Jim shook his head and put his weapon back in the holster.

"What have you got, Jim?"

"Luke was out front in his truck when Sarah went inside to get her purse and didn't come out. She's not here. Couldn't have been more than five or six minutes from the time she entered the house and she went missing."

Two doors slammed. A.J. took a step back to look around the corner of the cabin. Larry and Roland held their holstered revolvers against their sides as they ran toward him.

"Okay, men, two at a time. Luke and Jim, head up to the ridge, look for signs, clues Sarah may have had the presence of mind to leave if she was conscious. Larry and Roland, go down this path, weapons drawn, follow procedures. I'm staying here and checking every inch of this house, the attic, the basement. Meet back here in fifteen minutes. I have everyone's cell phone numbers. Go!"

# NINETEEN

With her tongue, Elva Lee shoved the carrot pieces to the inside of her cheek and answered the phone. "Search & Rescue, this is Elva Lee." She pushed the receiver up above her nose and hurriedly chewed and swallowed.

"Hello, Elva Lee. This is Miss Winnie Sue Jansen. We just heard from Carol down at the mayor's office that Sarah Morgan is missing. Is that true?"

"What do you mean 'missing'?"

"Well, Carol said the killer had Sarah, that he took her from McKenzie Cabin just a few minutes ago."

"I have to call Tommy and Buddy and send them out to the cabin. There's the alarm. I need to be at that meeting. Are you coming?"

"Why, yes, of course. Jim's parents, Jeb and Debra, are scheduled to pick me up. Miss Gertie's here so she'll come with me. We'll see you there."

Elva Lee called Tommy and Buddy, and then Jim.

"You stay at the office for now, Elva Lee, and search for information on Robbie or Brian. A.J. has Greta doing the same thing at the station. Let me know the second you find anything. Oh, and would you call Marilyn and Scott Morgan in Kansas and let them know their daughter, Sarah, is in trouble? Here's the number."

At Myra's Dress Shop, Irma cringed when she heard the alarm. She looked across the square. Mr. Norman fumbled to his feet and shuffled toward his home. She threw Myra's store money in the bank bag, locked it in the safe, picked up her keys, ran out the door, locked it, and raced to her car.

Penny hurried out of the restaurant next door, gritting her teeth as she tried to undo the knot in back of her soiled white apron. "Are you going to the meeting, Irma?"

"Yes, I'm an alternate leader. My George is a Team Leader, and I don't know if he'll be there or not. Do you need a ride?"

Pulling the apron off her shoulders, she nodded. "If you don't mind. I know A.J. will be there. Can my server—I mean, Francie—can she come, too?"

"Of course. You have any customers in there, Penny?"

"The last one just left."

"Did you turn off your grill?" At Penny's blank look, Irma said, "Run, girl! Get your purse, too. Catch the lights behind you."

Francie scampered out the door Penny held open for her. "I turned off the grill!"

Penny stopped and shook her head.

"Your door, Penny, honey," Irma shouted from the car. "Lock your door. Then jump in, both of you."

Penny's hands visibly shook as she followed Irma's instructions.

Fred and Myra's son, Trace, from the hardware store next door, watched as Francie eased into the back seat of Irma's flaming red, totally-rebuilt '67 Mustang. Penny sat in the front. "Y'all heading over to the high school gym?" he yelled from the doorway of Gally's Hardware.

"Yes. Is your daddy coming?"

Trace nodded. "Fred's a team leader. He won't leave Mama behind by herself, so Myra will be there, too."

"You keeping the store open?"

"Yeah." He looked around the town square. "If this is a search and rescue, people might need some things, so we'll stay open. Y'all be careful now."

All three women nodded and waved as Irma backed up and headed out.

"Wonder what's going on," Penny mumbled as Irma turned north and lead-footed the gas pedal.

Allison McIntosh flinched. A piercing alarm seemed to be right outside her car windows. She drove slowly around the town square as people scurried about, stopped to talk for a moment, then waved and jumped into their cars. Every single one of them headed north on Ridge.

She frowned as she drove up to Jodee's Salon, but Jodee was just coming out, nails wet apparently because she held her fingers up as if she hoped the breeze would dry them.

"We're closed, honey!"

Why were they all in such a hurry? What was that alarm? She opened her mouth to ask, but Jodee was already inside her car and backing up. Allison drove the full square. It had turned into a ghost square in mere minutes.

Annoyed, she headed down Main Street. The library was across the street from Miss Winnie Sue's house. A sign boasted "Spelunker's Club Meeting" tomorrow night. It might be interesting to see what a caver's meeting was like. Maybe the library had a book on caving. She pulled in and parked and was grateful the door was not locked.

The library was empty but for the woman behind the reservation desk. Allison walked to the counter and expected a friendly yet hushed greeting. But the woman behind the counter was efficiently ignoring her and continued to work on her computer. Allison rested her arm on the counter and drummed four long fingernails impatiently, with her head cocked.

She lustily sighed. The woman still ignored her.

"Excuse me?"

The librarian didn't bat an eye. Her fingers clicked away as if she had nothing better to do than to ignore a library patron. Finally, she popped one key particularly loud and turned toward Allison, brows raised, and offered not a word.

"I'm visiting here in Little Texas for a few weeks and wondered if I could get a library card."

"Identification?" The librarian's lips barely moved.

"Yes." Allison reached into her purse and drew out her wallet.

The woman slapped a white card on the counter and turned back to her computer.

Irritated, Allison filled out the card and slid it over the counter toward the woman.

She picked it up and set it beside the computer, punched some keys, and glanced back at the card. "Name?"

"Allison McIntosh."

The woman gasped. Her hand flew to her mouth as her face paled. Wearing this shocked expression, she stared at Allison as if she were an alien with two heads. Then the woman looked down at the card, picked it up, studied it, looked at Allison again, and promptly hurried out the front door of the library.

What was that all about? *Did that woman know me?* Allison frowned at the door. She hadn't looked familiar. *Strange.* "Hello? Is anyone here?"

The water fountain gurgled behind her, and she jumped.

A head appeared around a corner. A short frumpy woman was attached to it. She came into full view and looked at Allison as if she were a chicken dressed for Sunday dinner. What was it with these people, reacting to her that way? Was something on her face?

A replica of a pile of gray cow dung roosted on top of this woman's head. Her mouth rounded into a perfect O as if helping a customer was as foreign to her as eating grass.

Irritated, Allison said curtly, "Can you help me here?"

"Why, where's Laura?"

"She's sick, I think. She left the building in a hurry."

"Her ulcer must be acting up. How can I help you today?"

"I filled out this card." Allison pointed to the one beside the computer. "I wanted to get a library card."

The old woman twisted her plump freckled hands at her waist as her worried gaze looked at the computer, then at Allison, then back at the computer. "I'm the archivist. I've never been trained to do this. Maybe if you could come back in an hour or so, Laura will be feeling better by then."

"What time do you close?"

"Eight o'clock. Sharp."

"Thank you." Allison left the library, thinking the librarian had to be the rudest person she'd ever dealt with. She backed out of her parking spot and headed north on Ridge to see where most of the people of Little Texas had taken themselves to earlier.

Within fifteen minutes of the alarm sounding, most of the people of Little Texas were standing inside the gym, two blocks down from Barrett's Auto Repair, waiting for instructions from Mayor Terry.

He picked up the bull horn and spoke into it. "Thank you, everyone, for responding so quickly to the Little Texas Emergency Alarm. Team leaders, find your reference points. If you don't remember your reference points,

Team One stands in front of Section One. Team Two, Section Two, and so on. There should be ten teams. If you don't remember what team you're on, Team Leaders, hold up your cards. Folks, find your Team Leader now. Quickly, quickly."

Josh Daniels jogged in, searched the room, and ran toward the mayor who was pointing someone toward a man holding up a K-P sign above his head.

Terry shook his hand. "Josh, good to see you."

"I was at Penny's restaurant, Mayor. Came as quickly as I could."

"Just stand by. We'll get everyone's attention, and you can talk to the group searching around the Gem's Peak Park cave area." Terry held up his hands. "Okay, folks, listen up! Sarah Morgan was taken from the McKenzie's cabin about twenty minutes ago. Based on the evidence, we believe she was taken by the killer of the other women."

A widespread gasp and mumblings ensued.

"Time is our enemy. Remember the things we discussed at our town meeting. Your Team Leaders have your stations. Get to them and good luck."


Josh Daniels and five team members squatted next to the crevice where the three bodies had been found. It had been sealed with a thick, blue plastic covering. It was still in place. Two-man teams searched the area, in and around trees and brush.

Jim Banks' twenty-member team met him at McKenzie Cabin and scoured the area east of it for a quarter mile. Will Pollard and twenty-two others searched north of the ridge above the cabin and beyond. Tommy and Buddy's team of twenty explored the stream area below the cabin and circled around for a quarter mile.

Allison took Miss Gertie and Penny around town, posting flyers of Sarah Morgan at all major intersections, churches, grocery markets, the library, Barrett's Auto Repair, Gally's Hardware, Penny's diner.

Officers Larry and Roland went door-to-door along McKenzie Road, asking if anyone had seen anything.

Miss Winnie Sue stayed in the gym with seven other senior ladies and helped serve hot drinks to returning team members.

After five hours of exhaustive searching, all teams stood in the gym, tired, thirsty, hungry, discouraged, and with absolutely nothing to report. No one had seen or heard a thing.

The media showed up in droves. Reporters were not allowed inside, but they dogged weary searchers, asking unanswerable questions, pointedly reminding everyone that one of their own was not being recovered in anything like a timely manner.

Miss Winnie Sue supervised seating the team members at tables loaded with food and drinks. Pastor Clay thanked the Lord for the food and the people's generosity in lending a helping hand.

He asked for Sarah's safe return.

Then everyone ate quietly as they pondered where Sarah Morgan could be and why there had not been even a trace of a clue as to where he'd taken her.

Elva Lee had given Sarah's mother, Marilyn Morgan, perfect directions. Marilyn turned her rental car into the McKenzie driveway and parked behind a red truck, grateful she'd left Scott at the gym and her daughter Elizabeth and the family cat with Jodee's sixteen-year-old daughter Paige.

From the moment her family had arrived in Little Texas, its people could not have been kinder. She was surprised Jodee remembered meeting her on their last visit here.

"Why, of course, I remember you, Marilyn. It was two years ago at the rodeo. I had done your nails earlier in the day, and you went to the rodeo that night. You wore a yellow cowboy hat and rode Bullheaded the mechanical bull and lasted ten seconds as I recall." Jodee had made her sit beside Miss Winnie Sue, and they fussed over her.

She knew she couldn't hold it together if they did, so she asked if anyone had directions to the McKenzie cabin. She needed to see Luke McKenzie. She desperately needed that connection with Sarah.

And here she sat, in front of the cabin where her baby had last been seen. Marilyn made herself get out of the rental car. The front door of the cabin opened. A tall, utterly handsome young man with coal-black hair and, she could see even from this distance, stark blue but weary eyes walked toward her.

"Marilyn?"

Before she realized it, their arms were around each other. She was sobbing against him as if he was an old friend. She felt herself being led into the cabin through the front door and seated at a kitchen table.

A chrome napkin holder sat in the middle of the breakfast table. She fumbled for a napkin and yanked it out. "I'm so sorry. I hadn't intended—"

"That's all right, Marilyn. Here, would you like some ice water or something else to drink?"

She thought she'd die if she had to concentrate on getting something to her mouth. "No, no, I'm fine. You're exactly as she described." Another bout of crying, and she dabbed her face and blew her nose.

His eyes clouded, and he abruptly stood, left the room, came back with a box of Kleenex and set it on the table between them. "There, that should take care of both of us for a while."

"Tell me what happened."

He frowned as he stared out the windows. "We were ready to leave, everything was packed. She forgot her purse and went inside to get it. After a few minutes, I thought, I hoped, she was dawdling so I came in. She was gone. The back door was wide open."

"It had been locked?"

"Yes. I ran outside, screaming her name, ran everywhere. She was gone, vanished. He had such a slim start that I thought we'd have found them by now. And here I sit, doing absolutely nothing. A.J. said I should stay at the cabin in case she comes back."

Marilyn yanked another Kleenex out and pressed it against her eyes as a sob caught her unawares. "She—she's in love with you."

Luke stared at her. "I hoped she was, but she hadn't told me. She'd been hurt by the Darkslayer and didn't think she could ever—" He shook his head and searched her eyes.

"She's a strong young woman, Luke. Not many women can go through that experience and come out of it as determined as she is to let it go. But it catches her sometimes, when—" She sniffed and blew her nose. "—when she doesn't expect it to."

She looked outside. "The littlest things frighten her about people. She told me she should've been scared to death of you because of your size but she wasn't. She trusted you from the moment you helped her with her twisted straps."

Marilyn looked around the kitchen. "She loves to cook." She brushed her cheeks with a tissue. "Are they sure it's not the Darkslayer who took her?"

"They don't know, for sure. But evidence points to the killer who's stalking small women here in Little Texas." He abruptly stood and walked to the sliding glass doors. "I'm afraid of what he's doing to her. Or planning to do. Or-or—"

She got up, walked over to him, and touched his arm. "Keep praying. It's our best shot at getting her back alive and safe."

Scott appeared with A.J. Banks in the back yard. "Let me introduce you to my husband, Scott. Sarah's father."

Luke opened the glass door and stepped outside. "Mr. Morgan? I'm Luke McKenzie, Sarah's friend. I'm sorry we're meeting—"

Marilyn watched her husband reach for Luke and hug him. His shock of white hair stood out against Luke's black hair. Scott was a much smaller man but his arms easily enveloped Luke.

Her husband pulled away, reached for Marilyn, and folded her into his comfort. They both wept and rocked and unashamedly held onto each other.

"Luke brought tissues," Marilyn said as they moved toward the back door.

Scott patted Luke's back. "Let's go inside, son, out of this cold wind, and you can catch us up. A.J., will you join us?"

"In a few minutes. Luke, do you have a private room I could use?"


Luke called his brother, Mac, and told him about Sarah.

"I can fly there, buddy. Be there in a couple of hours at the most."

"Stay home for now. We have plenty of help. I'll keep you posted, then you can give updates to the rest of the family."

"Will do. If you change your mind, call me."

"Pray, bro.' Just keep praying."

"We all are."

Luke couldn't sleep. He had to get outside. He quietly tiptoed through the house and opened the sliding glass doors. He ran full-throttle up to the ridge and sat in the Indian paintbrushes Sarah had admired. The house was dark except for the light in the kitchen.

It began to snow, a light snow at first. He didn't care for himself.

But he worried about Sarah being out in it.

# TWENTY

Gertie couldn't sleep. Gentle folds of Winnie Sue's long blue gown wafted around her legs as she paced the kitchen in her sister's fuzzy house shoes, rubbing her arms as if she were chilled. But she wasn't cold. She was worried sick.

It had always been there at the back of her mind—the rape, the overwhelming anger, the doctor's grim face when he said a pregnancy had resulted, the decision to leave, the decision to give the baby away.

Winnie Sue and she had hoped and prayed that he'd have a better life than the one they could give him.

No one knew when she and Winnie Sue had left. An ailing aunt had sent for them, a worn-out excuse that no one questioned because they were well-respected in Little Texas.

But something had happened the night they gave the baby away. A part of Gertie had died. She withdrew inside herself—the part that could give and receive affection and love unconditionally. She had become a cold woman. Oh, caring, certainly. She'd give the shirt off her back to help someone. But touching, hugging, loving had been stripped from her when she'd allowed them to take the baby away.

A part of Winnie Sue had died, too. She'd become rigid and orderly, as if she could protect herself from anything bad ever touching her if she presented herself properly and lived by a strict code and schedule—if she could control her life.

And now his seed was here, doing far worse than his grandfather had done. How was a soul to bear it? Gertie picked up her coffee, glanced outside at the moon-cloaked night.

And looked into the somber face of the young man with the backpack!

She gasped, dropped her cup, and cringed as coffee drenched Winnie Sue's house slippers and gown. She slapped her hand over her mouth and tried to squelch the whimpering scream as she tiptoed out of the mess. She looked back up. He was gone. She looked at the back door. It was locked.

She patted her chest, so like Winnie Sue, as her heart pounded like it was drilling a hole in her bones.

"Miss Gertie, what happened?" A sleepy Winnie Sue, hand over her mouth, looked down at the floor. "Are you all right?"

Gertie's heart settled down as she turned toward the broom closet. "Yes. I'll get the broom. I'm sorry I woke you. I just had myself a little fright." She glanced over her shoulder at the window. "I'll get this, Sister. You go on back to bed now."

"What do you mean 'a little fright'? Are you in any pain?"

"Oh, no, no, no. I'm fine."

The coffee smeared on the floor as she swept up the cup pieces. Winnie Sue opened the broom closet, picked up the trash basket and a mop, and presented them to Gertie. "Is there more coffee?"

Gertie swept the pieces onto the dustpan and shook them into the basket. "There is, but it's three o'clock in the morning. You shouldn't be drinking coffee at this time of night."

"Don't tell me what I should and should not be doing at three o'clock in the morning, Miss Gertie. I'm perfectly capable at sixty-three years of age to determine what I should and should not be doing at three o'clock in the morning."

Gertie gaped, plain and simple. Winnie Sue Jansen had never talked back to her big sister like that. "Suit yourself," she muttered as she wiped up the coffee with a mop. "Pour me a cup if you don't mind. I don't think either of us is going to get any more sleep tonight."

Winnie Sue put the broom and mop away. "More? I haven't slept at all."

"Me neither. The third shift of searchers is due in at seven o'clock. We'd better be ready. They're going to be tired, cold, and hungry."

As she quietly shut the closet door, Winnie Sue said, "Who do you think is behind this, Miss Gertie?"

"I'm not sure. But I think it's Jansen blood."

"It's that monster's blood, not Jansen blood!"

Not once in the past fifty years had Winnie Sue referred to the rape or the perpetrator or the baby they'd given away. Gertie was more than a little surprised at the passion of her words.

Winnie Sue fussed over pouring the coffee, puttered over the percolator's insides as she dumped the grounds and cleaned out the strainer. She carefully avoided her sister's eyes as she handed her a cup of coffee and turned toward the napkin holder, shimmied two out, and handed one to Gertie.

Their eyes connected.

Gertie smiled.

With her gaze flickering between the coffee cup near her mouth and Gertie's eyes, Winnie Sue smiled and blushed.

Lord o' mercy, she blushed at her own sister.

Gertie reached out a hand. Winnie Sue hesitated, then she took it and squeezed. "You are a treasure to me."

It was apparent her sister didn't quite know how to act. But somehow, she found—in her vast repertoire of good manners—a proper response. "And you are to me, Sister."

Whether or not the young man watched them, Gertie didn't know. She was not so much afraid of *him* as she was the fact that someone could stand outside her sister's home and watch her.

She and Winnie Sue sat at the kitchen table, the special moment gone but still on their minds. They sipped and considered and worried over Sarah Morgan and wondered if she could possibly still be alive.

The next morning, Elva Lee was up before the sun. Too afraid to stay in her own home, she'd spent the night with her parents. By five-thirty, she was showered, dressed in her new size two jeans, and ready to go to the high school gym to help with serving a light pastry breakfast to the searchers.

She stepped over the rolled-up morning newspaper, saw the word "Joy," slipped off the rubber band, and spread it out. The headlines stated that Joy Martin would be flown home to Texas on Monday.

Elva Lee slipped the rubber band back on and threw the paper behind her onto the front porch.

The morning was bitter cold. A light snow dusted everything. She was scraping the snow-covered ice off her windshield when Jim Banks' truck pulled up behind her car.

Smiling, she raised her ice scraper in a wave.

And froze.

He certainly looked none too happy to see her. She took a step back at the fierce anger on his face as he slammed his truck door and marched over to her.

"Why didn't you tell me you weren't going to be home last night?"

At the vehemence and anger and, yes, concern in his words, Elva Lee's mouth dropped open. She took another step back. When her widened eyes blinked, her mind simply drifted out her ears like wind through a tunnel. "I—"

He pointed a stiff arm down the street and jabbed a pointed finger at absolutely nothing. "Didn't you think I'd go by your place and check on you?"

No, the thought had never entered her mind. "Well, Jim, to tell—"

He grabbed her shoulders, and she had to tilt her head back to find his eyes.

"You scared me half to death, Elva Lee! I thought..." He tightened his grip and gave her a little shake. "I thought he..." He closed his eyes and lifted his head toward the heavens. "Elva Lee, don't..."

She didn't—couldn't—and braced herself as he sputtered, "Ah, great," and lifted her—lifted her!—off her feet and kissed the absolute wits out of her.

After the initial shock of discovering Jim Banks' mouth on hers, she poured herself into the kiss. Where there was anger, she soothed. Frustration, she cooed. Weariness, she encouraged.

With no embarrassment or shame, Jim lowered her to the ground as if it was the most natural thing in the world for him to be kissing Elva Lee Ward at dawn on Faircrest Drive and lifting her plumb off her feet in the process.

He searched her eyes as his mouth lowered again, gentle this time, soft. When he let her go, he rested his forehead on hers and sighed. "Next time, let me know where you are."

She could only nod, barely able to hold back the bulging whimper clogging her throat.

He grabbed the ice scraper and attacked her windshield. He finished all her windows and handed her the scraper as his gaze locked on hers.

Her heart stopped. She had a vague sense of his face lowering to hers, of her chin lifting to meet his mouth.

"Been wanting to do this for a while," he said and kissed her again, a long and lazy kiss that caused her knees to buckle.

His strong arms gathered her up as he grinned at her. "Can you stand,

Elva Lee?"

She nodded. He set her against her car and turned on his heel toward his truck. Leaning on the open door, he said, "I'll see you at noon," and, with a satisfied nod, he hopped into his truck and left.

She couldn't move. Thinking was out of the question. As morning light arrived in her parents' neighborhood, Elva Lee stared, unmoving, at the spot behind her car where his truck had been parked.

And smiled.


Winnie Sue was in her element. At seven o'clock on this sad but beautiful Saturday morning, coffee needed to be made again. A new batch of searchers came in; stomachs were empty and needed to be filled.

Busy about her work, it was then that she noticed the straight-backed gentlemen of elderly years standing near the back wall, down from the serving table, staring at her.

She fumbled the cup of steaming coffee she was handing to Eduardo. He smiled, nonetheless, shook the coffee off his hand, and thanked her for her kindness.

The man at the library! The one who had stared and *winked* at her! Why, Winnie Sue had never had a man stare at her before and thought him far too bold to be doing so.

Certainly, she was nothing worth staring at, and she shouldn't even be considering whether she was or was not, with Sarah missing. But a hand fluttered to her neck anyway, and her fingers stroked across her lips.

She must have something on her face. She mumbled an "Excuse me, Penny, Irma," and made her way to the ladies' room and checked, but nothing seemed inappropriately placed on her face. He must have mistaken her for someone else.

Satisfied, she returned to the beverage serving table.

The gentleman was no longer against the wall.

He was waiting in line for a cup of coffee, with his gaze boldly on Winnie Sue.

Well, forevermore! She would simply pour his coffee and send that old man on his way.

Will Pollard handed her his empty coffee cup. "Good morning, Miss

Winnie Sue."

She smiled and poured his coffee. "How is Casey doing, Mr. Pollard, after that vicious attack in the park?"

"Better. She's at home now," he said, thanked her, and left.

The old goose was still staring at Winnie Sue.

Determined to ignore him and not blush, she smiled warmly as Tommy Blakesly took a cup from her. "Miss Winnie Sue, you're an angel. Thank you for the coffee."

Buddy Washburn mumbled, "Got anything to go in that, Miss Winnie Sue?" At her disapproving look, he looked a tad remorseful and thanked her anyway.

Then the gentleman stood in front of her. "A refill, if you please." His base voice seemed to reverberate through every bone Winnie Sue owned as she kept her eyes on his large hand. "Young lady."

Young lady, indeed!

"I haven't had the pleasure of making your acquaintance, ma'am."

Winnie Sue couldn't bring herself to meet his eyes. "Miss."

"Beg your pardon?" He cocked an ear and raised his brows.

Her eyes down, she whispered, "It's 'Miss' and no, I don't believe we have met, sir."

His stuck out a large, thick hand. "Name's Carl Jefferson."

Winnie Sue was beside herself with embarrassment. She took his hand, shook it, and couldn't get a word past her dry throat.

He leaned forward and smiled. "And whose hand do I have the pleasure of holding, miss?"

Blushing and trying very hard not to, she said in a low voice, "Winnie Sue Jansen, Mr. Jefferson." Very graciously and with as little discomfort to him as possible, she eased her hand out of his and looked behind him at a smiling Keith Liboski.

"A pleasure, Miss Winnie Sue Jansen." Carl Jefferson tipped a non-existent hat, smiled, thanked her for the drink, and went to stand in his spot against the back wall.

"Miss Winnie Sue, I do believe you have an admirer."

"It would seem so, Mr. Liboski." She gave him a cup of coffee and glanced over at Mr. Jefferson.

He saluted her with his cup and smiled.

She frowned and wiped her hands on her apron. "Forevermore."

The mayor blew a whistle to gather all the teams together and begin the day's business. Mr. Jefferson stayed where he was and watched them, *and her*, and she wondered why he was in Little Texas and just what that old man was about.

It wasn't a long walk from Gertie's house to the McKenzie's cabin, and she'd enjoyed the crisp early morning and the quiet. She was glad to see A.J.'s patrol car parked in front. It was seven-thirty, and she wondered if he'd been here all night. She knocked.

A disheveled Luke opened the door, squinting against the cold breeze. "Come in, Miss Gertie, and have some fresh-made coffee. We were just talking about you."

"We were?" She walked down the hallway to the kitchen. A.J. and Jim rose from their chairs.

She flapped her gloved hands at them. "Sit, boys. No account of getting out of those warm chairs this early in the day. Any news?"

Luke shook his head. He looked the worse for wear as he poured her coffee and gestured for her to sit beside him.

Will Pollard's father, Truman, a psychologist who helped the police out from time to time, continued where he'd obviously left off when Gertie knocked.

"He's a hermit, a recluse, likes to hole up where no one can find him. Hence, the pit where he dumped the bodies. He's meticulous. Driven. He hasn't killed Luke because he's on a mission to kill Rosie. He won't kill indiscriminately. That's why Luke is still alive, although he could have killed him and taken Sarah—or 'Rosie' as he believes she is."

Gertie set her purse on the table and got out of her winter things. "I think you're talking about my kin, Truman. I also think I know how to get that gopher to come out of his hole."

"Now, Miss Gertie."

"Don't you 'now Miss Gertie' *me*, A.J. Banks. I know what I'm about. That boy believes he's killing *me*, but when he sees a woman that looks like me, he thinks Rosie isn't dead, that she got out. So he kills again. In his damaged mind, he's obeying his father and doing what he was told to do. This is totally beyond his control now. That being said, I'm willing to use myself as bait to get him to come after me. Provided, of course," she nodded at A.J., at Jim, "that you boys are ready to get him when he does. I've got some living to do yet."

A.J. glanced over at Jim, who raised his brows and cocked his head. "Well, Miss Gertie."

"I can tell by that look that you're not buying what I've said, A.J. You've got a psychologist fellow here—no offense, Truman—who's gonna tell you about someone he doesn't know. I don't know him either, but I think I know more about him than anyone here."

She walked in front of A.J. and Truman. "I don't mean to be disrespectful of your job, Truman, but I've got a stake here. I intend to use whatever advantage I have to get him to set Sarah loose if he hasn't killed her already and maybe save himself in the running."

A.J. picked up a pencil and let it fall back to the table, picked it up, let it fall. "All right, Miss Gertie. Let's hear this plan of yours."

Raw, hammering pain radiated from the crown of her head into her neck. She moaned and tried to move her arms, but every part of her body screamed out in torment.

Sarah struggled to open her eyes and keep them open. Complete blackness engulfed her. Sharp points of pain dug into her left shoulder and arm. Unable to keep her eyes open, she drifted along black corridors of agony. Where was she? Was she in the cave?

She remembered being groggy, and a voice saying, "There ya go, Rosie. Dead and buried. Finally!" Then he'd shoved her, and she'd fallen a good distance onto dirt and into sudden, excruciating pain.

She tried to turn on her side, but spasms of unbearable anguish racked her left foot and shoulder. She cried out and made herself be still. Even without moving, pain stabbed her body, radiating in every direction. "Help me," she whispered and then drifted away.

A cameraman entered the gym, followed by several other people. In minutes, he said, "On my mark, five, four, three, two, one." A red light came on and the anchorwoman for Channel 11 News smiled into the camera.

"This is Toni Pruett, live from the Little Texas high school gym in Little Texas, Colorado, where hundreds of volunteers are still searching today for twenty-five-year-old Sarah Ann Morgan, who was abducted from the home of Luke McKenzie yesterday morning.

"Many volunteers help to make things flow smoothly in a search and rescue. One of those volunteers is with me today: Rosie Jansen. Miss Jansen, how many people are here today helping with food preparation and serving?"

Gertie looked at the camera. "Approximately thirty."

"And you, Miss Jansen, have helped several times through the years with such efforts?"

"Oh, yes," she laughed, "many times. I was born here in Little Texas, and my mother would say, "Rosie, someone needs our help." I remember the rescue of a man and his wife right behind our cabin there on Bear Camp Road. He had a broken leg, and she had a broken collar bone. So, yes, my sister and I have helped on many rescues."

"Do you still have hope, Miss Jansen, that Sarah Morgan will be found alive?"

Gertie focused on the camera. "Of course, that's our hope. My mother used to say to me, 'Rosie, if you need to find someone, stay with it until they're safe.'"

"We also have with us today A.J. Banks, chief of police here in Little Texas. Chief, what are your plans today?"

A.J. shifted his feet. "Same as yesterday, Toni. We have team leaders in constant contact with command control, scanning the area where she was last seen as well as other areas in and around Little Texas. We couldn't do this without the help of people like Rosie Jansen and the other volunteers."

"How many searchers do you have, Chief?"

"Around two hundred fifty."

"Do you think she'll be found alive?"

"None of us would be out here working this hard if we didn't."

Toni Pruett smiled into the camera. "This is Toni Pruett with Rosie Jansen and Chief A.J. Banks in Little Texas. Back to you in the studio." She stared at the camera until the red light went off and then turned to Gertie. "I sure hope this works."

"Me, too. I sounded like an absolute dingbat, tooting my own horn like that. A.J., thanks."

"Nothing to it, Miss Gertie. I think the talk of the town will be why in the world we called you Rosie."

Within minutes of the interview, Jim Banks walked into the gym and scanned the room. Elva Lee's heart skipped a beat when he spotted her talking to Penny.

She couldn't breathe as he walked toward her, eyes intent, teeth set. He edged behind the serving table, wrapped an arm about her waist, pulled her up to his mouth, and kissed her thoroughly.

Penny's mouth dropped open. Irma giggled. Miss Winnie Sue Jansen blushed and glanced back at Carl Jefferson who nodded and smiled at her.

The whole room quieted.

Jim stepped back. Both he and Elva Lee blushed. He bent over, kissed her again. "One for the road," he muttered, and then turned to Miss Gertie. "Are you ready to leave, Miss Gertie?" He headed out with her but sent one last glance over his shoulder at Elva Lee.

Irma grinned and hugged Elva Lee. "It was that dress we picked out, girl!"

Penny smiled. "It's about time that man opened his eyes."

And, in general, Little Texas had something to smile about. News traveled fast. Everyone felt heart-warmed about Elva Lee and Jim, especially with the prospects getting better of finding Sarah—well, no one could say the d-word yet. It was almost as if they were afraid it would come true if anyone said it out loud.

# TWENTY-ONE

Holed up in a tiny closet inside Miss Gertie's house, Officer Larry Traylor smelled musty shoes and stinky socks and just plain 'old' around him. He figured her grandfather had stuffed an old pair of well-used socks in a corner, and no one had ever discovered them.

Something crawled on his arm. He wanted to swat at it but couldn't. Not when a murderer might be sneaking into Miss Gertie's cabin right now and hear him. He wasn't ashamed to say that he was terrified. He'd never even fired his gun, much less pointed it at a human being with that intent. He hoped he'd be able to aim and shoot when he needed to without dropping it.

In Miss Gertie's basement, Officer Roland Graves peeked over the rickety worktable, grateful he wasn't allergic to dust. For crying out loud, the floor was made of *dirt*. If he so much as breathed on the lopsided table next to him, it would crumble at his feet. His knees and his back ached—neither liked being in a constant bend. But A.J. said he had to be ready to fire his weapon. And he couldn't be ready sitting on the floor, knotted up like a pretzel.

A.J. looked through a slit in the wall of Miss Gertie's old worn-out barn, searching the house and grounds for any activity. His fingers cramped on his weapon, so he set it on a dusty crate near his foot and sat on an old bench where he could keep his eye on the cabin.

It had been an hour since the interview. Channel 11 said they would run it three more times today. It was a long shot that the killer had access to a T.V., much less that he was watching the news.

At McKenzie Cabin, Sarah's mother, Marilyn, glanced at Luke. He was asleep at the kitchen table with his head on his arms. She fixed peanut butter and jelly sandwiches while Scott watched the TV for any news of Sarah.

She closed her eyes as exhaustion pressed in on every cell in her body. She'd lain wide awake all night, not even a little drowsy, the hurt and worry too deep for sleep.

She was rinsing her plate when a knife fell off it and dropped into the sink. Molly barked at the intruding sound.

Luke jerked awake. "Wha—?" He looked around the room and sighed. He rubbed his eyes and glanced outside. Sadness sat heavy on his heart as the afternoon sun waned and still no news of Sarah.

He wearily stood. "Marilyn, I think I'll take a walk outside, see if I can, you know, see anything. Come on, Molly."

He needed to be outside, where Sarah had last been.

Two days. And another night approaching.

Did she have any water? Was he giving her food? Was she tied up? Was she alone?

A surge of desperation seized him. He ran like a madman up the ridge, welcoming the raw pain in his chest and legs as he topped it, spun around, and groaned like an animal in pain.

He could see for miles and wondered if his gaze skimmed over the man's hiding place.

"SARAH!" he yelled as loudly as he could. He turned in a circle and looked down at the cabin nestled comfortably in tall trees, the pool house below the cabin, the gazebo, the path leading down to the stream.

He couldn't for the life of him figure out how the killer had made off with her so quickly. Luke had long legs that ate up distance in a hurry. Stubby little legs couldn't cover much ground even if the guy was fast, especially if he was carrying someone his own size.

He hadn't had that much of a start on Luke, considering how fast Luke had run. "So why didn't I catch up with him?"

How was the man able to outdistance him?

A bike? Impossible in this terrain.

A dirt bike? No, he hadn't heard anything, and they were loud, and he couldn't have carried someone limp on it.

Luke searched through the trees. Thick brush was everywhere. How had he made it through the brush?

He turned around. The man couldn't have gone in front of the cabin. "I would have seen him."

Luke looked toward the stream. Too much underbrush.

He glanced past the gazebo. Same problem—underbrush with a single path through it toward nothing but more trees and brush. So how had the killer done it? How had he—?

Luke's body and mind froze. He stood on the ridge, stunned to the bone. Of course!

She was still here. She was still here!

Luke stumbled over himself getting down the slope, gained his feet, and made it the rest of the way down. She's still here!

Why hadn't he thought of that earlier?

Frantic, he walked around the house, hunched over, searching the ground for a storm cellar or a root cellar. There had to be some sort of an underground room on the property. This was old property, dating back to the 1890s. People built root cellars back then. It was accepted practice for preserving foods, for protection.

He pulled out his cell phone and punched in Mac's number.

"Mac, it's Luke. Do you have the original plans to this property?"

"The original plans? My architect can get them. Why?"

"I need to know if there's a storm cellar on this property, a root cellar of some kind. Probably where the original house or cabin was built in the 1890s. I think Sarah might be in it."

"Okay. I'll call Calvin and get him to email it to you. You can print it off in the downstairs office."

Luke told him he'd keep him posted and disconnected the call. He kept searching the ground. He could hear Marilyn yelling upstairs, "Scott? Scott! Luke's onto something. Go outside and help him."

In minutes, Sarah's father was rushing outside.

Luke bent over, scraping old leaves and mulch away from the gazebo with his foot.

A little out of breath, Scott said, "What are we searching for?"

Luke's gaze was riveted on the ground. "A root cellar, a storm cellar, an underground room. He couldn't have outrun me, Scott. My legs are much longer than his, and he was carrying Sarah." Luke looked up. "She's still here. I can *feel* it! She's still here. Come on."

Luke raced to the garage and pulled down two rakes and handed one to Scott. Both started working on the yard.

"Look for an indentation or an opening. You start here. I need to go inside and get into my email. Mac's architect is sending me the original plans. Marilyn can watch for his email for me."

He took Marilyn to the office and opened his email. "Come get me when it gets here. Then we'll print it off." He thanked her and rushed back outside. "Scott, I'll search over here. We'll increase in five-foot increments until we hear from Calvin, the architect."

They worked in silence for twenty minutes until Marilyn hollered at him that the email had arrived. They printed the blueprints.

Nodding, Scott quietly studied them for a few moments. "You're right, Luke. Isn't that the root cellar right there?"

"It is."

"Give me a minute to figure this out. Do you have Calvin's number? I need his input."

Luke gave it to him.

"Okay," Scott said as he joined Luke outside a few minutes later. "Calvin thinks we're going to have some difficulty finding it. The easiest way to do this is for him to talk us through it. Calvin?" He put the phone on speaker. "We can both hear you now."

They listened to the architect for a few moments as Luke led Scott down the path toward the stream. "It's exactly 310.78 feet from the west end of the property, going east. That means you have to find the west end of the property first. Look for a large boulder. That's where you start."

Sarah awoke to complete darkness.

Her head hurt. Her left arm and shoulder hurt. Her left ankle hurt. She was chilled but so grateful she'd started the day off in warm clothes.

She had the presence of mind to know that tape covered her mouth and secured her wrists. Dusty. Dirty. Old. She was underground. A cave? *Oh, God, no. Please.*

She tried to move and screamed from the pain radiating up her left arm. *It must be broken.* With swollen, stiff fingers, she tugged the duct tape off her mouth. "Hello? Is anyone here?"

She was alone; she could sense it. She chewed on the strips holding her wrists together. Her left arm dangled unnaturally when she held up her hands. Pain seared through her arm and shoulder as she continued to nibble at the tape. Sweat dripped into her eyes, burning them.

Gasping for air, her head fell back against the dirt surface. She was so tired, she wanted to close her eyes again and escape into the darkness.

But she couldn't go back to sleep. She had to get out before he came back. *Sit up, Sarah. Sit up! Stay awake!*

She struggled into a sitting position and gently patted her lower leg. Everything felt normal until she touched her ankle. It was hot, swollen, and incredibly tender. It didn't feel like her foot. *Oh, Lord, please help me. Too much is wrong with my body. I don't know if I can do this.*

Because she couldn't pull against her left hand without causing more pain, she had to gnaw through the tape on both sides of her hands. She rested. She nibbled. She breathed. She rested. She chewed. She gasped for air.

After what seemed like an hour or more, her hands finally broke free. She screamed at the throbbing pain radiating through the left side of her upper body and wept uncontrollably for a few minutes.

"Okay, Sarah." She tried to maneuver to her good knee and shrieked. Moaning, she whispered, "Get on your right side, Sarah. Come on."

She tucked her left hand into the waistband of her pants to secure it and then scooted on her bottom, using her right arm as an antenna to figure out where she was and what could help her escape. Time dragged by. She screamed as her foot dragged on the dirt floor, throbbing in pain. Gritting her teeth, she reached out again and touched something. Wood. A rung! He had left an upright ladder for her.

But why?

Of course, it was for his convenience in getting down, not for her to get out. But where was she? She would have to climb the ladder to find out.

Okay. She'd head up backwards.

She reached for a higher rung, tugged her bottom up to the first rung, and wept. Everything hurt too much. She couldn't do this.

*It's just a matter of time now.* Luke's words, at the cave.

"I can't, Luke. I can't."

*You roared like a lion.*

*I didn't, didn't I? A lion. I like that.*

"A lion. A lion." She hoisted herself to the second rung using her right arm and leg. She kept herself from falling forward by digging into the ground with her right foot. "And I thought the dark was my worst enemy. That's nothing compared to this."

Her left hand wriggled out of her pants and sent stabbing pain all over her body. She cried out as she lifted her useless, broken arm and stuffed her left hand back into the band of her pants. "Father?" She sobbed. "Help me. Please help me get out of here."

She rested for a while. She thought she might have fallen asleep, draped over the ladder rungs.

Then she pushed with her right foot on the bottom step, and she eased herself up to the next run. She couldn't tell how tall the ladder was, but her strength was ebbing. "I can't do this...much longer, Lord. You know I can't."

*My grace is sufficient for you, for my strength is made perfect in weakness.* "Perfect... strength," she muttered. "The lion has perfect strength."

She reached for the next rung and slowly hoisted herself up. Her swollen left foot grazed the ladder. Oh! She sucked in a breath and set her teeth against the crushing pain. Suddenly nauseous, she thought she might throw up. "Perfect strength, Sarah. Perfect strength."

She stopped and rested.

Time crawled by.

Another rung. She rested.

Then another. And another until she was dripping wet with sweat. Every muscle in her body was shaking. The air was getting thinner.

Her chest was hurting.

Everything hurt.

"Luke, find me." She wept, hard. "Father, help him find me."

Time meant nothing. Once, she thought she'd stayed in one position for more than an hour. Another time, she'd rested so long that her muscles seized up. She tried to shift her working foot, but it wouldn't obey her.

*Just relax. Rest a moment.*

*Perfect strength. Perfect strength.*

She closed her eyes and listened to time ticking away. Then she reached for another rung and touched something hard. She was at the top! She felt wood, like a trap door. "Oh, Father, we did it!"

She wanted to cry, but she didn't have the energy. No light shined around the small door, but she pushed against it anyway. It didn't move. Okay. Okay.

"Get your back against it."

She heaved herself up one more rung and stooped over. With her back, she shoved hard against the wood.

It didn't budge. *Come on, Sarah. Push!*

She did. Nothing happened.

"It's too heavy for me." Was there something on top that prevented her from lifting it? "Come on. Try again."

She took a deep breath, marshaled every bit of strength she had, and pushed as hard as she could against the door.

It shifted, letting in some light.

Her whole body was shaking uncontrollably.

She was dripping wet. In horrible pain. Nauseous. Weak.

"Don't fall, Sarah." She looked up. Dirt fell into her eyes. She blinked furiously and wiped her eyes with her wet shoulder. Shoving again, the door lifted a little more. She pressed as hard as she could against it, shoved back with her head, and the door gently fell open.

Sunlight!

Little white dots danced. She closed her eyes and grabbed a clump of grass and weeds. Whimpering, she shoved with her foot and tugged herself up, an inch at a time.

With one last push of her right foot, her body passed the door. She fell to her back in tall weeds.

She saw Indian paintbrushes before the encroaching blackness made them disappear.

Miss Gertie had been in her cabin about an hour and a half, A.J. guessed, as he looked at his watch in the dimly lit barn.

If the killer was waiting on her to settle in before he made his move, A.J.

sure wished he'd make up his mind to do it. His allergy to hay was kicking in, and he needed to sneeze something fierce.

Gravel popped. A.J. looked out the slit in the barn wall. A late model white SUV crept down the lane toward Miss Gertie's house. A young man sat at the wheel. His gaze darted around Miss Gertie's yard as he parked and slowly opened the driver's door.

He was a short fellow who wore his blondish-brown hair a little long and pulled back in a stub of a ponytail. A.J. thought he spotted a dangling earring in his left ear.

As the man crept up the wood steps, a board creaked.

Gertie had been primed as to how to get the man into her house.

She'd heard the car pull up, stood at the closet door and told Larry to get ready, that someone had just driven up.

He whispered, "Okay, Miss Gertie, just keep your head, all right?"

She nodded. "I will. Just be ready for anything."

She walked to the edge of the living room as she held onto a well-worn dish towel as if her life depended on it.

Her mouth was dry. Fear did that to a person.

The young man stood on her porch and looked around the yard. He raised a knuckled fist and knocked three times on the wood frame of her front door.

She swallowed hard. This was it.

She made herself move one foot forward, then the other, again and again, until she stood in front of the door.

The man rubbed his knuckle and looked right at her as she smiled at him, opened the screen door, and looked into the face of a killer.

Within fifteen minutes, Luke and Scott found the general area of the root cellar but no sign of a break in the ground where a door had been lifted.

Luke rubbed his burning eyes and looked around his feet. "Let's spread out about fifteen feet, Scott. Yell if you see anything."

But after another twenty minutes of searching, Luke threw out his hands. "Something's wrong. It's not here. There has to be another one." He called Calvin back. When he answered, Luke said, "We need to check for newer blueprints. Hiram Jansen's wife's parents lived in this area, on this very property."

"I'll do a search right now."

"I'll wait for your call. Thanks." Luke hung up.

"He's looking for them, Scott. On the same online site where he found the first set."

It didn't take long for him to find them.

Luke put the phone on speaker. Calvin said, "You're right, Luke. Another one was built up above the ridge. Pretty much right smack in the middle of that original pasture."

Luke's heart pounded hard like a fist fight rolling down a flight of stairs. "Come on, Scott." He heard Calvin say, "I'll give you the parameters—" but he didn't wait for them. He raced up the ridge with Scott somewhere behind him and headed toward the field of Indian paintbrushes. As he got closer to the center, he spotted something in the tall weeds. "I see her! I see her!"

He ran as fast as he could and landed on his knees beside her. "Sarah? Sarah?" He reached for her but stopped. "Don't touch her. She's—Oh, God." He gasped as tears flooded his eyes. "She's broken. Look at her arm, her foot, her face. She's broken. Bruised. Where did the blood come from?" He gently moved her matted hair aside that covered a gash on her forehead.

He touched her neck and then stilled as he struggled to feel a pulse. "She's alive. Call 9-1-1, Scott. Get an ambulance over here!"

But Scott's hands were shaking too much.

"I got it." Luke called A.J., told him the location, answered some questions, and hung up. "Ambulance is on its way."

Behind them, Marilyn stifled a scream when she saw Sarah. Her frantic gaze searched Luke's face. "Is she—?"

"She's alive." Luke touched Sarah's cheek. "Sarah, can you hear me? Sarah?"

Scott knelt beside her. "They're on their way, honey. No more than a couple minutes. The ambulance has been on call since yesterday." He stroked her face. "Sarah, honey? It's Dad. You're all right now. Stay with us, honey. Stay with us."

Luke's phone rang. "Yeah, A.J." He listened and said, "That's good news, man. Thanks for telling us. Yes, she's still alive. I hear the sirens now. Talk to you in a bit."

Leaning over Sarah, he said, "The police just arrested the Darkslayer. He's in custody, sweetheart." His heart ached for her. "Sarah," he whispered, "I love you. Please stay with me."

Sirens screeched loudly outside the cabin. Two EMTs raced up the ridge and over to them. Luke, Scott and Marilyn backed off and let them try to save Sarah.

"She did it all by herself," Luke said as he hugged Marilyn. "With a broken arm and a broken foot, she crawled out of that hole by herself."

"She's amazing."

In the bright sunlight, the EMTs gently and competently prepared Sarah for transport to the hospital.

Scott said, "How did the killer find this cellar?"

"Probably the same way the architect did. Blueprints were online. Did you hear me tell Sarah that the police have captured the Darkslayer?"

"That's great news," Scott said as he watched the EMTs work. "Now, they need to concentrate on finding the Little Texas killer."

Nodding, Luke said, "One down. One to go."

## TWENTY-TWO

A shout of joy rose from the bleachers at the gym when Mayor Terry Mason announced that Sarah Morgan had been found alive. Winnie Sue hugged several of the women as team members straggled in, exhausted and ready for the evening meal. But when they heard the news, discouraged expressions changed into happy ones.

"How is she, Mayor?"

"EMTs are working on her right now to take her to the hospital. That's all we know at this point, Miss Winnie Sue. She's unresponsive but her vitals are strong." A collective sigh flew across the crowd. "Chief Banks believes she was unconscious when she was thrown ten feet down into a root cellar that he believes was used by the killer as a hiding place. Bones were broken. She sustained other injuries but, folks, we have a lot to be grateful for tonight."

"Where was this root cellar?"

He told them everything Luke had told him. "Sarah managed, with at least a broken arm and a broken foot, to get herself up a ladder and out of that root cellar by herself. Now, that's one very brave and very strong woman, folks."

Winnie Sue was decidedly uncomfortable when Carl Jefferson entered the high school gym during the announcement and stood right behind her. Lord o' mercy, what was a good Christian woman to think about such boldness?

"—pray for her recovery, and Search & Rescue wants me to pass along a great big thank you for all your help! Give yourselves a hand, folks!"

Elva Lee's mother, Heather, leaned over her daughter. "Would you like to stay with us again tonight, honey, seeing as that man hasn't been caught yet? You're more than welcome, you know that."

Elva Lee smiled at her. "Maybe one more night, Mama. This time, I think I'll let Jim know where I am."

Myra's sister, Irma, heard her. "A good shaking up was good for him. Look where it got you." She nudged Elva Lee with her shoulder, and they both laughed.

Winnie Sue cast what she hoped was a surreptitious glance over her shoulder and discovered that Carl Jefferson was leaning toward her.

She gulped. The whiskers on his mouth tickled her ear as he said, "May I have the pleasure of taking you home, Miss Jansen?"

She backed away from his mouth as hot as an August house-a-fire and feared she might be close to swooning. But she gathered her wits about her and glanced over the crowd for her sister. "Oh, my," she whispered. "I can't seem to locate my sister, Mr. Jefferson. She's staying at my home this evening."

"I'd be more than happy to take both of you home."

"No, no. That's not the point, sir," Winnie Sue said as she shook her head. "I don't see my sister anywhere."

With every ounce of courage she possessed, Gertie grinned at the man cupping his hands around his eyes and peering through her screen door.

"Howdy, young man. What can I do for you?" Bold as brass, she pushed the screen door open. She tried not to react to the slight bulge in the nice blue shirt he had loosely tucked into his dress pants. "Are you lost, then?"

"Are you Rosie? You can't be Rosie. You don't look like the picture."

A chill raced from her neck clean down to her toes. She stepped back and made herself look surprised. "Why, how'd you know my name, young fellow? Did you see my picture there on the TV?" She thought she was doing a fine job of acting addle-brained as A.J. had suggested.

"So, you *are* Rosie. I couldn't find you." He pulled a paper rose from his pocket and stuck it to the glass in her screen door. Then his hand moved so quickly, Gertie couldn't react. In a second, he had a gun in his hand, and it was pointed right at her. "I couldn't find you. You're old. Nothing like the picture."

"Why, no call for a gun. Nobody's gonna hurt you here." She backed up as he stepped inside with a glint of something way past anger in his eyes, past being human.

"Rosie, Rosie. You can't know how long I've searched for you, how long I've needed to see you." Tears filled the young man's eyes, but he quickly sobered—too quickly—and bared his teeth. "How long I've needed to kill you." A deeper voice. "I've tried. I've tried and tried to kill you."

He shook the gun at the sofa. "Sit down, Rosie. I want you sitting down."

Gertie obliged him and sat primly, as if Winnie Sue was watching.

"Feel my heart, Rosie." He leaned over with the tip of the weapon square between her eyes. "Feel my heart, how excited I am to see you."

Her trembling hand touched his chest. "Yes," she whispered. "I can feel it, Brian."

"Don't call me that!" In an instant, his voice was higher. "DON'T CALL ME THAT!"

The young man sat on the coffee table and hugged his head with both hands, the gun pointed straight at the ceiling.

"He never could do it." The young man wept and wiped his eyes with the back of the hand holding the gun. "He'd just sit in the corner and curl up like a cat. And take it, and take it, and TAKE IT! Over and over and over and over and over, again and again, he'd just TAKE IT!"

His whole body shook. The man jerked up and lunged toward the north window, gasping for air.

"But *you* didn't, did you, Robbie?"

He spun around with noxious hate in his eyes and quick-stepped to the sofa. "How do you know my name?" He snarled as the barrel of the gun slapped her forehead.

She'd seen it coming and leaned away as he hit her, but still the stars came, the gripping pain. A drop of blood ran down her temple. "Allison told me, Robbie. She's my friend."

"NO!" He jumped up and down like a fit-throwing two-year-old. "She doesn't understand! You're in Brian! I'm going to kill you."

He sat on the table again, suddenly quiet. "He said you were in Brian, that you had to come out of him. I-I was a little boy. I didn't know how to do it then." He glared at her. "But I do now." The deeper voice was back. *A split personality.* "Oh, Rosie." He laughed as if they were at a dinner party and he was telling an old story among friends. "You're finally going to die today."


Officer Larry could hardly breathe. If he took a good breath, Robbie might hear him. He covered his mouth and breathed into his hand as his heart galloped. The confession had to come first and then he could step out. A.J. had been very clear about it.

"Robbie, don't."

Gertie hadn't heard a car. Nor had she heard the librarian, Laura Langston, walking up her steps. She opened the screen door and stepped inside, glanced over at Gertie, and then placed her attention on Robbie.

"Who are you?" Robbie swung the gun and aimed it at the woman. "I *said,* who *are* you?"

"You were my quiet child. Always acquiescing, always in the shadows, hiding, afraid. But you don't look afraid now, Robbie."

Gertie agreed. He looked evil, depraved, insane. His eyes were gripped in the blank look of madness.

"I'm your mother, Robbie."

It was pathetic watching his face scrunch up like a little boy who didn't want to cry but couldn't help himself. Big gasping gulps filled the air as his wrist pushed away the moisture on his face. With the gun in his hand, he stared at this woman who was his mother. His bottom lip quivered.

A young boy's voice said, "No, my mother's dead. He said she was dead."

"Well, I'm not, Robbie. I'm alive."

Robbie's eyes glinted, and he growled. He squinted at his mother and, in a grand sweep, pointed the gun at Gertie. "Did you do this?" He flicked his head toward Laura. "Did you put her up to this?"

Gertie's mouth had gone completely dry. "No, Robbie. It *is* your mother. She's the librarian here in Little Texas." Keep it smooth and easy, A.J. had said. Don't upset him. "I've known her for many a year."

"Robbie, I came here where Rosie lived because I knew you would eventually find her. You were always so inquisitive. I wanted to be here, in Little Texas, to give you answers if you needed them. I've been here since I left you."

Angry eyes bored into Laura as Robbie raised a straight arm with the gun pointed right at her face. One side of his mouth lifted. His head dipped. He looked down the barrel at her.

Utter silence filled the room.

Gertie could not get a breath. Robbie smirked, and his gun arm swayed. Then he made little circles with the gun, outlining Laura's face. He stopped and reversed the path of the circles. His eyes closed as his right eye began to twitch.

"You're dead, Mommy." Quick as a snap, Robbie sneered, squeezed the trigger, and the gun popped. Wide-eyed, Laura stared at her son, swayed, and fell to the floor.

Robbie spun toward the large window and stood there, so still.

In a flash, Gertie thought of the note she'd left on Laura's kitchen table and regretted leaving it. Lying on the floor, Laura looked at her, sent her a "thumbs up," and then closed her eyes. The bullet hadn't even touched her.

The closet door opened a bit. Gertie slowly shook her head at Larry and winked, the signal not to come out of the closet. She mouthed, "She's alive." Larry nodded. She knew he was sending A.J. a quiet text right now, as instructed.

A.J. put away his phone. So, Laura Langston was unharmed. Good for her for faking being shot. That might come in handy later.

In the waning light outside, A.J. bent over, scurried across the front yard, and squatted at Gertie's steps. She had purposely left the door open so he could hear everything.

Slowly, slowly, he crept up the steps, hoping Larry wouldn't get antsy and jump out of the closet and get himself killed.

Roland backed away from the cabin, craning to see what was happening above him. A.J. caught his attention and shook his head. Roland disappeared under the overhanging porch. A.J. lifted his head enough to see that Robbie was standing at the north window, looking out. A.J. bent over and headed under the rectangular window above the sofa. He could get off a good shot from here if he had to. He decided to move to the south window and watch through the tall potted plant he'd stationed there after the interview.

The signal for Larry to exit the closet and capture Robbie was a shot fired in the air. A.J.'s safety was off. His finger rested against the trigger. Now, all he could do was watch and wait.

Robbie hit Miss Gertie, and A.J. cringed.

Robbie pointed his gun at his mother on the floor. "You're gonna die just like *her,* Rosie!" He swung around and slapped Gertie again.

The blood on his hand caught his attention.

Panting, he brought his hand close to his face as he stared at the red streaks. He wiped his hand on Gertie's shoulder. She wanted to cry over the loss of this precious young man who was her blood, to weep over the injustices done to a child unable to fight against the terror in his own home.

The pain in her head was raw and unforgiving. When Robbie grabbed her hair and yanked her head back, she groaned and opened her eyes.

"Now that's better." Robbie spoke in a deeper voice. He shoved her away, backed up, and sat on the windowsill. The gun dangled from his right hand. "You don't know what happened, do you, Rosie?" Still, the deep voice of an older man.

With her head buzzing, Gertie didn't know if he wanted her to answer him, so she said nothing.

"Well, you're gonna listen to all of it!" The child was back. "You're gonna know what you did to me! What you did to your own flesh and blood." At the word 'blood,' a dazed look crossed Robbie's face. He held his hand up in front of his face again. "It's all gone," he whispered in awe.

"Robbie, I-I didn't know you."

Wildly, he shook the gun at her. "Don't call me 'Robbie,' Rosie! I'm not yours!" He jumped up and down. "I'm not yours!"

Gertie figured she'd better keep her mouth shut. Robbie was past being able to be soothed, past understanding. Her head ached. Her stomach was queasy. She reckoned it didn't really matter that much, seeing as how she wasn't going to be alive to have to deal with any of it.

"Are you listening to me?"

When had he moved? He was so close, she could feel his breath on her face. "Your eyes are so much like your sister's."

"Robbie?"

He stiffened as his head jerked toward the front door. Allison stood on the other side of the screen door.

"Robbie?"

Shaking, he rubbed his eyes, tilted his head to one side, and looked again. The little boy was back. "Allison?"

The screen door opened, squawking as if to warn her off. Her face was pale as she looked at the gun in his hand. "Robbie?"

Then she saw the woman near the television and gasped, "Oh, my God, Robbie!" and started to crouch beside her.

"No, Ally, NO! You can't be here!" He wildly waved the gun at her. "Get back. Rosie's not dead yet." He looked at Gertie, then at their mother sprawled in a heap, and started to sob. "GO, Ally! Rosie—"

"Robbie, stop it! Why did you do this?"

Wide-eyed, his glazed eyes stared at his mother. "Mother's dead now, Allison. Mother's dead."

"Mother?" Allison shook her head, glanced at Gertie. "Gram?"

Robbie screamed, jumped up and down as he pointed the gun at Allison. "Don't call her Gram! She's Rosie! Rosie hurt all of us."

"Robbie."

At the sound of his voice, Robbie jerked as if he'd been shot. He slowly turned toward the kitchen, his breathing quick and shallow, his eyes glassy. Tormented, he closed his eyes and shook his head and looked again at the man standing in the back door with a gun in the hand that rested casually against his pant leg.

Robbie swayed, wiped his forehead with his gun hand and, with a wan smile, took a step toward him.

Gertie knew it was his brother, Brian, just as she'd known somehow that it was Brian in the truck and Brian at Winnie Sue's window. Instinctively, she wanted to warn him, shield him, but there was no shielding anyone tonight.

He made no move to use his weapon as he stepped into the dining area. "Robbie," he said gently, quietly, soothingly. "I'm here. Everything's going to be okay now."

Gertie couldn't believe the transformation. From a raging bull to a little boy and back again, from black eyes filled with anger to brown eyes filled with obvious love.

"I tried, Brian. I tried to kill her, but she wouldn't stay dead." Robbie gasped and held his breath as tears streamed down his face. "Rosie won't stay dead, Brian."

Carefully, Brian took two more steps toward his brother, stopped at the open closet door, turned and looked into the eyes of a policeman. Their gazes connected for a second, then Brian kicked the door shut with his boot.

Robbie jumped and swung the gun up. Seeing only his big brother, he whimpered and lowered his arm.

Allison eased down beside Gertie Jansen and grabbed her hand.

Brian took another step toward his brother. "I know you tried." He wanted to wrap his arms around his little brother and soothe him and tell him that the world wasn't a bad place, that all fathers didn't abuse and beat their sons. He was very much afraid it was too late for Robbie to hear any words of truth.

Brian glanced at the woman lying on the floor and recognized her from pictures. He hoped Robbie didn't notice the pulse throbbing in their mother's throat or the lack of blood on her. He took another step toward him.

Robbie snarled as the shadows of evil crawled back into his face. He pointed the gun at Gertie. "She won't stay DEAD!"

Robbie swung his straightened arm at Brian, the gun cocked, his hand shaking. "Don't come any closer. It's Rosie. It's Rosie!" Frantic again, he pointed the gun at Gertie, then at Brian, then Gertie.

"I know, but I didn't come to see her. I came to see you."

"Me?" His face softened. A little smile tipped up the corner of his mouth. "You came to see me?"

Brian cursed himself for leaving his brother and sister when he was younger. He'd had no choice but to get out. But at what price? He'd abandoned Robbie and Ally just as their worthless mother had and left them to deal with their father alone.

He'd just been a kid himself at fourteen and didn't know the first thing about saving his siblings from the man. He knew now that he shouldn't have been put in the position of having to choose between *them* and *living*. He'd actually thought that if he left, then the abuse would end, since he was his father's favorite target. He didn't know, one way or another, what had happened after he left.

But he knew now, with his father's madness in Robbie's eyes, that the violence hadn't stopped. "Yes, just you, Robbie." He was almost there, just another six feet.

Robbie took one step back, his straightened arm swinging from Brian to Rosie, back and forth, as if he couldn't decide which one needed his attention. "Allison?"

"Robbie, I'm right here. I'm always here for you, Robbie."

"I—" Frozen like a deer caught in a truck's headlights, Robbie stared unseeingly at his brother's slow approach, then flicked his gaze to the old woman. "Allison?"

"I'm here, Robbie."

One more step, and Brian would be close enough to touch him. "It's okay, Robbie. I'm here just for you, buddy."

But Robbie shook his head and stepped back with a pathetic sob. "I can't, Brian." The hand holding the gun on Brian shook uncontrollably. "Too much... the pain... too much."

For a moment, his pleading gaze met Allison's, then rolled to Brian's, then slashed to their grandmother as the change ripped through him. In a split second, his arm straightened as he pointed the gun at Gertie Jansen.

Brian lunged and cried, "NO!" Allison screamed as she shielded Gertie with her body, and, smiling, Robbie's gaze flicked to Allison's just as he turned the gun toward his own head and fired.

Glass shattered. Robbie slumped to the floor.

Allison screamed. With her hands violently shaking over her face, she screamed and screamed and screamed.

Larry jumped out of the closet, arms straight, gun at eye level.

A.J. opened the screen door. "Drop your weapon, Officer. Mr. McIntosh?" A.J. held out his hand, with his other hand holding a gun aimed right at Brian. "Your weapon, son?"

He handed it to A.J., then turned and bolted out the back door.

"Let him go!" A.J. yelled at Larry. "Just let him go. Miss Gertie? You all right?"

She couldn't say. She touched Robbie's cheek. It was still warm, still tear-streaked. He looked like an angel lying on her floor, his face relaxed, his eyes closed, his mouth soft as if he dreamed of cotton candy fields.

She wished she could have given him—all of them—anything but the life they'd lived.

"We need an ambulance at Gertie Jansen's cabin immediately. Two victims. One gunshot wound."

Allison looked up. "Wounds? You mean my brother's still alive?"

"Yes, as is your mother," Gertie whispered, still stroking Robbie's cheek. "A.J. shot him through the window. Robbie just grazed his head."

"I thought he—oh, Gram—I thought he killed himself."

Gertie shook her head, so grateful he hadn't. "Maybe now, he can get the help he needs. I'm willing to do whatever it takes to get him help. I just wish Brian hadn't run away."

"Stop fussing over me, Winnie Sue. I'm fine. Really." But truth be told, Gertie's head was pounding ruthlessly.

"But it's my fault. If we'd only told the truth—"

"And what? Have Robbie hurt you instead of me? That's ridiculous."

"But you wouldn't have been—"

"No, Winnie Sue." Tears gathered in Gertie's eyes. Must be all the trauma to her head. She never cried. Unless, of course, someone hurt her little sister. "I would never have done that to you. The truth is that I took care of the baby. I did my best by him."

Winnie Sue placed her hand on Gertie's arm. "And by me."

"You were only a child, barely thirteen. I wanted to kill that man. I wanted him to die for what he did to you that night. I'm ashamed to say it, but it's true. It took me a long time to forgive him, but I did."

Winnie Sue nodded. "I don't know if I ever told you—" She slipped a hankie out of her sleeve and dabbed at eyes spilling over with heavy tears. Her bottom lip trembled. "How much... it meant to me... that you were with me during the darkest hours of my life."

"I loved you. You were my baby sister. Family sticks together."

"But you took all the blame, all the shame."

"Shame? There was no shame. None of it was your fault. All the fault belonged to that monster!"

"But now A.J. and Jim know. They think *you're* the one—"

"They'll never check out my story. Rosie Jansen never existed. All will be well. You'll see." Gertie looked over at her and took her hand. "You are dear to me, Sister."

"You've proven that to me so many times."

"Well, then."

"I bought you something." Winnie Sue handed her the small box that had been sitting on the kitchen table all day.

Gertie lifted her brows. "What's this?"

"Just a little something to help me sleep at night."

Gertie opened the box and looked at a shiny white cell phone. She lifted it out of the box. "Well, I'll be."

"I have one, too. It's easy to use. Here, Sister, let me show you how it works."

The next morning, Brian stepped stealthily over the gravel and crossed to the grassy borders of Gertie's driveway. He headed up to the familiar, perfectly flat tree stump and shooed away the ground squirrel sitting on top. "Mine, little fellow."

He glanced down through the trees at her cabin as he sat. The early-morning light lay atop the mountains like a halo.

He couldn't count the number of times he'd come here to wait for her, to watch her, to be a part of her life. To remember.

Not long after he'd run away from home, he'd written a letter to 'Rosie Jansen, Little Texas, Colorado.' Accusing words from an angry and withdrawn fourteen-year-old struggling with life.

But she'd written him back, signing the letter, 'Gertie.'

He'd read that letter so many times, he'd memorized it. He wrote her again, on the streets, tired, hungry, and weary of life.

Another letter addressed to "Brian McIntosh, General Delivery, Pueblo, Colorado," arrived, and she'd asked him to come to Little Texas and stay with her. It took him months to answer that letter. But when he did, he told her everything about his family—his father, his mother's death, and his own torment.

She'd written him again, with another invitation to come to Little Texas—and her. And then the letters flowed between them; so many, he couldn't count. He'd even sent her the one picture he had of his parents. She'd told him about his father's ugly letter to her, how it had crushed her not being able to answer his hurtful questions.

Brian glanced at her cabin.

His father had been totally wrong about his mother.

Through the years, she had, quite simply, nourished Brian's soul.

He only wished Robbie could have had her love during those horrible years of living with their father. Brian was sure it would have made a difference for him, too. At least now, he would get the help he so desperately needed.

Her screen door screeched a rusty *'Good day.'* His grandmother stepped out, coffee steaming from her cup as she scanned her yards. She walked to the corner of her porch and faced the coming sun. Full of her, Brian watched, holding his breath.

Gertie knew he was there, behind her, sitting on a tree stump. It thrilled her that he had come here after last night's horrors. Did he blame her for what happened? Was it at all possible that Brian would let her love him and not just in her letters to him?

A yearning deep inside her had been born last night when Robbie was shot. After the rape, she'd become a woman unable to draw people into her heart. But she wanted a chance to prove that she could do just that, with Brian—even if he wasn't her grandson.

It was a shame that Brian's mother left Little Texas last night without a word to her children. Gertie shook her head at the thought as she went back inside, picked up the basket of wet things, and headed outside to the clothesline.

Brian moved to the right, the better to see her.

She stretched up to the line, pinched a corner of the towel over the wire, slipped a clothes pin on it, slid her hand across to the other side, pinned it. Her fingertips glided down the length of it.

Next, she popped a wadded sheet, tucked the corners, pinned it. Then she hung another towel, a pillowcase, a fitted sheet.

Life here breathed a sense of permanency. The line itself, the pins snug over it, knowing what would happen next, how she'd fold, pin, touch each piece, pause to look at the mountains, begin again.

When she finished, she eased her two fists onto her hips, faced the mountains, and didn't move a muscle for a good two minutes.

Then she picked up her basket and walked inside. Always, it was the same ritual. And always, it soothed him to watch her.

For an hour, Gertie watched him. He picked up a pebble, tossed it, kept an eye on it as it rolled a few feet. Then his gaze would fix on her cabin as he frowned like a little boy unable to gauge whether his mother was happy or unhappy with him.

He picked up another one, tossed it, glanced at her home the same way he'd looked at her at Winnie Sue's house, sad but expectant, as if he'd bust a gut if he couldn't say what was on his mind.

Biscuits were ready, as was the bacon, white gravy, scrambled eggs, coffee, and preserves. Gertie wiped her hands on her apron, walked back to the front door, and peered up. He had a stick in his hand now, scribbling in the dirt. What was traveling through his mind? She figured it was high time she found out.

Brian couldn't explain why he stood and headed down the hill toward her house. He wanted to stop at every step but couldn't. He needed something. *From her.* Or maybe he needed to give her something. He didn't know.

Almost to her yard, the screen door opened. "Hello, Brian."

He pulled back as she stepped out. Tears stung his eyes.

She took a step toward him. "You're welcome to come in and have some breakfast with me."

His feet seemed concreted to the dirt. Weariness swept over him. His heart pounded a heavy beat, and his throat tightened. Bone-tired in his soul, he flicked a glance at her again, this woman he'd never actually met. This woman his father had hated.

This woman he loved.

"Biscuits and gravy, bacon, fresh-made coffee. Blackberry jam I made myself."

For some reason he couldn't explain, Brian glanced over his shoulder, his heart swelling as he stared at the stump he'd just left. Years of pain and abuse had taken a part of his soul from him.

But now, the words of a psalm entered his mind: "He restoreth my soul." Brian no longer stood in the shadow of the father who had taught him to hate himself, because *she* had taught him about acceptance and love.

"Come in, son, if you've a mind to. Stay as long as you'd like."

The screen door groaned open, and he glanced toward the cabin. She held the door open for him, a look on her face that spoke of expectancy, joy, and sorrow all at once. She smiled and nodded at him, as if telling him he could do it. He could come to her, and she would wait until he did.

But it took more than he could manage to take that first step. Tears overflowed. A little sob escaped from behind his hand as he tried to hide his face and his shame.

The screen door slammed.

He looked up.

She was coming toward him. Tears fell down her face as she walked down the steps with a sure foot.

Brian stepped back—and still she came. He sobbed. Tried to stop but couldn't. Then she was in front of him. All the years of hate and pain and grief washed over him as she held out her hand.

For a moment, he simply stared at it through his watery gaze.

Then he looked into her eyes. For the first time in his life, what he needed, what he'd yearned for and never had, stood before him.

He reached out. Almost touched her. And then, before he knew it, she was tugging him toward her cabin. Not a word was spoken as they walked up the steps. She reached to open the door, but he nudged her hand away and opened it for her. She looked up and smiled at him.

When they walked inside, she headed for the north window so they could admire the glorious view of her world. He stood there, soaking in the vision he'd seen so many times while she went into the kitchen and fixed their plates.

"Here, Brian. Sit, now son. Let's enjoy this bounty the Lord's given us today. And after we do, we'll visit with my sister, Winnie Sue. She wants to tell you a story."

## TWENTY-THREE

Luke heard her car coming up his driveway. August was a terrible time of the year for Sarah to see the panhandle for the first time. It was hot and dry and miserable. He'd stayed at her parents' home for over five weeks while she healed from her injuries, and it had been a month since he'd seen her. That was a month too long.

He rushed to the front door in time to see her get out of her car. Man alive, the sight of her made his heart go wild.

He whooped, ran out the door, jumped over the steps, scooped her up, and spun her in a circle. Laughing, he stopped and kissed her like a madman. "I've been waiting all day for that. One more." He took it slower and deeper. "Just what I needed." He was pleased when she melted against him and pulled his head down so she could enjoy another long kiss.

"I've missed you so much."

Words he needed to hear. "I've missed you more. How did your arm and foot make the trip?"

"An occasional twinge of pain but that's it. Almost one hundred percent healed." She turned around. "Your house is beautiful. And big. I've always loved log cabins. Where's Molly?"

"She's at my brother's ranch. She goes there every day. We'll see her later."

"Good. What's the construction?"

"A surprise." He walked with her to the skeleton of a small building in the back. "A shop for a glass maker, just in case, y'know, one happened to be here and needed—umph!"

She'd grabbed him in a tight hug. "Oh, Luke! I love it! Thank you for this. You're so thoughtful."

"Well." He was embarrassed. Her reaction was exactly what he'd hoped for. "I wanted you to have your special place to work when you're here."

"It's perfect. Thank you."

"Come on. Let's get you out of this sun." He led her into the barn where a mist promptly cooled them off.

"A misting system in a barn?"

"It's for my horse, Pepper. He was restless earlier today, so I turned him out for just a few minutes. It's too hot for him to be out long. The mist is above his stall and at both ends of this aisle." He flipped a switch, and the barn lit up.

Sarah looked over at him. "It was in the darkest blackness that I first realized I loved you."

"The cave."

She nodded. "You held me after we saw Robbie." She reached for his hand. "And when I was in the cellar, I was terrified at first. It was worse than any nightmare I'd ever imagined. But God helped me out of there, and you found me. I'm not afraid of the dark anymore."

"And you taught me about forgiving myself for my Dad's death. We've come a long way, Sarah." He drew her close. "I knew I loved you the moment I saw you."

"That's a bunch of hooey. You thought I was a brat."

"Any direction I head after that remark will get me in trouble." He led her past some trees and stopped. In the far distance, his brother Mac's two-story, ten-thousand-square-foot log cabin sat in a wide valley. The chapel his family built in the 1880s was situated down from the house at the edge of some trees, with a gazebo sitting near the huge lake in front of the chapel.

Luke gestured toward Mac's property. "Did you notice the lake?"

"Oh, yes. It's lovely."

"Mac's house?" He picked her up.

"Magnificent." Laughing, her arms encircled his neck.

"The chapel?" He lowered his mouth and kissed her.

"It's beautiful," she whispered against his mouth.

"It's functional."

"Is it?"

"Church services on Sunday, Bible studies, funerals."

"We don't like funerals."

Luke shook his head and kissed her again. "Weddings."

She gasped playfully. "Not weddings, *too*?"

"Yep."

"Any while I'm here?"

"Yours, if you'll have me."

"Is that a proposal, Mr. McKenzie?"

"Yes."

She grinned up at him.

"Is that a yes, Miss Morgan?"

"Yes!"

He war-whooped and swung her around and around. "I love you, Sarah." He kissed her again.

"I love you, Luke. You, uh, you didn't name your ranch 'The Sweating Like a Pig Ranch,' did you?"

"You've already said 'yes,' so it's too late to change it."

Grinning, he carried her toward the house. "We've been invited to the main house for dinner with Mac and Marianne. They're excited about meeting you. Marianne's pregnant with their first baby. It's due in November."

"I'm looking forward to meeting them. Do you want me to call my parents and tell them to come on down to Texas?"

"Yes." An impatient man, he stopped. "When?" He caught her scent and nuzzled her neck. He was, quite simply, totally lost in her.

"Well, time's a-wastin', McKenzie. How about Friday, four days from now?"

"Don't you want a big wedding with all the trimmings?"

"No. I just want you. Now tell me what you really named your ranch."

"The L & S Ranch."

"Oh!" She hugged him warmly. "I'm a ranch!"

Laughing, he opened his front door. "I'll carry you over the threshold when you're my wife and not a second sooner." He set her down and led her inside. "Welcome home, Sarah."

***

All of Little Texas was gearing up for the wedding of Miss Winnie Sue Jansen and Mr. Carlton Mitchell Jefferson. The week before, Jim and Elva Lee had tied the knot, and many were thinking something suspicious could be thriving in their drinking water, especially with the news that Penny and A.J. Banks was expecting their first child in the spring.

Miss Winnie Sue's wedding dress arrived at Myra's Dress Shop. It had come in two days before the wedding and, of course, the bride had to try it on, friends had to fuss over it, and the hang of it had to be just so.

"Miss Winnie Sue, I declare," said her friend Myra as she tugged on the lace sleeves and straightened the floor-length white chiffon folds. "You are a beautiful bride."

The wedding day finally arrived. Gertie was beside herself with joy at having her new teeth firmly in her mouth and having Carl Jefferson take her sister off her hands. And him a younger man, at that. Three years younger than Winnie Sue.

Gertie laughed as she remembered the angst her little sister went through after discovering their age difference.

"Why, people will think I'm desperate."

"Well, truth be told—"

"I am *not* desperate to be married, Miss Gertie, but," her eyes grew soft, "I am so desperate to marry this particular man. We have two new grandbabies and another on the way." Winnie Sue sighed wistfully. "Oh, Miss Gertie, he is a dear, isn't he?"

Gertie couldn't help but snicker. The woman was a goner. But he was worse, unashamedly singing her praises everywhere and truly believing the sun rose and set in his Winnie Sue.

And Gertie supposed it did.

For when the newlyweds came out of the church beaming and blushing with flowers falling around them and Mrs. Jefferson's white veil pulled back so that everyone had a clear shot of her husband devouring her right there on the steps of Mountain View Church, her smile was as bright as any sun Gertie Jansen had ever seen.

Brian sat on his stump and admired the yellow ribbon of light outlining the mountains. There was no other place he'd rather be than right here, watching the sun rise.

Aunt Gertie opened the screen door and waved at him.

He stood and headed down to her as the door slammed shut behind her.

"I didn't hear you get up, son."

Brian nodded. "I tried extra hard to be quiet this morning."

"Well, you were." She glanced toward the mountains for a long moment or two. "Breakfast is ready."

"Good. I'm starving." He walked up the steps. "After we eat, I thought I'd chop some more wood. We sure go through the firewood."

"It's been cold at night, and you like your fireplace."

"Especially when you sit with me and tell me stories about my family." He joined her at the edge of the porch and draped an arm around her shoulders. She settled close to him, and together, they admired the morning's glory.

"Oh, your cousins Walter and Mike called. They want to hire you again for another project. A renovation near the bank. Said your carpenter skills are the best. And, God help us, your grandmother called. She says it's time to prune the roses."

"Oh, no." He chuckled. "Not the roses again."

"She's determined that we learn how to tend to them. Well, we better get this breakfast eaten so we'll have the strength to face them." She grinned up at him.

He grinned back and opened the door for her. "After you."

*From Tamara:*

I hope you enjoyed *Rosie Won't Stay Dead*. If you did, please post a review of it on the review site of your choice. Reviews are so important to authors! To post on Amazon, click HERE.

Now, on to Kyle and Natalie's story: Book 3, *Deception at Fairfield Ranch*. Kyle McKenzie is deceived by the person he loves the most, and the master of disguises who tore his life apart isn't finished with him yet. 5-Star Review: *"You can't help but love these characters. This book had me laughing, crying, and turning pages. I want to visit Fairfield Ranch ...but I think I'll lock my door."* Grab your copy of Book 3, Deception at Fairfield Ranch, today!

## Books by Tamara G. Cooper

### Brothers of Texas Series
Who Killed Brigitt Holcomb?
Rosie Won't Stay Dead
Deception at Fairfield Ranch

### Sophie O'Brion Mysteries
The Vacant House
The New Neighbors

### Romance
Love, Again

## About Tamara G. Cooper

Born and raised in the great state of Texas, Tamara lives with her husband, sons, and four dogs in a small town in Texas. She enjoys fishing, swimming, hiking, camping trips, picnics, reading, and, of course, writing.

Made in the USA
Monee, IL
07 March 2025

13646205R00142